MISSING IN ZANZIBAR

A GREENE WOLFE THRILLER - BOOK 2

DOUGLAS PRATT

NICHOLAS HARVEY

HarveyBooks LLC

Printed in the United States of America

First Printing, 2024

ISBN-13: 978-1-959627-26-5

Cover design by Nicholas Harvey and David Berens

Edited by Chelsey Heller

1

ZANZIBAR, AUGUST 27TH, 1896

Teddy held the spyglass to his eye, bending his knees to absorb the gentle rolling of HMS *Thrush* beneath him. He scanned the grounds of the palace, several hundred yards off their starboard side, and satisfied himself that the defenses remained the same. On any other day, the captain would have enjoyed the tranquility of the morning, hearing the water lap against the hull of his ship and the sun beating down between wispy clouds. But not today. He knew this day would be different.

Swinging the spyglass to stern along a row of four British navy vessels, he settled on the mast of HMS *St. George*, from which Rear-Admiral Harry Rawson commanded the small fleet. Signal flags were being hoisted. On shore, Brigadier-General Lloyd Mathews of the pro-British Zanzibar army had made his last attempt at a peaceful resolution, which, from the message being sent, Teddy knew had failed.

"Prepare to open fire," he ordered calmly, though it was relayed far more boisterously through the chain of command.

Teddy picked out the captains of HMS *Sparrow* and HMS *Raccoon*, who looked his way from their respective ships. All three men raised an arm, and as Teddy swept his downward, the others followed suit. The morning calm was shattered by the booming of HMS *Thrush*'s six four-inch Quick Fire guns launching two-pound shells at the wooden structure of the sultan's palace. Like echoes all around him, Teddy heard the other naval ships unleash their weaponry on the shores of Zanzibar. Their combined mass of fire-power rained down on the three thousand defenders, who were mainly servants and slaves.

The palace's only significant cannon succumbed to the first wave of shells before ever firing a single shot of its own, and many of the defenders, surviving the initial onslaught, hastened their escape into the waiting arms of General Lloyd Mathews' men.

Off the port side, the sultan's only naval vessel, HHS *Glasgow*, opened fire with a Gatling gun and its nine-pounders. Teddy couldn't decide if it was brave or stupid of the sultan's men, but either way, they were rewarded with return fire of higher-caliber weapons with better aim. He watched as, within minutes, the wooden hull of the *Glasgow* was so badly holed, she sank to the seafloor of the shallow harbor, leaving its masts and funnel protruding above the waves.

"Retrieve those men," the captain ordered as the vessel sank, sighting the stricken crew hoisting a British flag, indicating their surrender.

While the big guns of the British ships continued to destroy the sultan's palace and surrounding buildings, rowboats were launched and plucked the men from the sea. A pair of hopelessly small steam-driven boats neared the fleet, with the occupants optimistically opening fire with rifles. It was suicidal, and Teddy redirected one of the *Thrush*'s four-inch QF guns in their direction, quickly destroying both launches and all aboard.

"Damn it," he muttered to himself, annoyed by the senselessness of their effort.

The shelling had begun at 9:02 am, and at 9:40 am, the signal flew from HMS *St. George* to cease firing. As the smoke began to settle over the ships in the harbor, Teddy looked at the palace and surrounding buildings ablaze. Brigadier-General Lloyd Mathews' men swarmed the sultan's compound, where the remaining defenders surrendered without further resistance.

"Landing party with me," Teddy ordered, then handed command of the *Thrush* over to his lieutenant before descending the netting to a launch alongside the ship.

His men rowed them to shore, where the chaos was beginning to calm, and the slaves and servants who'd hopelessly attempted to defend the palace were now tasked with putting out the fires. Teddy strode across the grounds, past the lighthouse. His post-surrender orders, whether following a peaceful or bloody victory, had been made clear, and time was a key element.

Maintaining order after the conflict was a logistical nightmare, with a few uniformed and so many un-uniformed combatants involved. Friend or foe had become blurred and muddy as every man claimed to be loyal to the British crown now that the undesirable sultan had been overthrown. But that was the brigadier-general's problem to solve, and Teddy ignored the pleas and questions as he advanced with purpose.

Entering the palace from the east, staying clear of the burning harem building and the west end of the palace, Teddy followed the instructions he'd been given and scaled the stairs to the upper floor. The sultan's private chambers should have been heavily manned, but only one soldier remained.

"Step aside," Teddy demanded.

The man, who wore the uniform of the sultan's personal guard, appeared confused, but wisely kept his rifle at his side.

"Speak English?" the captain barked, which the guard met with a blank stare.

Teddy waved a hand to his interpreter. "I don't have time for this. Ask him if Sultan Khalid bin Barghash is inside."

The interpreter stepped forward and spoke to the guard in Arabic. Terrified, the guard shook his head and babbled until the interpreter held up his hand.

"He says the sultan left, sir. There's nobody left inside."

"Damn it. You stay with me," the captain ordered the interpreter. Presuming the guard was telling the truth, Teddy told his men, "The rest of you, take him with you, and make sure no one comes up these stairs."

Teddy pushed open the ornately painted double doors into the sultan's chambers and stepped inside.

"Close the doors, Kassim," he told the interpreter, his voice relaxing from his authoritative tone around the other men.

The interior was lavish, featuring decorative arches along every wall and colorful rugs running across hand-painted tile floors. Plush seating upholstered in gold and red fabrics formed a gathering area around a large, low table carved from exotic wood.

In contrast to the opulence, a wind blew through the upper floor from where the captain knew a corner of the building had been destroyed by his own shells. The yells and commands of men could be heard as they fought the fire.

Teddy hurried through the reception room, searching for the sultan's private quarters, which he prayed were not at the devastated east end of the structure. Sultan Khalid bin Barghash's brief occupancy of the palace had only lasted two days following the death of his cousin, Sultan Hamad bin Thuwaini. With the absence of power, Khalid had inserted himself into the position without the blessing of the British authorities. That the British leaders suspected him of poisoning his own cousin hadn't endeared the self-proclaimed sultan to the English regime.

"Here, sir!" Kassim called out from the rear of the building.

Teddy joined his faithful servant, valet, and interpreter. With the chaos surrounding the sultan's arrival, the British officer doubted Khalid bin Barghash had enough time to move his own clothing into the palace during the past forty-eight hours. However, the captain's objective was for something far more valuable than Barghash's belongings. An archway led from the anteroom of the sultan's bedchamber to a small space where Kassim held a bundle of silk curtains aside, revealing a safe atop a stone pedestal. Beside the safe, a narrow spiral stairwell led down, and the captain assumed it was how Khalid had made his escape.

Teddy rushed forward and began turning the dial of the safe, using the numbers he'd committed to memory. Just as he tugged the heavy metal door open, footsteps echoed from the stairwell. Teddy stepped back and drew his Webley Mk II revolver, holding a finger to his lips, making sure Kassim remained quiet. His servant drew a similar weapon and aimed the barrel at the gloomy hole in the floor.

From the drumming of boots on the wooden steps, Teddy knew more than one man was approaching, but the narrow stairwell meant they could only arrive one at a time. He waited, his heart thumping in his chest and adrenaline surging through his veins. A red fez appeared from the shadows.

"Halt!" Teddy shouted, bringing the man to a stop as he peered up at the Webley aimed between his eyes. "English?"

"Yes," the man replied with a heavy Arabic accent as he slowly raised his hands.

"Those with Khalid bin Barghash have surrendered, and British order has been restored," Teddy barked. "State your allegiance and your business in the palace."

"We are following orders, sir," the soldier replied. "We serve the sultan. If this is no longer Khalid bin Barghash, then we serve the new sultan."

Teddy recognized that the man had little choice other than to say that, unless he'd prefer to die where he stood in the name of his former employer. The captain remained aware and suspicious.

"Why are you returning here?"

"We are guards of the palace, sir. Our post is here," the soldier replied, glancing down the stairwell below him.

When his eyes returned to the Royal Navy captain, so did a hand clutching a revolver. A shot rang out from the stairwell below, and Teddy instinctively pulled the trigger. The guard's head kicked sideways, then backwards as blood splattered the walls in several directions. The man's body slumped to the steps, crashing against the wall as he fell down the steps with a thud.

"Cease fire, sir!" a man called out. "I am with the sultan's guard, faithful to the British, sir!"

"Show yourself," Teddy demanded. "Hands raised! Are you alone?"

The second man tentatively stepped over the corpse and looked up, a revolver dangling from the fingers of his raised hand, his other empty and in view. He wore a similar red fez to his compatriot.

"I am alone, sir."

Teddy frowned. "Did you shoot him first?"

"Yes, sir," the guard replied. "He was one of Khalid's men, sir. I am truly with the sultan's personal guard."

"Where's Khalid?"

"The German consulate, sir. He ordered us to escort him there after the shelling began."

"Why did you two return?"

"We were sent back for what's in this room, sir," he replied.

"I dare say you were," Teddy replied. "Continue up. Slowly."

The guard came up the steps until he joined them in the confined space of the room.

"Kassim, escort our friend here to the front entrance and see he's reunited with the true sultan's guard," Teddy ordered, taking the soldier's firearm from him. "You'll have a new, British-sanctioned sultan to protect by end of day."

The guard nodded.

"Sir, I would prefer not to leave your side," Kassim said, hesitating.

"I'm fine, Kassim," Teddy replied. "Take this fellow away. I'll meet you downstairs shortly."

"Sir," Kassim reluctantly acknowledged and led the guard away through the palace.

Teddy returned his attention to the safe, staring at the ornately decorated jewelry boxes packed inside. Pulling them out one by one, he quickly raised the lids and checked the contents. Precious gems and fine jewelry sparkled and gleamed from inside each container, and the captain found himself captivated by many of the fine treasures.

With a jolt, he reminded himself of the precarious nature of being alone on the upper floor of the palace, where he could still hear men dousing the last of the flames nearby. Teddy ran into the sultan's chamber, hunting for something he could use to carry the jewelry boxes, reluctant to empty them out and risk damaging anything. Searching through wardrobes and drawers, he found nothing but robes and silk blouses. Without a better option, he grabbed the plainest robe he could find, and when he returned to the safe, he tied a knot in the lower section.

Feeding the boxes through the neck hole of the garment, he quickly filled the makeshift bag, leaving just enough room to tie the arms together, forming a strap. As Teddy rose to leave, he noticed a box he'd accidentally knocked aside and cursed under his breath. The wooden box was too large for his uniform pocket, but, reluctant to unwrap his newly formed carrier, he lifted the lid and was immediately struck by the beauty of the piece within. In awe, he gently lifted the perfectly crafted treasure.

The sound of a door flinging open and voices resonating from the reception room prompted Teddy to cram the piece in his pocket, tossing its box down the stairwell, where it clattered and bounced off the curved wall and narrow steps. He hauled his makeshift bag over his shoulder and, Webley in hand, ventured through the anteroom and carefully checked before stepping into the sprawling lounge.

"Brigadier-general, sir," he greeted Lloyd Mathews.

"The rogue flee?" the army officer asked in a thundering voice.

"To the German consulate, I'm told, sir."

"He left the sultan's treasures?"

"We were timely, sir," Teddy replied. "The man sent back for it lies dead in the secret stairwell."

"That all of it?" the brigadier-general demanded.

"Yes, sir," the captain replied, holstering his firearm and handing his sack to one of the soldiers. "I emptied the safe, sir."

"Good, good," Mathews muttered. "We'll keep it under guard until this ridiculous nonsense is dealt with."

"Yes, sir," Teddy responded, slipping a hand into his pocket and clutching the contents before taking his leave.

2

____

LONDON, ENGLAND: PRESENT DAY

Charlie Greene dropped onto the living room sofa in her London flat and let out a long sigh. Her cat, Stanley, briefly lifted his head from the chair he'd claimed as his own before returning to disinterested sleep. From the kitchen, she heard her brother, Grant, talking in whispers to his girlfriend, Angie. Charlie was too tired to put any effort into making out what they were saying, although she *was* curious.

The build-up to the day had been exhausting, and although their father's funeral had gone smoothly, it had sapped every last drop of Charlie's energy. There had also been two rather strange interactions she was still trying to process.

Grant walked into the living room, contemplated moving Stanley from the chair, then settled for the other end of the sofa. Until a month or so ago, neither Charlie nor Grant had known the other existed. Each had been raised by a single parent two continents apart. Their lives had been turned upside-down by the deaths of the mother Charlie had never known, and then her dad, whom she'd adored. For Grant, it had been the opposite. First, he'd lost the mother who had raised him, and then the father he'd only just met.

The funeral had been for Keith Greene, despite having no body to cremate. Instead, they'd placed Fiona Wolfe's urn in the family columbarium. She'd been murdered by a Russian mobster, and when Keith had helped Charlie and Grant track down Dragan Lazović on his mega-yacht, their father had been lost in the explosion from the charges he'd set himself. Charlie and Grant had only narrowly escaped.

Keith had been pronounced "assumed dead" based on a match to his blood type found on a piece of wreckage. Charlie had finally accepted her father was gone… until she'd seen a man lurking in the shadows at the funeral.

"Are you sure it was Keith?" Grant asked, looking her way.

Charlie nodded.

"What did he say?"

"I didn't talk to him," she admitted, her voice more defensive than she'd intended.

"Why would he leave and not talk to you?" Grant questioned.

Charlie shrugged her shoulders. "How would I know? I guess he's trying to stay under the radar. Can't really blame him, right?"

Unbeknownst to the siblings, their parents had been undercover agents, and while Fiona had retired to a regular life in the Florida Keys, Keith had remained active to at least some degree.

Grant fidgeted and took a few moments before asking his next question. "How close did you get?"

Charlie frowned at her brother. "What do you mean?"

"I mean exactly what I asked," he snapped back, then took a breath. "How far away was the man when he took off?"

Charlie flippantly waved a hand in the air. "I don't know, exactly. A little ways off, I suppose."

As a former Scotland Yard detective—although her career had been brief due to an overzealous arrest—Charlie was accustomed to paying attention to details, a fact she knew Grant was also aware of. She cringed inside, knowing her vague response was unpersuasive. Grant's look of doubt grew stronger.

"Did he wave, acknowledge you, or indicate he'd seen you in any way?" he asked.

Charlie sat up straighter, about to give her brother the brunt of her frustration, but reined herself in. His seeds of doubt weren't misplaced. In the moment, she'd been convinced it was her father standing in the shadows of the trees, watching the funeral proceedings, but that could have been wishful thinking. Sneaking away from the service at the columbarium, her heart had been pounding in her chest with the idea that Keith Greene had somehow survived the blast. Now, as she sat in the large London flat she'd only recently returned to sharing with her father, her visual recollection of the figure was already blurred. She hadn't been close enough for a positive identification.

"He moved like Dad," she offered, which was still a stretch.

At best, she was pretty sure it had been a man rather than a woman, but the person had melted away into the stand of trees, then evaporated by the time she'd arrived where he'd been watching from. A tall hedgerow bordered the edge of the cemetery, with a street on the far side lined with homes on large lots beyond. Whoever had been spying on them had skillfully vanished.

Grant raised an eyebrow.

"Shit. I know," she confessed, her own doubt quickly spreading. "I swear it *felt* like Dad, but I don't know why he wouldn't have at least spoken to me once he knew I'd seen him."

Grant relaxed into the sofa and nodded. Charlie was glad he was content to leave it at that, but she also knew what was coming next. The other strange interaction they'd had. A man named Cecil Bamford had approached them with a job offer to track down a precious family heirloom that had been stolen from his family's country estate. He'd thrown out a tempting finder's fee, but Charlie had little enthusiasm for doing anything beyond mourning her father. Especially now that her fleeting hope for him still being alive was dwindling.

"We promised that posh guy an answer by the morning, Charlie," Grant said. "We have to talk about it."

Charlie groaned.

"It's a lot of money," Grant pressed. "Twenty-five grand just to get started. Maybe you're sitting pretty now, but I still have no idea what Mom had tucked away, so I need the money."

Charlie let her head fall to the back of the sofa and closed her eyes.

Grant's voice softened. "This will be good for us both, Charlie. We need the distraction. Something to take our minds off the shit we've just been through. Besides, maybe we'll actually find his missing… whatever it is that's been stolen and make two-hundred-and-fifty grand."

Bamford had been tight-lipped about what they'd be looking for, but he'd been clear in the point that he wanted it handled discreetly without law enforcement involved. Charlie had taken that as suspicious, but she knew Grant was caught up in the idea of making enough money to get by for a while.

"I don't trust Bamford," she said.

"I thought you knew his family?"

"Dad knew his family," Charlie corrected. "He kept his old Austin-Healey at their place as there was nowhere to park it in London without spending a fortune. I've never met any of the Bamfords before today, and I think Dad was friends with Cecil's father. I've never heard him mention the son."

"I wonder why the father wasn't at the funeral if he was a friend of Keith's?" Grant responded.

"He has to be pretty old," Charlie replied. "Cecil's probably sixty by the look of him."

Grant nodded. "I suppose." He leaned forward again. "Our flight is the day after tomorrow. Why don't we go meet Bamford at his place in the morning and see what he has to say?"

"So you two can fly back to Florida and leave me to work on the case?" Charlie complained. "How's that going to work?"

"I told you, I have one job I have to wrap up back home, and then my schedule is clear."

Charlie recognized this was another reason her brother was so keen on new income. He didn't have any work on the books.

"He already said he can't tell us anything more unless we take the job," she countered. "What will we learn that we don't already know?"

Grant enthusiastically patted the sofa with his hand, and Stanley raised his head, staring irritably at Grant, who frowned in return before returning to his sister.

"You know he'll tell us something else if we're actually there," he said. "He approached us, remember? He won't be able to resist if he thinks he's selling us on the gig."

"And why is he having to *sell us* on the gig?" Charlie asked. "That stinks of dodgy, doesn't it?"

"I think so," Angie said, walking in from the kitchen with a tray of wine glasses and cookies. "But surely there's no harm in listening to what he says."

Grant snatched up a dark brown cookie and took a bite. "Exactly," he said, crunching as he spoke. "What are these?"

"Bourbons," Charlie muttered.

"They're good cookies," Grant said, grabbing another from the tray.

"They're biscuits," Charlie corrected.

"That's another English thing, isn't it?" he said, staring at the snack in his hand. "Biscuits come with gravy and turkey and stuff. This is a cookie."

"It's an English thing because you're in bloody England, you plonker," Charlie retorted, sitting up and taking a glass of white wine from the tray. "And we were making biscuits long before you lot killed all the locals and renamed biscuits 'cookies' for no good reason." She frowned at her brother, then nodded to Angie and raised her glass. "Thanks for the drink."

"I couldn't find much, I'm afraid. The fridge is bare," Angie replied, picking up a glass herself. "I did throw out the milk that expired a week ago."

"Let's drive up there and talk to the guy," Grant said, clearly attempting to get the conversation back on track. "What can it hurt?"

"Stanley needs me here," Charlie grumbled, balling herself up as though she was about to be dragged from the flat.

Grant scoffed, pointing at the sleeping cat. "He's barely acknowledged your presence since you got here."

"He's introverted," Charlie countered meekly. "See how relaxed he is now that I'm here?"

"All he ever does is sleep," Grant said, shaking his head.

"He does sleep a lot," Angie added, leaning on the back of Stanley's chair.

The cat ignored them all.

"Bollocks," Charlie muttered to herself as she realized her only valid excuse for not meeting with Bamford was her own lack of interest in anything the outside world had to offer. Which was a thin excuse. She had to find work and an income stream at some point. "Fine. We'll go and talk to him."

"Great," Grant enthused, pulling Cecil Bamford's business card from his pocket. He paused, card in hand. "Can I use your phone?" he asked with a grin, looking at his sister. "I don't have an international call plan."

3

They left the flat at 8:30 am in their late father's Jaguar F-Pace SVR. Despite the engine's throaty rumble, they crept along in heavy traffic, making slow progress for the first hour. After that, Charlie zipped along the A41, interspersed with periods of stop-and-go through every village and town. Drizzly rain dampened the roads for the early part of their drive, giving way to peeks of sunshine between clearing clouds.

"There's no freeway?" Grant complained after almost two hours of driving.

"Motorways," Charlie replied. "And the M40 would take longer. It's too far west from where we're going."

"I like this way," Angie said. "The countryside and little towns are pretty."

"At least we're in a cool car," Grant commented, running a hand over the plush interior of the Jaguar SUV. "What engine does this thing have?"

"One that takes petrol," Charlie quickly replied, then softened a touch. "Dad told me, but I don't remember. It's some fancy model with lots of power."

She wished she'd paid more attention. Not because she cared

what horsepower the car had, but because her dad had cared, and she'd give anything to share that with him now.

"If you had freeways here, we could use some of that awesome power," Grant joked.

Charlie trudged along at thirty miles per hour through a little village called Padbury, then pushed the accelerator once a sign indicated the speed limit had changed. The Jag leapt forward, and Grant grabbed the armrest on the door. Angie let out a gasp from the back seat, and Charlie couldn't tell whether it was from fear or excitement. Within a few seconds, they were rocketing down the two-lane road at eighty miles per hour, and Charlie didn't slow for the curves, adeptly using the full width of the road to open up the radius of the turns.

"Yup, lots of power," Grant muttered shakily. "Charlie!" he added with more volume as they rapidly approached a van.

Charlie pulled out and passed the slower vehicle, easing back into her lane as the Jag topped 100 miles per hour. With a sharper right turn corner approaching, she smoothly braked much later than Grant seemed comfortable with, from the way his fingers dug into the armrest. Charlie softly released the brake pedal as she entered the corner, keeping the vehicle's weight transferred to the front tires as she coaxed them into biting the asphalt. Once the low-profile sports rubber pointed the SUV at the apex, she squeezed into the throttle, accelerating off the turn.

Grant hung on for dear life as the cornering force thrust him against the passenger door. "I can't tell if you're really good or just a maniac," he grunted.

Charlie slowed as they passed a sign for a roundabout, dropping back to a sedate thirty miles per hour.

"We did a bit of driver training when I joined Scotland Yard," she said nonchalantly. "Oh, and Dad took us both to a racecar driving school at Brands Hatch for my eighteenth birthday."

"Shit. I would have liked that," Grant commented.

Charlie figured they could both add that to the myriad of experiences and events they'd missed with their respective parents. And now with them both gone, there'd be none to look forward to in their future. Well, she corrected herself, with one of them gone, although she was becoming increasingly skeptical about her cemetery sighting.

"I went on to do a few races with the school, too," she added.

"Then you really are good at driving," Angie said from the back.

Charlie glanced over her shoulder. "I won a few races."

"Why didn't you stick with it?" Grant asked.

"They kicked me out for being too aggressive."

Grant grinned at his sister. "You? No way."

Charlie rolled her eyes.

"Hey," Grant blurted, pointing at a sign. "This is Buckingham? Like the palace?"

"No."

"I thought the king lived in Buckingham Palace?" Grant pressed.

"He does."

Grant looked over at her. "Right. So why can't we drive by the palace?"

"Because it's not here."

His expression showed more confusion. "There's another Buckingham?"

"No," she replied, becoming annoyed. "Buckingham Palace is in Westminster."

"Isn't that where we just came from in London?" Angie chimed in.

"Yes. Westminster's in London," Charlie replied.

"You have a town within a town? That's not confusing," Grant muttered sarcastically.

"Where's Manhattan?" Charlie asked.

"New York," Angie answered with a laugh, and Charlie gave Grant a knowing look.

"Okay. Fair enough," Grant conceded. "But that still doesn't explain why Buckingham Palace isn't in the town we just drove through."

Charlie sighed. "Because it was originally built *by* the Duke of Buckingham, then later bought and expanded by the royal family."

"So why didn't the duke dude build his palace here in his own town?" Grant asked as Charlie drove through a narrow section between old buildings with shops on the ground floor and offices or apartments above.

"Stop being so bloody…" she began.

"So bloody what?" Grant barked back.

"American."

"What do you mean by that?" Grant asked defensively.

Charlie just shook her head.

"Seriously. I'm just being curious, that's all."

"No. What you lot like to do is ask all this stuff, then tell us how it's so much better in America."

"Land of the free," Grant replied, lightening his tone. "Fighting for democracy anywhere we can stick our nose in," he added with a laugh.

"I don't think your citizens had much of a vote in 1700," Charlie pointed out.

"We had to get rid of your people first," Grant countered.

"I was talking about the indigenous people," Charlie replied.

"Oh. Well, yeah," Grant muttered. "Wait a second here. How about all the countries England conquered and took over?"

"That's beside the point," Charlie replied, then slipped into a laugh. "Think of it more like embracing nations under one flag instead of conquering."

Grant laughed with her. "So, seriously, why didn't the Buckingham guy build Buckingham Palace in Buckingham?"

"Because it didn't have much to do with the town," Charlie replied, making a right turn down a narrow lane. "Duke of Buckingham was just a title he was given by some other toff."

"Toff?" Angie queried.

"Yeah, you know, some hoity-toity royal or lord somebody or other."

"How did the people of Buckingham feel about that?" Grant asked.

"They didn't have a say," Charlie chuckled.

"Speaking of not very democratic," Grant pointed out.

"Our citizens didn't have much of a vote in 1700, either," Charlie responded. "It was a work in progress."

"Yeah, we still are," Angie ribbed. "This is pretty," she added, looking out the window as they drove down a steep, hedge-lined hill with a view of a small village in the valley below. A river meandered through the fields, and homes speckled the landscape in no particular order.

After two sharp turns, the narrow lane crossed an old stone bridge spanning the river before ascending the hill on the other side. On their left, large brick or stone homes sat nestled amongst stands of oak and sycamore trees, while on their right, a field of tall grass swayed in the breeze. They passed a village shop, and Charlie wondered how on earth the tiny place had stayed in business in such a small village.

She followed the road around a sharp right curve, then slowed to a stop by an impressive stone entryway with a pair of open wrought-iron gates.

"Shit. You sure that's not a palace?" Grant murmured, staring at an impressive stately home at the end of a long, straight driveway surrounded by perfectly manicured lawns and flower beds.

"That's Bamford Manor," Charlie said, easing the Jaguar forward and trundling up the driveway.

"Do you think they'd let us stay in the servants' quarters?" Angie joked, leaning forward between the front seats.

"The good news is it looks like this guy has the dough to pay us the finder's fee he talked about," Grant said, letting out a low whistle. "This is some crib."

Charlie parked off to the side and turned the ignition off. "Hold your horses, cowboy. Most of these old estates became far too expensive to maintain years ago, unless they turned them into some kind of destination for tours or events. That, or they simply sold them to foreign billionaires who wanted a fancy old English home to impress their billionaire friends. This doesn't look like either, so I wouldn't assume Bamford has deep pockets."

The front door to the home opened, and an older man dressed impeccably in tails, waistcoat, and a bowtie appeared on the broad steps.

"You have to be kidding me. We've landed in an episode of that Downtown Abbey shit you made me watch," Grant said, shaking his head at Angie.

"*Down-ton* Abbey," she corrected him as they all got out of the car.

"Here to see Cecil Bamford," Charlie said to the man as they approached the steps.

"He's expecting you, madam," the butler replied in a posh English accent. "I'll show you to the drawing room."

"Damn it, I forgot my pencils and paper," Grant joked in a whisper. Angie elbowed him in the ribs.

They followed the butler through a high-ceilinged vestibule with grand, curving staircases to either side, then down a wide hallway past several doors to a large entrance into a room overlooking the pastures behind the manor. Cecil Bamford's plump form rose from one of the many sofas and luxurious antique chairs spread around the enormous room.

"I can't tell you how pleased I am to see you," he greeted them, enthusiastically shaking their hands.

Charlie introduced Angie, then Bamford ushered the three of them over to a pair of sofas on either side of an ornate wood and glass coffee table.

"Tea? Coffee? A cocktail?" he offered.

"Coffee, please," Charlie replied, to which the other two agreed, and the butler quietly left.

"I'm delighted you've decided to take the case," Bamford gushed.

"We decided to come and speak with you again," Charlie clarified. "Then we'll decide about taking the case."

"Oh, well," Bamford bumbled. "What more can I tell you?"

"I think that's our question, sir," Grant replied. "What more *can* you tell us? We don't even know what's been stolen from you."

Bamford reached beside the sofa and retrieved a briefcase, which he opened on his lap.

"I have taken the liberty of preparing non-disclosure agreements," he explained. "Which I must insist on you signing. I had planned for us to take care of this after you'd agreed to help me, but I don't see why these documents couldn't be executed beforehand. Then we may speak freely about the case, and you can decide whether to accept my offer or not. If you decline, then the NDAs are still in effect, and you'd be restricted from revealing anything we discuss today."

Grant looked at Charlie and shrugged. "Not sure who we'd tell, anyway, so I don't see a downside."

The police were the one entity that came to Charlie's mind, but she stayed quiet.

"Can we read the NDA?" she asked.

"Of course, my dear," Bamford replied, handing a copy across the coffee table. "Take your time." He passed a second copy to Grant. "Forgive me, but I only prepared two copies," he said to Angie. "I'll be back in a jiffy with another one."

"That's okay," Angie said. "These two will be working your case. I have to be back at work in two days."

"Were you intending on waiting outside?" Bamford asked, his tone turning more serious. "And not discussing a word of it with your beau?"

"Well… I don't know…" Angie began.

"Just sign it, Ange," Grant said. "Or it'll be a long and boring ride back to Westminster, where the Buckingham guy built a palace."

Bamford looked confused, but left to print another copy as the butler arrived with a tray of everything you could possibly want involved in a cup of coffee. And a plate of biscuits.

Eyeing a bourbon on the tray, Grant waited to speak until the butler left. "This looks boilerplate to me."

"The dollar signs are blocking your view of everything at the moment," Charlie replied.

"You see a problem with it?" Grant asked through a mouthful of biscuit.

Charlie picked up a pen Bamford had left on the table, signed the form, and handed the pen to her brother. He grinned and signed his NDA.

By the time Bamford returned with the extra copy, his guests had helped themselves to coffee and Grant had wiped out the biscuit selection. Angie signed her copy, then they all looked expectantly at the man on the other sofa.

"What you'll be looking for is an antique necklace," Bamford said, taking a photograph from the briefcase. "The centerpiece is a thirty-six-carat ruby," he added, sliding the picture across the table.

"Fuck me," Grant muttered, spitting crumbs as he stared at the ornate piece of jewelry.

4

"Can we see where the necklace was taken from?" Grant heard his sister ask, and his mind immediately switched over to work mode.

"When was the robbery?" he asked as Bamford led them into the hallway.

"Yesterday," the man replied. "The day of your father's funeral."

"Was anyone here at the time?" Charlie asked.

Bamford plodded up the curved stairway, breathing heavily with the effort. "I was away. My father was here, but unfortunately, he doesn't know much about anything going on these days. Regardless, he would have been asleep."

"So, it happened at night?" Grant asked.

Bamford paused on the landing for a moment. "I'm presuming so. I returned mid-morning, and that's when I discovered the har..." he bumbled, then corrected himself. "The stone was missing."

"Where was the help?" Grant asked.

"You mean Braithwaite?"

"If that's the butler's name," Grant replied. "I'm sure you have other staff who clean, cook, do laundry and things."

Bamford raised an eyebrow. "Not like the old days, but yes, we have staff. Braithwaite lives in the staff quarters above the garages," he continued, moving down another wide hallway to a pair of tall double doors, which he opened. "His wife works part-time as cook, and we employ a cleaning lady, but she lives in the village. We use a service rather than a staff groundskeeper."

Grant took a moment to admire the room they'd entered, a study that was about the same size as his whole home in Key Largo. A coffee table and two sofas dominated the center of the room, with antique oak desks to either side. Floor-to-ceiling bookshelves ran down both walls behind the desks, and original oil paintings hung between the three windows. He walked around the table and whistled at the magnificent view of the English countryside.

"Breathtaking," Angie commented, standing beside him.

"Yes, it is," Bamford said with a touch of sadness. "In the early days, my father ran his businesses from the offices in London, but as he aged, he preferred to work from home and held many meetings in the conference room next door. You'd be amazed to hear some of the names who've crossed our threshold for business or pleasure. Bamford parties and gatherings were held in high esteem."

"I see cameras," Charlie noted, pointing to all four corners of the room.

"From those positions," Grant added, "they should capture every inch of this room, including all access points." He looked up, but couldn't see any loft hatches, which meant ingress and egress would be the main door and the windows.

Bamford nodded and sighed. "A few years back, before my father's dementia left him incapacitated, he equipped the house with a state-of-the-art security and surveillance system. It's nearly ten years old now, but still very capable. Unfortunately, the yearly contract for recording, maintenance, and monitoring is very expensive, and with things being what they are, we were forced to let it lapse."

Grant caught Charlie's *I told you so* glare from across the room.

"You're saying the cameras are off?" he asked.

"They're on, but not recorded or watched live," Bamford explained. "They feed to monitors in a basement room."

"Alarm?" Charlie asked.

"We do have an alarm system," Bamford replied.

"They circumvented the system?" Grant asked.

"No. I didn't set it," Bamford admitted sheepishly. "Father wanders sometimes and trips it off."

"The necklace was in that case?" Grant asked, looking at a glass display with a black velvet-covered base shaped like a human neck and shoulders.

"It was," Bamford confirmed.

"So, tell me if I've got this right," Charlie began. "Two nights ago, at an unknown time presumed to be during the night, your prized family heirloom went missing, which was discovered by you in the morning when you returned home. Your father was here, but can't tell us anything, and none of the other staff were in the building or noticed anything strange going on. The alarm wasn't set, the cameras weren't recording because you can't pay the bill, and the scene wasn't secured so it's doubtful we can pull any evidence from the site. Sound about right?"

Bamford stammered for a few moments and rocked uncomfortably from one foot to the other before replying. "Yes, I suppose that about sums it up, although my father's nurse was also in the house. But she didn't hear anything, either."

"Perfect," Charlie muttered before raising her voice again. "Then I have two questions."

"Ask away," Bamford replied, and Grant guessed what one of his sister's queries would be.

"How many people would know about the details Grant just spelled out?" Charlie asked.

"I can make you a list," Bamford replied. "And the other question?"

"If you can't pay your bills, how will you pay us a two-hundred-and-fifty-grand finder's fee?"

That was the one question Grant figured was coming, and he couldn't blame her for asking. Chances were a family or staff member had taken the necklace, so it was possible they could track it down relatively quickly, but that wouldn't do them much good if the guy couldn't pay them. Although, they could hold the gem until he did.

"Good question," Bamford replied, surprising Grant with how well he took Charlie's challenge. The man walked over to one of the bookshelves behind the desk and to the right of the glass case. He removed two sections of books and placed them on the desk, leaving a pair of empty shelves. Pulling on the middle shelf, it slid from the bookcase, bringing a section of the wall with it, revealing the door to a safe.

"Not as good as a secret door, but that was pretty trick," Grant commented, and even Charlie smiled.

"We have a secret door on the other side," Bamford replied as he entered a code on the touchpad. When the safe beeped, he pressed his thumb to a fingerprint reader, and the door unlocked.

Grant wanted to see the hidden door, but was more curious what the contents of the safe might be. Bamford stepped to one side and let them look. The space was stacked full of neat bundles of cash.

"My father prepared us for difficult times and rainy days," Bamford announced. "Should I hand you your twenty-five thousand now?"

Grant went to step forward, but Charlie held out a hand and stopped him.

"Your money doesn't mean we'll break the law, Mr. Bamford. If you truly knew my father..." she began, then checked herself. "*Our* father, then you'd know that's not how we operate."

"I thought your services were *no questions asked*?" Bamford replied.

"I didn't ask if *you* had, or plan to, break the law, sir," Charlie countered. "I'm telling you *we* won't. There's something not right about this deal, so I'm letting you know upfront there's a line we won't cross."

"What makes you think this is shady?" Bamford asked defensively. "I just want my family's heirloom back from whoever stole it."

"Why won't you go to the police?" Charlie shot back.

Bamford looked uncomfortable once more.

"It's not insured, is it?" Charlie asked.

"It's insured, alright," Bamford quickly retorted.

"But they won't pay because the security was turned off and the required protections weren't in place," Grant finished for him.

Bamford nodded. "Precisely. And if I go to the police, they're obligated to contact the insurer, and I'll never get the policy reinstated."

Charlie let out a groan. "If we can retrieve your stone, that is."

"Exactly," Bamford agreed. "I'm in a bind, and I need your help, Miss Greene. Your father would have been the first person I'd turn to, and I know we all wish I still could. But you two are the next best thing. So, what do you say?"

Grant caught Charlie's eye and could see she was dropping her defenses.

"Fine," she said. "The twenty-five buys two weeks of our time. But if this is a total dead end, or it turns out the job requires something illegal from our side, then we're keeping the money and you're on your own."

Bamford reached inside the safe, then handed Grant a bundle of £100 notes held together with a currency strap. "We have a deal. I'll make you that list."

It was midafternoon by the time they'd finished speaking with the first three people on Bamford's list. The hospice nurse, Braithwaite the butler, and his wife, Agnes, the cook.

"I think the butler did it with a candlestick in the library," Charlie grumbled as they walked down the steps from the servants' quarters above the garages.

"None of these people strike me as master jewel thieves," Angie said as Grant stood on tiptoes to peer through the wide but shallow glass window of the first garage door.

"Didn't have to be," Charlie pointed out. "All they had to do was stroll into the study and walk out with the necklace."

"Is that Keith's Austin-Healey?" Grant asked.

Charlie stretched to look in the window. "Yep. That's the Sprite."

"Our father sure liked green cars," Grant said, lifting Angie up to see.

Charlie looked at him like he was an idiot.

"What?" he blurted.

She kept staring at him.

"Oh, right," he mumbled, setting Angie down. "Last name's Greene. Duh."

"It's so cute!" Angie exclaimed. "The headlights look like a pair of eyes."

"That's why they were nicknamed Frogeye Sprites," Charlie explained.

"How old is it?" Angie asked.

"1960… something," Charlie replied. "'61, I think. Okay, let's find the cleaner, or it'll be midnight before we get home."

They walked around the manor house to the Jaguar, avoiding going through the home and having to speak with Bamford again. The man had poured himself a cocktail with lunch and appeared ready to continue a long afternoon of drinking. Charlie drove them away from the house, turning right at the lane to go back through the village, watching out for house names on signs beside the driveways.

"Here!" Angie exclaimed, and Charlie parked in front of the little shop she'd noticed earlier.

As Grant climbed out of the SUV, he surveyed the front of the business with what he guessed to be a home above.

"Charlie," he said, pointing to a small metal box mounted to the corner of the building.

"Is that a CCTV camera?" she asked in reply.

"That'll be my first question," he said, entering the front door to a clanging of bells above his head.

"Be right there, love," came a female voice from the back with an English country accent.

Angie looked around the handful of aisles while Charlie and Grant waited by the counter. After a few moments, a middle-aged lady appeared, wearing an apron dusted with flour.

"Hello there," she greeted them. "How can I help?"

"We were wondering," Grant began, but Charlie took over.

"Does Heather Cartwright live here?" she asked, then added quietly to Grant, "Should probably start there."

"Aye, she does," the woman replied, looking at them blankly.

"May we speak with her?" Charlie continued.

"What for?" the woman asked.

"It's a private matter."

"And who are you three, then?"

"We're private investigators, ma'am," Grant replied, seeing if an American accent held more sway.

"Are you now?" the woman said, not appearing impressed.

"Is Miss Cartwright here, ma'am?" Charlie tried again.

"Aye. I'm Miss Cartwright."

"Oh, then why didn't you say that?" Charlie responded irritably.

"Cos I'm not Heather. She's my sister. I'm Amelia."

"Then can we speak to your sister?" Grant asked, noting Charlie was balling up her fists.

"No."

"Why's that, Amelia?" he responded, getting annoyed himself.

"Cos she's not here."

Grant laughed.

"You two are in a Monty Python skit," Angie chuckled from the corner of the shop.

"Amelia," Grant said pleasantly, "is that a CCTV camera mounted outside your store?"

"Yes."

"Does it record?"

"Yes."

"Could we take a look at the recorded footage from two nights ago?"

Amelia stared at Grant and Charlie, looking like she'd tasted something awful. Grant was about to try another tack, lying that they'd get a warrant from the local authorities to look, but Amelia finally spoke up again.

"This about whatever it was that got nicked from the manor?"

"How do you know about that?" Charlie asked.

Amelia gave her a wry smile. "You're from London, aren't you?"

Charlie nodded.

"This is a tiny village, love. We all know what's going on in Radclive."

"The footage?" Grant asked again.

"Sure. Come back here," the woman said, and a few minutes later, they were sitting in a small office, looking at a computer screen that showed impressively good-quality night vision footage.

Amelia continued her baking in the kitchen, Angie chatting away with her like they were old friends. Tea, coffee, and biscuits were also in process. Grant fast-forwarded from midnight on, based on Charlie's theory that no sensible thief would risk being on the prowl until after the pubs had closed and the traffic had died down. He paused for each vehicle, and she noted the make and registration plate, as she called them. They were both surprised by the camera, which had enough resolution to pick out the letters and numbers. After forty-five minutes, a cup of coffee, and too many biscuits, they had a list of thirteen vehicles.

"Amelia," Grant began, "could you look at these cars and see if you recognize any of them as local residents?"

The woman dusted herself off and stood behind them as Grant moved quickly to each timecode they'd noted. She was able to identify the first five cars, not only saying who each vehicle belonged to, but also approximately how long they'd had the car for, and which family member was likely behind the wheel, although the interiors couldn't be seen clearly in the dark.

"No clue," she said on the sixth vehicle.

"It's a hire car," Charlie noted, pointing to the company sticker on the front of the hood. Circling the license plate number on her list, she took out her phone and stepped into the shop while Grant continued searching with Amelia. After a few minutes, Grant had all but the one car accounted for, which they'd also noted left the village again only thirty-five minutes later.

"Any of these locals the thieving types, Amelia?" Grant asked.

The woman laughed. "I wouldn't leave a beer unattended around most of them, but pinching something from the manor is a different kettle of fish. We don't lock our cars or even our back doors half the time."

"And I assume your sister is a saint," Charlie said, walking back into the office.

Amelia scoffed. "Doubt our mother, God rest her soul, would have used that term, but Heather would wet her knickers if she did anything worse than park on a double yellow."

"In that case," Charlie said, "the hire car was rented to a bloke named Saleh Al-Maawali, under a company called Sunshine Gourmet Imports. It was returned midday yesterday."

Grant opened an internet browser on the computer and searched for the company name. "Who gave you that info? Your man, Froggy?"

"No, he hasn't returned my calls since we got back," Charlie replied. "I think he landed in hot water helping us out. This is another fella at Scotland Yard."

"Another fella with a crush on you?" Grant ribbed.

"Maybe," Charlie grunted, leaning over his shoulder to study the screen. "So, where are these Sunshine people based?"

"Hah! This might work out perfectly," he said, sitting back in the chair. "Sunshine Gourmet Imports are located in Miami."

Charlie squeezed his shoulder. "Looks like you've got someone to visit when you get home."

5

———

The plane droned on at thirty-four thousand feet above the Atlantic Ocean. Grant shifted in his seat as he tried to keep his ass from cramping. Angie dozed in the seat next to him. Her head lolled over onto his shoulder, and he envied her ability to drift off to sleep. After seven hours in the restrictive coach seat, Grant's leg throbbed. He'd been off the Oxycodone for a few weeks, and for the most part, he'd handled the withdrawals well.

Now, though, the damaged muscle in his left leg begged him to do something. If he could walk around, it would help. But the seat-belt sign remained illuminated, thanks to the rocky air the Virgin aircraft was bouncing through.

He arched his back slowly so as not to disturb Angie and fished into the watch pocket of his Levis for the pair of 1000-mg acetaminophen tablets he'd stashed there before the flight. The white pills hit the back of his throat, and Grant swallowed a gulp of water from the bottle he'd bought at the gate.

As his head came back down, he spotted the man at the front of the plane. He was about Grant's age, with dusky skin. Grant thought he looked Caucasian, but his bronze complexion could lead someone to speculate where the man originated.

It wasn't his skin color that troubled Grant, but the man's dark gaze was directed back at him. The stranger was standing at the lavatory between business class and coach. When Grant locked eyes with him, the passenger shifted his stare and moved through the curtain to the front.

Grant straightened up, stirring Angie.

"What's wrong?" she muttered, sensing the change in his demeanor.

"Some guy was just watching us," he murmured.

"Are you sure?" Angie asked, now fully awake. "Where is he?"

"Positive," Grant acknowledged. "He was by the bathrooms."

Angie lifted her head over the seat to scan the forward cabin. "That guy's just waiting for the bathroom."

Grant looked again. An older gentleman stood where the other man had been a moment earlier.

"Not him, Ang. There was another dude there a second ago."

"Where did he go?" she asked.

"Up into first class," Grant noted.

"He was probably just waiting on the john. You're letting your imagination get ahead of you."

Grant shook his head. "I don't think so."

"Who would it be?" Angie questioned.

"I'm not sure. Maybe someone involved with the Bamford jewels."

"What about your father?"

Grant furrowed his brow. "Angie." His tone flattened, like a teacher signaling that the student gave the wrong answer.

"Charlie thought she saw him."

His head shook slowly. "Charlie wanted to see him."

"The Coast Guard didn't find a body," Angie pointed out.

"No, but that's not unusual. The boat exploded. What was left of it settled at the bottom. They didn't even bother to bring it up from that depth."

"You said he was on the top deck, though, right? He could have gotten free."

"The Coast Guard would have found him if he was on the surface. But he could have been sucked down with the yacht."

"But I thought the divers recovered bodies from the wreck."

Grant nodded. "Those were all below deck. Anybody on the top deck probably got picked up by a shark looking for a quick bite."

"Grant!" Angie barked. "Don't talk like that. He was your father."

"For less than a week," Grant reminded her.

"Grant," Angie scolded.

"Look, Keith was a nice enough guy, and I suppose I understand what he and Mom were thinking. But that doesn't change a lot, really. He wasn't around when I was a kid. No more than Mom was around for Charlie. Fuck, they couldn't even tell me I had a sister."

"But Charlie's great," Angie remarked.

"There he is!" Grant blurted out in a loud whisper, motioning with his head toward the front of the aircraft.

Angie looked up to see the individual Grant had spotted earlier. The passenger, who was of average height, appeared from behind the curtain blocking coach passengers from those in business class.

"I want to find out who this guy is," Grant said.

"What? Are you planning to barge up into first class and interrogate him?"

"Why not?" he demanded. Angie caught his wrist as he mindlessly massaged his aching leg muscle.

"Because you are getting grumpy."

"I'm not—oww!"

Angie released the hand that had just squeezed Grant's left leg muscle.

"You're hurting, and you're grumpy."

"It's this fucking coach seat. I should have splurged for first class."

Angie smiled at him. "Did I tell you how proud I am that you're getting off the oxy?"

"It's a blast," he grunted between gritted teeth.

"I know," she stated, massaging his leg more gently now. "Look, your spy left. He was just checking to see if the bathroom was free yet."

Grant glanced up again to see the man was no longer there.

"You really think Charlie's just seeing things?" Angie asked.

"I figure she saw someone, but let's be honest. Most of the men at Keith's funeral were pasty, white, middle-aged British guys. How easy would it be to catch a glimpse of one and mistake him for another?"

Angie snickered. "I would like to see you tell her that."

"Shit, she'd clobber me," Grant quipped.

"What do you think about this Bamford guy?"

Grant shrugged. "I think he might have stolen his own jewels. When he discovered insurance wouldn't cover them, he needed to find a way to recover them." Grant made air quotes at the word "recover."

"He paid you upfront, though." Angie continued to rub his leg, helping Grant lose focus on his discomfort.

"The hoity-toity Brits don't want to lose face. Old Bamford still considers himself some noble. He'd go into debt trying to look like he hadn't ripped off his own jewels."

"Why take his money, then?" she asked.

"It's still money," he reminded her. "Besides, I've been wanting to get away from the divorce and custody cases. Something like this could pan into bigger opportunities. With my and Charlie's backgrounds, we could build a global recovery company."

"It is nice to see you getting your feet back under you." Angie grinned.

"What do you mean?"

"There's a fire in your eyes," she explained. "I haven't seen it in a while. Not since before the shooting."

"You're saying I've just been a useless bum?"

"No, but connecting with Charlie has been good for you."

Grant nodded reluctantly. He had to confess that as he'd gotten to know his sister, he relished the idea of a sibling. As a kid, it had been lonely with just him and his mother. During the school year, he had his friends, but he'd longed for a brother to bond with. Never once had he imagined a brother would actually be a sister.

"I want to know who that guy is," Grant admitted, bringing himself back to the curious traveler he'd spotted watching them. Or rather, watching him.

"What if I go scope him out?" Angie suggested.

"It could be dangerous," Grant noted.

"On a plane? He had to go through security. The only thing another person can do on a plane is bore you to death, talking about their trip."

Grant didn't point out that there were plenty of people who could hurt her with just their bare hands. Not many could overpower all the passengers, but Grant was only worried about Angie.

She studied his face. "Look, I'll just take a look. I'm far less conspicuous than you are. And I'm a ton less grumpy, which means more people will talk to me than to you."

"Fine," he relented.

Angie's mouth turned up into a half-smile as she unfastened her seatbelt and moved toward the front of the plane. Grant twisted around to check on the flight attendants. All three for the coach section were away from the dividing curtain. He assumed there were at least two or three in business class, but Angie was right. She'd be less likely to be noticed right away than Grant. After all, he resembled a cross between a rugged cop and an out-of-work beach bum. Angie just looked like a legal assistant on her way to talk to her boss.

He watched as she disappeared behind the curtain. Nervously, Grant counted off the seconds as he watched the curtain sway with the vibrations of the plane.

"Ladies and gentlemen, we are beginning our final approach to Miami," the muffled voice of the pilot declared over the plane's public address system.

The fabric swept to the side, and Angie shuffled down the aisle toward Grant. As she buckled her seatbelt, Grant stared at her.

"Well?" he asked finally when she'd settled into her chair.

"He's sleeping," she remarked.

Grant raised an eyebrow. "Sleeping?"

"Laying his head back with his eyes closed. He didn't look like he was interested in anything but that."

Grant almost sighed. He didn't think he was wrong, but if Angie was correct, the man in first class was more relaxed than someone supposedly spying on him.

The plane groaned as it began its descent.

"Please raise your tray tables," the flight attendant requested as she swooped down the aisle.

Grant secured the tray in front of him. "Just sleeping?"

Angie shrugged.

"Folks, we'll be making our final descent now," the pilot announced. "Flight attendants, please prepare the cabin for arrival."

Grant leaned his head back as the lights in the cabin dimmed. With his eyes closed, he thought about the Bamford case, the man in the front of the plane, and his father.

When the wheels screeched against the runway, he opened his eyes, having discovered no answers. Seconds later, the plane slowed to a taxi, and the pilot steered the craft toward the gate.

People began moving around, and Grant was itching to get to his feet. His left leg ached, but mostly, he wanted to get off the aircraft before the man in first class got away.

However, as he stared at the twenty rows of seats between him and business class, he realized that was going to be a long shot.

After an interminable time, the crowd started moving forward. Angie and Grant pulled their carry-on bags from the overhead compartment before shuffling along with the line of other passengers.

"Come on," Grant urged under his breath.

"What is it?" Angie asked, turning to stare at her boyfriend's exasperated face.

"I'd like to get off the plane," he replied.

"Babe, he'll be in baggage claim," she stated.

Grant tilted his head to look at her. *Damn, she's right.* He visibly relaxed, and Angie smiled at him.

"I'm exhausted," she remarked. "It's like 8:30, but I feel like I've been up for days."

"London time is like almost two in the morning."

She yawned in response. "I'm too old for these late nights," she quipped as the pair reached the sky bridge.

A minute later, the couple poured out into the Miami International Airport. The pair followed the crowd to United States Immigration. Grant began scanning the area for the man, but there was no sign of him.

I should have checked his seat on the way by.

He shook his head. What would he have found there? Probably the trash from the snacks the crew had passed out.

"Let's get to baggage claim," he urged Angie, grabbing her by the hand as soon as they'd been cleared by the immigration officials.

The two hurried down the escalator with the rest of the passengers. When they reached the conveyor belts, Grant paced around the tracks, looking at faces.

The man from first class was nowhere to be seen.

6

Sitting in heavy traffic on her way back to Westminster, Charlie wondered why she'd insisted on dropping Grant and Angie at the airport herself. They could have taken the Tube and been there in the same amount of time, saving her from bumper-to-bumper hell. But she knew the answer to that question. It delayed her facing the empty flat, Stanley aside. Her father was gone, and now so was her brother, leaving a void in her life that felt like a gaping hole.

After an hour and ten minutes on the M4 and then the A4 into Central London, Charlie finally made it home. She parked the SUV in a permitted space on Morpeth Terrace, the narrow street between the back of her building and Westminster Cathedral, adding the permit cost to the list of things she needed to find out about. A list that was growing at an alarming rate. The task of discovering, understanding, and then managing everything her father had always handled was daunting, and making her feel like a privileged kid.

Locking the car, she walked toward the arched entranceway to the historic building, but, glancing at her watch, slowed to a stop. It was late afternoon, or early evening. Charlie's current viewpoint had her spinning around and walking past the Jaguar to Francis

Street, where she turned left. Ten minutes later, after two more turns and a stroll past Westminster School's playing field, she entered The Royal Oak pub on the corner of Rutherford and Regency Streets. There were several fancier bars and gastropubs closer to the flat, but The Royal Oak was more her style. A casual, traditional watering hole dating back to the late 1800s.

"Charlie," the bartender greeted her with a nod and an Irish accent. "Been a while."

"Hey, Liam. I was in America for a bit," she replied, taking a seat at the bar.

"What yer having?"

"Maker's and Coke," she replied, and Liam raised an eyebrow.

"Yeah, yeah, don't give me any stick," she added. "I've had a shitty week."

Liam grinned. "I like having you come by, is all, and I believe it started with Maker's and Coke last time."

Charlie rolled her eyes. "It started with that wanker spilling my Maker's and Coke."

"I have no doubt," Liam said as he poured her drink while still grinning from ear to ear. "But the boss'll make it more than a six-month ban if you get to brawling again."

"It wasn't a brawl," Charlie complained, looking around to make sure no one was overhearing their conversation.

It didn't matter. She recognized every face in the place, so they all knew, anyway. A few raised a glass in her direction, and she nodded in return. Liam slid her drink across the bar.

"Don't suppose it was, at that. Fella went down like a sack of potatoes."

Charlie held up her glass. "*Sláinte.*"

"*Sláinte is táinte,*" Liam replied, completing the traditional Irish toast.

She ordered a basket of chips and chatted with Liam when he was between serving customers. After a second whisky, Charlie switched to straight Coca-Cola and moved to the end stool to make room for more patrons. Shooting the breeze with the bartender was the distraction she needed, but he soon became more occupied as the place filled up. A young woman joined him in serving drinks, taking over Charlie's end of the bar.

Charlie's mind wandered, finding its way back to her father and his funeral. The glimpse of the man in the trees was already a vague recollection that refused to stay in focus. She knew from her police work that memory was an unreliable tool—even for her, who'd been trained to lock in observations. A person's imagination was quick to fill in missing details and omit others based on outside comments and expectations of the scenario. It was not uncommon for eyewitnesses to have no idea what color jacket a suspect wore until a red coat was brought up, spurring their memory to recall—or imagine—a red coat.

"You look like you could use some company," a man's voice came from beside her, accompanied by a warm waft of beer breath.

"Not interested," she replied without turning.

More beer breath and a laugh emanated from the man. "That's because you don't know me yet, love," he persisted. "Note the time. I bet yer in ten minutes, we'll be getting along like Romeo and Juliet."

"They both end up dead," Charlie replied.

The man laughed again. "They did?"

Charlie could see him in the mirrored backdrop between the bottles of booze behind the bar. He was a good-looking guy who undoubtedly had success, with his cheesy lines and carefully quaffed hair, but she wasn't the easy mark he was hoping for.

"Move on, mate," she said, trying to keep her voice civil.

The guy banged into Charlie, and from the way he turned around, she figured someone else had knocked him. She took a deep breath and told herself to stay calm.

"Be careful," her suitor snapped.

"Fuck you," came a reply, and Charlie was bumped into the bar as she felt the two men shoving each other behind her back.

She glanced up and saw Liam looking at her with an eyebrow raised.

"I didn't do anything," she said, but her words were drowned out by the loud chatter in the pub.

A body slammed her against the bar this time, and she pushed back, whirling around and dropping from the stool. The two men were facing off, just out of arm's reach of each other, and the crowd around them had stepped back. Several voices told them to knock it off, and a couple more encouraged them to get it over with. Both men were taller than Charlie and outweighed her by a large margin. She recognized Romeo from his reflection in the mirror. The other guy was lean, with long dark hair held in a man bun atop his square-jawed head.

Choosing Romeo, who was now pointing a threatening finger at his opponent, she grabbed his outstretched wrist and twisted as she pulled down. He yelped at the pain in every joint, and Charlie spun him by the shoulder and kicked the back of his knee. Romeo crumbled to the floor. From behind her, she sensed Man Bun stepping in to either attack her, help her, or take advantage of his foe while he was down. Whatever his intentions were, Charlie didn't care. With a quick thrust, she caught him in the solar plexus with her elbow and heard the air rush from his lungs in a pained wheeze.

"Charlie!" she heard above a mixture of cheers and gasps from the crowd.

Liam's voice made her look up, and she released Romeo's wrist like a dog dropping the slipper they'd stolen.

"I broke up the fight," she said as the two men moaned and groaned on the floor.

"She did that all right!" one of the locals shouted. "I'm buying that girl a drink."

Several others cheered and echoed their intentions to keep Charlie's glass full all evening.

"Bloody hell," Liam grumbled as he began shepherding the brawlers out the door.

Charlie sat back down on her stool, trying her best to be polite and smile at the people slapping her on the back and shouting at the barmaid for drinks. It took a while for the dust to settle and the place to return to normal, but as soon as it did, Charlie figured she should leave.

"What do I owe you?" she asked Liam when he came down to her end of the bar.

He laughed. "I owe you three more Maker's and Cokes. Your tab's been cleared and then some."

Charlie managed a smile. "Then make sure the boss knows I stopped this fight for you. I want to be able to come back and claim my credit."

"I didn't plan on mentioning it at all," Liam replied. "But I know a few of the club managers around here. I'd be happy to give you a recommendation as a bouncer."

The look on his face told Charlie he was serious.

"Now you're not a copper anymore," he added.

"Thanks, but I have a job," she said, leaving a ten-pound note on the bar as a tip.

"Ta, love. What is it you're doing now?" he asked.

"Private investigator," she replied, saying the words aloud for the first time. "With my brother."

"I didn't know you had a brother," Liam said as Charlie made her way into the crowd.

"Neither did I until a few weeks ago!" she shouted over her shoulder.

It was still daylight outside, but the temperature had cooled into the mid-sixties. Charlie instinctively looked around to make sure the threat had cleared—meaning, either of the two guys who'd been ejected and might hold a grudge. Rutherford Street was busy with pedestrians, but she couldn't see anyone lurking, so she set off for home, where Stanley would be impatiently waiting for his dinner. And she would finally have to face an empty flat.

Forcing herself to think about Bamford and his missing necklace, Charlie moved along with other pedestrians, most of whom were either on their way home from the office or heading out for dinner. As she crossed the street to turn onto Vincent Square, she nonchalantly glanced back to see if anyone was following. One man caught her attention as he checked for traffic before crossing Rutherford. He was in his forties, wearing a lightweight jacket, jeans, and a flat cap. He definitely wasn't either of the two men thrown out of the pub, but she made a mental note to keep an eye on him.

Passing the playing field, she checked again, but there were too many people between them. Or he'd just happened to turn shortly after her and had now gone on with his evening, heading a different way. Her mind drifted back to Bamford and what her next steps could be while Grant chased down the Miami lead. She wondered if an old contact in the Flying Squad group at Scotland Yard would still speak with her. The department, nicknamed Sweeney Todd in Cockney rhyming slang with squad and made famous in TV shows and movies, handled serious, high-value robbery cases. They'd have a watch list of known jewel thieves, so she'd try reaching her tomorrow. The worst that could happen would be the woman ignoring her call.

Reaching the corner of Vincent and Rochester Row, Charlie continued straight, then crossed to the left-hand side, giving her the opportunity to look back down the road. She spotted Flat Cap. He crossed over before reaching Rochester, and Charlie nipped into the doorway of a business under renovation. Peeking around the brick-work, she watched the man turn on Rochester and disappear from view. Coming out of the doorway, she walked back to the street corner and checked he'd not doubled back. The man continued without as much as a brief look over his shoulder.

Charlie laughed to herself. After being chased around the Florida Keys and having a mysterious man show up at her father's funeral, she was becoming paranoid. Walking on, she took another five minutes to turn left along Francis Street, where the crowd had thinned, then right on Morpeth Terrace. Wishing she'd eaten more at the pub, she remembered the cupboards in the flat were still shy of food, so she took out her phone and thought about what she could have delivered quickly without costing a fortune. Pizza sounded perfect, but she knew she'd appreciate a healthier choice when her stomach ached in the morning.

What hit her, she had no idea, but the back of her legs suddenly screamed in pain, and she buckled to the ground. Charlie's first reaction was to defend herself against a second blow, but a knee landed in the small of her back, pinning her to the sidewalk and knocking the air from her lungs.

"Where's the necklace?" a man's voice growled from above her.

"Good question," Charlie gasped, wondering why he'd think she'd know.

"Don't play dumb. You're in on it with Bamford," he said, and Charlie took a moment to process his words, noting a hint of a regional accent.

"He hired us to recover it," she groaned, wriggling to get herself free, but the man was too heavy.

"We know that's a cover-up," he responded, his knee digging in harder as he reached to secure her arms. "Where is it?" the man repeated.

Keeping one hand free, Charlie swung her elbow up, but hit the man's thigh with no effect. He was struggling to grip her right arm as she could feel something solid in his hand, presumably whatever he'd used to club her. Her left leg was also pinned, but with his right knee in her back, her right leg wasn't restrained.

She whipped her heel, nailing him in the back. The force rocked him forward, which dug his knee in even harder, but she knew he'd be slightly off-balance. Swinging her elbow again, Charlie rocked the man left, shifting his weight to the hand holding her left arm to the sidewalk.

Pushing off the ground with her right hand, she was able to draw her right leg up enough to use her knee as a lever. She roared, putting every ounce of energy into throwing her assailant aside. His weight shifted, and Charlie started to roll with him when the club gave her a glancing blow across the top of the head.

She dropped limply to the sidewalk, her world spinning in circles and her stomach threatening to heave. His body was gone from on top of her, but Charlie willed her hands to cover her head, readying to defend against the next strike. But nothing came. She rolled to her side and saw no one.

It took a few moments for the nausea to pass, and she sat up. The street was empty of pedestrians. He couldn't have gotten far. It would be easy to hide behind parked vehicles or hop the wall to the playground of the Catholic prep school across the road by the cathedral. Charlie struggled to her feet. It had been a clumsy attack, but the man had certainly caught her off-guard.

Slowly making her way to the front door of the building, she ran over what he'd said in her mind. Plenty of people had faked the theft of their own valuables, but that made no sense with Bamford. Insurance wouldn't pay a penny without a police report. Which further begged the question of who had sent the thug after her?

She'd never gotten a look at her attacker, but Charlie tried her best to recall the features of the man wearing the flat cap. Her gut told her it was him.

7

____

Grant stood in the entryway to his mother's house. *No, it was his house now.* Angie had already crashed out after their long day, but Grant had wanted to collect his dog, Wrench, from the neighbor who'd been looking after him. With apologies for the late hour, he'd walked back home, unsure who was more excited to see each other, man or dog.

Wrench trotted into the kitchen to inspect his bowl. He returned a few seconds later and stared at Grant from the door. Apparently, the dog had already adjusted to the fact that Grant's mother wasn't home. Grant hadn't yet allowed himself the time to process their new circumstances. *When could, or should, he do that?* He hadn't even made it to the funeral in Key Largo, which already felt like a lifetime ago. Well, he went, but then Charlie arrived, followed by a slew of gunmen, and he hadn't made it back inside to the service.

Of course, what had he missed? The funeral director hadn't known Fiona Wolfe. He'd have talked about how she had friends at the salon or around town. There'd have been talk about how she enjoyed gardening or helping down at the community center. Nothing would have been said about Keith Greene, Charlie, or the fact that she'd once been an American spy.

Hell, the funeral director might not have known her, but then neither had Grant. As he stared at Wrench, he wondered if his mother had ever confided in the dog. Perhaps that's why Wrench seemed so nonplussed.

He's a dog.

Grant walked into the kitchen and pulled a cold Iguana Bait beer from the refrigerator. He cracked the can and walked to his mother's bedroom. He needed to adjust to the idea that this was now his home. He'd lived here off and on since he'd graduated high school, but he'd always considered it temporary.

He stared at a pile of papers on the bed. Grant and Angie had begun going through some things before the funeral—before the chaos that Charlie had brought with her to the States.

It wasn't Charlie's fault. The blame fell directly on their parents.

Still, he needed to sort out his mother's financial records. He had no idea how much she owed on the house or even how much money was in her bank account. It was a task he'd put off, thinking that it would be something he could tackle after the stress of the funeral.

So much for that plan.

He picked up the pile of pages and carried them with his beer to the kitchen. Wrench stood beside the empty food bowl and stared at him.

"Fine, give me a sec," Grant told the dog as he set the beer and papers on the table. Finding an almost empty bag of Blue Buffalo kibble in the pantry, he looked down at the Wrench. "You're going to need more food."

Wrench only stared at him as if to remind Grant that it was his job to get that.

"Right, I'll get some later." Grant dumped the cup of food into the stainless-steel bowl.

Wrench dove nose-first into the bowl and gulped a bite. Grant noted that the dog always ate like he hadn't had anything in a week.

When he returned to the table, he took a swallow of beer and flipped through the pages. His mother had a strange way of keeping her important papers. It was something that had always annoyed him. In retrospect, it made more sense. He'd searched offices and homes during investigations, and the more organized a suspect was, the easier it was to find the evidence he needed. He wondered if Fiona Wolfe's apparent disorganization was, in fact, a method to hide vital information.

He found the latest bank statement. Fiona had $2,735 in her checking account and only about half of that in her savings accounts. Grant started stacking papers into various categories: bank, house, car, and retirement.

When he ran out of papers, he went to the bedroom and returned a few minutes later with another stack. Wrench, finding the task boring and pointless, stretched out on the tile floor. When Grant returned, the dog lifted his head long enough to determine that he wasn't about to be fed again.

Grant finished his beer and stared out the window at the lights flickering on the canal. With four stacks of paper, he still hadn't determined much of anything yet. Of course, he'd taken the time to sort the mess, but he hadn't read past the current bank account balances.

His phone buzzed, and he glanced at the screen. Tony Macabee.

"Mac, sorry it's so late. How's it going?" Grant asked.

"That's okay. I'm still up and just saw you called. You back from across the pond?"

Mac had been a fellow deputy with Grant. Unlike Grant, the Monroe County Sheriff still employed him.

"Yeah, just this evening."

"Were you calling to pay me back with that fishing trip?" Mac asked.

Grant chuckled. Mac was one of those Keys people who had figured out that the best way to have a boat was to have a friend who had a boat. That worked out for Grant, too. He'd hit Mac up when he needed something like a license plate number or an address to a subject he was investigating in exchange for a trip on the water. Secretly, Grant preferred Mac's company, anyway, so it was a win-win for him.

"All you have to do is come on by," Grant told him. "You know I'm always ready to hit the water."

"So, that's not why you called?"

"No, but come out this weekend if you're off work. We can run out and find some tuna."

"I'd love to, but I'm on six days this week. How about next weekend?"

"Let's do it," Grant agreed. "But I need a bit of info asap if possible."

Mac groaned a bit. "One day, you'll get me in trouble."

"But it won't be today."

"Yeah, yeah. Whatcha got, Grant?"

"There's a guy I saw on the plane back. I think he was following me."

"What do you know about him?"

"He was in first class. Think you could get me a manifest?"

Mac laughed. "You're kidding, right?"

"Not really," Grant admitted.

"You know that's not even remotely possible. I'd have to get a warrant for that kind of information."

"Damn, I guessed as much. What about running anything on a company called Sunshine Gourmet Imports?"

"That's more likely," Mac admitted. "Hold on while I wake up my work laptop."

Grant heard keystrokes through the phone.

"They don't have a big digital footprint," Mac told him after a minute or so. "I doubt I've got anything more than you'd find in an internet search, to be honest, but I have an address. It's odd. It might take a deeper dive. Some of these foreign companies bury their details in layers. I'm sure it's a tax thing. You know, these companies that come in to take our money without paying taxes."

"Just give me the address," Grant said, ignoring his friend's rant. "I'll go have a look."

Grant jotted the street number down as Mac recited it to him.

"Next week, then?" Mac asked.

"Yeah. If you want to bring a sleeping bag, we can camp out."

"Or we can come back and drink some beer over at Sharkey's."

Grant laughed. "Whatever, man," he replied before hanging up.

Wrench heard him end the call and rose to his feet with a long stretch. Grant stood up and walked to the front door, opening it. The dog bolted down the steps in the dark, and Grant turned back to the table of papers. He picked up the empty beer can and shook it.

It was almost midnight. He could crack open another beer and work for another hour. Or he could call it a night. The latter sounded better. He stacked up the papers, keeping the categories separate by placing a blank piece of paper crosswise between the groups. Turning off the kitchen light, Grant opened the front door and watched Wrench wearily plod up the steps.

"Bedtime, buddy?"

Wrench meandered toward the bedroom, taking one glance back to make sure Grant was following.

8

______

Charlie's head hurt. So did the bruises on her back and the scrapes on her knees. She'd settled for a bowl of cereal the night before after locking herself safely in the flat, and now repeated the meal for breakfast while she drank coffee and thought about her next move. A small, emergency carton of UHT pasteurized milk in the back of the cupboard had saved her, but grocery shopping needed to be a priority. Yet, her mind was stuck on Bamford and his missing necklace.

After pushing the empty bowl aside, Charlie slid her laptop closer and scrolled through the search results on the screen. The Bamford family produced endless results, mostly about Benedict Bamford, the earl, a title Cecil would inherit when his father passed away. Benedict's wife had died of cancer fifteen years ago, and, according to Wikipedia, the earl had two sons. Charlie's interest piqued, and she typed in a search for Edmund Metcalfe, the second son mentioned. From a handful of news articles, it appeared he was the illegitimate offspring of the earl's tryst with a maid at the manor. He used his mother's surname.

Results for Edmund were far fewer than the legitimate Bamfords, mixed amongst hits of multiple individuals with the same name, but several articles on one subject stood out. The earl's lovechild had been arrested, convicted, and sentenced for embezzling money from a dot-com company he'd formed with two partners. Charlie couldn't find any reference to the man after the fuss over the trial had died down. She stopped scrolling and searched for "Edmund Metcalfe release."

According to a handful of mentions on various internet sites, none of which Charlie recognized as being affiliated with major press, Edmund was set free after serving nine months of his seven-year sentence.

"Something's fishy here, Stanley," she announced to the cat, who ignored her.

Picking up her phone, she texted Julian Haines, her friend at Scotland Yard who'd run the rental plate for her. While she waited for his reply, Charlie dialed the cell number of her contact at the Flying Squad.

"Izzy," she said in surprise when the call was answered.

"Charlie Greene," came a London accent. "What have you been up to these past few months? Last I recall, you owed me a drink or three."

Great, Charlie thought. She'd been hoping the woman had forgotten about the last favor.

"I'm sure you know I'm no longer with the force."

"Yeah. Raw deal, I'd say," Izzy replied. "The upstairs crowd are overly sensitive about that shit these days. How were you to know the bloke had a dodgy back, right?"

Charlie scoffed. "And a ferret of a lawyer. Once the bastard got his teeth into me, he wouldn't let go."

An awkward silence fell over the line.

"What are you up to now?" Izzy asked, saving Charlie from having to discuss her dismissal any further.

"PI work. Turns out I have a brother in America. He and I have teamed up."

"That's great," Izzy said. "No problem getting the PI license, then?"

Charlie balked. She hadn't gone beyond thinking about looking into an official license. Mainly because she knew her dismissal from the Metropolitan Police wouldn't help her application slide through without a major hitch.

"Application is in," she lied, hoping her friend wouldn't take the time to check.

"Great," Izzy replied, but Charlie knew her response was dripping with doubt. "I have a feeling you're not calling to catch up on those drinks, Charlie," Izzy continued. "What can I help you with?"

"Thanks, Izzy. I would like to pay you back when we have the time, but yeah, we have a case with a missing jewel. I was hoping you could give me a few names to look at."

Izzy sighed. "Am I to assume the person you're working for doesn't want to involve the police?"

"Correct."

"Is the gem hot?"

"Not to my knowledge, Izzy, or I wouldn't have called you. Or taken the case," she added, then hesitated. Charlie couldn't believe they hadn't discussed that possibility. Bamford had told them it was a family heirloom, and they hadn't questioned his word. But perhaps they should have.

"What sort of jewel are we talking about?" Izzy asked.

"Antique necklace. Bloody great big ruby in it."

"Other gems?"

"Yeah. Sapphires, I think. All pretty big themselves, but the ruby's a whopper."

"Antique stuff is tricky to fence. Women want to wear their vintage Tiffany, which is hard to do if it's on our recently pinched list. Major named pieces can move amongst private collectors, but they're few and far between. If some rich bloke buys Charlemagne's amulet, he usually wants everyone to know it."

Charlie didn't know what Charlemagne's amulet was exactly, but she got the point.

"Okay, so what if it's the gem that's the real value?"

"If the ruby's as big as you say, then it would usually have provenance, and that adds value," Izzy explained. "Gems that size are rare and get noticed. But if the piece was put together from several antique gems and settings from different periods, that could be different. The Nazis did all kinds of things with the gems they stole during the war. Their provenance is what you might call tainted. Most people aren't keen on wearing jewelry taken from condemned souls during the Holocaust."

Charlie chewed the information over for a second. Bamford hadn't mentioned the necklace's history, but they hadn't asked, either.

"Okay, so with the little I've been able to give you," Charlie said, "any names spring to mind who might be good for this job, or fence a necklace like this?"

Izzy laughed. "A month ago, I would have said yes, but Jimmy Fingers dropped dead of a heart attack outside a Chinese takeaway on Battersea Park Road."

"Jimmy Fingers? Seriously?"

Izzy laughed again. "I know, right? James Finch, known for the past forty years as Jimmy Fingers. This would be right up his street, but unless it happened more than four weeks ago, he didn't do it."

"Anyone else spring to mind?" Charlie asked.

"Not really. What was security like?" Izzy asked.

"Practically nonexistent."

"Well, that opens the door to anyone. I'd start with whoever had knowledge and access," Izzy suggested.

"We questioned the staff," Charlie replied. "I can't say anyone stood out as likely."

"Family?" Izzy asked. "Look for the dodgy friend or relative who dropped by recently."

"Yeah, working that angle now," Charlie said. "Let me know if anyone springs to mind, or you hear about a ruby the size of Wembley Stadium showing up."

"Will do," Izzy replied. "And that's four drinks you owe me now, Charlie."

"I'll pay up soon. Thanks, Izzy."

Charlie hung up and realized a text had come in while they'd been talking. The message held an address, which she opened in her maps app. Llangollen was two hundred miles away in North Wales. She zoomed into the route and noticed Buckingham wasn't too far east of the M40. She quickly discovered that selecting Bamford Manor as an additional stop would take twenty more minutes, but would hopefully give her the opportunity to casually quiz Cecil more about the necklace. While not mentioning to him that her final destination was his stepbrother's house in Wales.

Charlie typed "thank you" and sent the reply to Julian at Scotland Yard.

Leaving London on a Friday could be a nightmare as people scattered to their country homes, family visits, or weekend jaunts, so Charlie hastily grabbed a few things in case she had an overnight stay. Stanley dropped from his chair, did a lap of the auto-feeder she set on the kitchen floor, then looked up at her in disdain.

"Sod off. It's work, and you don't really care if I'm here or not," Charlie told him as she grabbed her bag.

Stanley sauntered away with his tail in the air, giving her an unobstructed view of his exposed butt.

"Yeah, love you, too," she muttered before rushing downstairs to the Jaguar.

What began as an overcast, dreary day slowly improved to partly cloudy and mid-60s. Hardly the Florida Keys, but a pleasant English early summer day, and Charlie was happy it wasn't raining for her drive. It took two hours to reach Radclive, and as she drove into the valley, sunshine bathed the pretty village, lifting her spirits to one of guarded optimism.

Which were soon dashed when she parked at Bamford Manor and met Braithwaite at the door, where he informed her that Cecil was away for the day.

"Is Heather Cartwright here by any chance?" she asked, hoping the stop wouldn't be a complete waste.

"She is, miss," Braithwaite replied, and his neutral tone left her wondering whether he'd let her in the door or not.

But Charlie was never one to worry about such details. "Perfect. I need to have a chat with her, and I'd kill for a cup of coffee," she said, sidestepping past the butler into the vestibule.

She paused inside and waited. Braithwaite closed the door.

"This way, miss," he said in the same vanilla tone, and led her to the sitting room where they'd met Bamford on their first visit. "I'll see if Miss Cartwright is available."

Charlie stood by one of the tall windows and gazed at a small river winding through the bottom of the pasture beyond the garages and staff quarters. After a few minutes, she heard a voice from the doorway.

"You wanted to see me?"

Charlie turned and saw a woman she intuitively knew was Amelia Cartwright's sister. They shared the same round face and slightly plump but shapely figure. Unlike her sister, Heather showed no signs of gray in her hair, which she'd pulled back in a disheveled ponytail, and Charlie decided she was a few years younger than Amelia.

"Hello, Heather. We popped in the shop to see you the other day, but you were out."

The woman stood in the doorway clutching her hands together as though she were terrified of setting foot inside the room. She didn't respond. Charlie noticed she wore no makeup at all, her pleasant features stopping just shy of what most would consider pretty.

"As a matter of routine, we're talking with all the staff about Monday night," Charlie continued.

Heather didn't move or speak.

"Would you like to come in and sit down?" Charlie asked, indicating one of the sofas.

The woman timidly walked over and sat down, carefully perching on the edge of the seat.

"We have to start with the standard stuff, I'm afraid," Charlie began. "So, can you tell me where you were on Monday night?"

"Home," Heather replied, as though it was madness to think of being anywhere else.

It was painfully clear to Charlie that Heather Cartwright couldn't pinch a slice of bread from her employer, let alone an antique necklace worth more than she'd make in her lifetime. Either that, or she was a shoo-in for an Oscar as best actress. Which Charlie doubted.

Braithwaite returned with a tray of coffee and biscuits, which he placed on the coffee table.

"Thank you, Mr. Braithwaite," Charlie said. "Would you mind staying for a few moments as I have a couple of questions for you both?"

The man took a few paces back and stood beside the sofa. Charlie sighed. Maybe this was how these people lived their lives, but the perpetual awkwardness was driving her crazy.

"Okay. What can either of you tell me about the stolen necklace?"

Two pairs of eyes widened, and Braithwaite's mouth dropped slightly open.

"I beg your pardon, miss?"

Charlie thought over her question. "Shit. Sorry. I wasn't asking what you'd done with the necklace, I was asking what you knew of its history," she clarified. "But if you did pinch it, I'd appreciate you telling me that, too."

Charlie smiled, and they both visibly relaxed. At least compared to their prior levels of not being relaxed at all.

"It's a family heirloom passed down through generations dating back to the 19th century," Braithwaite said in what sounded to Charlie like a well-rehearsed and repeated speech. "It was brought to England by the current earl's grandfather, Theodore Bamford, who was a captain in the Royal Navy."

"Brought from where?" Charlie interrupted before the butler could ramble on.

Braithwaite looked at her blankly, and for a moment, she thought she'd broken his ability to play back historical verbiage about the family.

"From his naval travels is all we know," the man said, sounding defeated at being stumped for a better narrative.

It struck Charlie as strange that a necklace as valuable as the one stolen from the house remained of unknown origin. Surely, during the appraisal process for insurance, this would have been researched, and the style, craftsmanship, and gem quality been narrowed down to a region and time period. Regardless, the butler didn't seem to know, and she was wasting time.

"Can I get the coffee to go?" she asked, ready to be on her way. "And the keys to the garage?" she added as a fun idea came to mind.

9

The windows were down on the 1996 Honda Del Sol. The once candy-red finish lost its shimmer in the early 2000s, and by 2010, the intense Florida sun had faded the red paint, leaving speckles of white. Now, there was more white than red on the car, and Grant considered having it painted to bring it back to its splendor. But it would cost him a grand at the body shop, and it would do nothing more than slap lipstick on a pig. The little car would continue to miss if he skipped up to fourth gear too fast, and the air conditioner wouldn't work if the RPMs climbed above 2000.

Grant glanced at the passenger seat to see Wrench hanging his head out the open window. With how excited the brown lab mix had been to see Grant the night before, he didn't have the heart to leave him at the house while he traveled up to Miami. The dog kept his face in the wind as they continued north, letting the breeze flap his lips and tongue. It was clear that the dog was smiling.

Grant slowed on Highway 836 to make a left on NW 27th Street. Given the part of Miami he was driving into, Grant appreciated Wrench operating as a security system for the Honda. The alarm, which Grant got in 1996 when he bought the car brand new, had crapped out like the air and CD player. However, anyone who wanted to steal the Del Sol might think twice if they saw the big brown mutt standing guard.

While he should have tackled more of Fiona's paperwork, Grant was keener to start digging into the Bamford case. Before he did that, though, he spent two hours this morning compiling the pictures he'd taken of Clayton Thompson for his wife, Olivia. None of the photos were flattering of Clayton, mostly showing him leaving a motel in Marathon with a CrossFit instructor. Grant had to wonder what a fitness nut like this woman saw in the thirty-five-pound overweight Clayton. Grant didn't think the man had seen the inside of a gym, much less a CrossFit class, since his twenties. But he emailed the photos to Olivia along with an invoice.

Grant hated domestic cases. If this Bamford thing worked out, perhaps he could get out of the divorce game and focus on something far more interesting.

He turned west on North River Drive after crossing over the Miami River. It was difficult for him to reconcile that this dumpy section of waterfront was only an hour from Key Largo. On the whole, Grant preferred to avoid Miami. The city reminded him of a drain that let all the scum and shit wash through it. The section of riverfront warehousing on the edge of the Allapattah neighborhood made him think of a clump of hair that just wouldn't wash through the strainer.

Scrapyards lined one side of the street, while rundown buildings and overgrown lots filled with old excess equipment that someone had parked in the late nineties stretched along the opposite side of the street. Nestled between a mostly vacant lot and one wrapped in chain-link fencing that drooped down like the bags under an over-the-road trucker's eyes was a small red and white concrete building. One overhead door on the front was closed, and an office jutted out the front of the small building with a single window and a red entry door. The only signs on the business were a large placard reading the address "2901 N River Dr" and a "Please call 305-223-4699 for deliveries."

The address matched the one Grant had found for Sunshine

Gourmet Imports. The place would be easy to miss. The business had no cars out front, and if it weren't for the fresh paint on the exterior and doors, Grant might have thought it was vacant.

He checked the time. It was just past noon.

Maybe they went to lunch.

He pulled into the lot, anyway. "Stay here," he ordered Wrench.

The dog sat in the passenger seat and stared at Grant. Even if he wanted to jump out the window, the dog was fastened into the seat with a leash connected to the black tactical vest he wore and the car's seat belt buckle. During his days on the sheriff's department, Grant saw three car accidents in which the humans all survived, but their canine companions didn't. In each case, the dogs may well have survived if they'd been buckled in.

Grant got out of the car and walked to the door. The front window was just at his eye level, and he peeked in to see a computer screen glowing on a desk. No one ever turned their computers off.

He tried the door. It was locked. His knuckles rapped on the metal. No one came to answer it, so Grant tried again. Nothing.

With a quick glance back, he checked on Wrench, who stared out the open window at him. "Watch the front, boy," he told the dog. "If anyone comes, honk."

Wrench responded by watching Grant with more enthusiasm than Grant ever watched anything.

"Anyone there!" Grant shouted as he walked to the overhead garage door. When he beat his fist on it, the steel panels clanged in their tracks. After no one answered, he tried to lift the door by the handle. It budged an inch before stopping. Someone had secured the latch on the inside. Grant considered how simple and effective a three-to-four-inch piece of metal was in locking these types of doors. There was no way to defeat it discreetly. Sure, he could drive the car through it, but the damage to the Honda would be greater than the door.

He returned to the office door, which sported a traditional lock and knob. He squatted in front and examined it. The door was secured with a deadbolt. Grant recognized the name. It was a mid-range lock that fell into the not-too-expensive category. It was a security measure that defeated an honest man, or a lazy one. With a simple lock pick set, a novice burglar could penetrate the door in two minutes.

Grant considered himself a notch above beginner. A level two. He'd done a stint on the robbery squad and had seen his fair share of break-ins. The Keys were rife with them. Take rich people with nice houses that are often unoccupied for months at a time, and an industrious cat burglar will find his way inside. Sure, the alarms were deterrents, but like the locks, they could only do so much.

Was there an alarm here?

Grant couldn't see any sign of one. It was midday, and if they did man the shop on Saturdays, they'd probably gone out for lunch. Which didn't give him long, but he'd take advantage of the time he had.

In his glove compartment, he retrieved a lock pick set. Wrench watched him remove the pouch with wan eyes.

"Okay, you can come, but stand guard."

Wrench straightened in his seat as if he'd just received orders from the general.

Maybe he had.

Grant chuckled as he unfastened the dog's seat belt. The lab-pit mix leaped through the open window, landing next to Grant.

"Come on. We need to be quick," Grant said, kneeling again in front of the lock and retrieving a hook and a tensioning tool from his pack.

Wrench sat on his haunches, watching with intense scrutiny as Grant inserted both the hook and the tensioner. The deadbolt had four pins in the cylinder, and he began working from the back forward. The trick to opening any lock was to maneuver the individual pins up so the tumbler would turn. Of course, the right key did that automatically. With each pin he moved up, Grant applied more tension to the lock until the last one slipped upwards into place, and the tumbler completed its turn.

Grant turned the knob freely and looked at Wrench. "That was a little slow," he admitted to the dog. "I need to practice more."

Wrench popped up on all fours as if he agreed. Grant straightened, pocketing the small pack of tools, and stepped inside the office.

Stale tobacco air hit him as the door opened, and Grant wrinkled his nose at the odor. If someone had told him he'd just walked into a 1970s used car salesman's office, the light-tan wood paneling would have sold it as such. The newer-model Dell computer on the desk and the artwork that reminded an ignorant simpleton like Grant of Middle Eastern culture suggested otherwise.

The click of Wrench's nails followed him across the room as Grant rounded the desk carefully. The sweet nicotine smell grew more familiar with each passing second.

"Keep your ears open," he told Wrench.

The dog did a circle, as if checking the room for perpetrators, and then walked to the brown leather couch covered with ripped cushions. The dog jumped onto the sofa, curled up in a ball, and watched Grant.

Shaking his head, Grant muttered, "As long as you keep your ears open."

Papers cluttered the desktop, and Grant rifled through them. Most were in a language he didn't recognize. There were a few with a mixture of English and the unknown language. He could muster some Spanish and thought he could recognize most of the Romance languages, even if he couldn't read them. Somehow, this didn't feel quite like those. However, they resembled shipping manifests, bills of ladings, and other customs documents. *Bureaucracy seems to look alike in any language.*

He pulled out his cell phone and snapped several pictures of the paperwork. No point in getting bogged down looking at it here. Grant lifted his eyes to check on Wrench, who hadn't moved from the couch. He was counting on the dog to alert him if anyone pulled into the drive.

Grant then looked at the Dell computer. The desktop was open, and again, he smiled at the laziness of people. With a sweep of the mouse, he opened the email icon on the taskbar. Microsoft Outlook opened, and he stared at a list of emails. Several of the subject lines were in the same language. He opened the first couple, clicked the Home menu, and found the "Translate Message" option.

Immediately, the message turned to English. A small box at the top flashed for a split-second, stating that the original message was Swahili.

Swahili?

Grant scanned the text. It was an innocuous email about an order of cashew nuts coming into New York. Grant moved to the next one. The message translated again, and Grant's eye caught the email signature at the bottom. Uhuru Global Exports. He scanned up the text to the body of the email.

The door swung open, drawing his attention to the figure who appeared in the opening. The Miami sun streamed in behind the man, blinding Grant to his features.

"What the hell are you doing here?" an accented voice demanded.

Before Grant could react, the man's hand swept down, and despite the bright light, Grant saw the glint of metal from a small pistol. As his eyes quickly adjusted, Grant instantly recognized the man in the door. It was the suspicious guy from the plane.

"The door was open," Grant lied to the man, cutting his eyes to the sleeping dog that hadn't pricked up an ear at the gunman's approach.

The man stepped inside, letting the door swing close behind him. "And you helped yourself to the desk? You are already too much trouble."

Grant pushed away from the desk, rising slowly to his feet.

"Don't move!" the other man snapped loudly.

Wrench opened his eyes somewhat lazily, seemed to take in the situation, and in a split second, decided he didn't like what was going on. There was a low, nearly inaudible growl, followed by a brown blur flying off the couch.

The gunman caught what his brain registered as a couch cushion lunging at him. He twisted around as the dog's canines buried into his forearm.

"Oww!" he howled, dropping the gun and flinging his arm around as he tried to throw Wrench off.

Grant raced around the desk, throwing his shoulder into the man in a modified tackle. The three figures crashed into the wood-paneled wall with a resounding crack.

Grant grabbed the door, throwing it open. "Wrench! Car!" he shouted as he dashed into the bright sunshine.

The dog released the man, who slid to the floor. As Grant jerked the driver's side door open, Wrench bounded through the still-open passenger window.

The Del Sol's engine fired up, and Grant was already in reverse when he saw the man coming out the office door. A second later, the faded red Honda sped down North River Drive.

Now that he had a second to calm down, Grant took a breath and turned to Wrench. "I think we need to talk about what keeping watch means," he told the mutt.

10

Charlie's ponytail swished in the wind as she downshifted the manual transmission into third gear and swept past a delivery van. The little Sprite felt gutless after the Jaguar, but it was still exhilarating to drive and begged her to go faster. The motorway wasn't much fun, with trucks blowing the little Austin-Healey all over the place, but once Charlie cleared Birmingham, she chose the two-lane A41. It would take a few minutes longer, but the smaller road winding through the West Midlands countryside was far more pleasurable.

At Whitchurch, she turned left onto the A525 and soon crossed over the border into Wales, marked by a small road sign peeking above the overgrown grass. As Charlie sped along with the smell of fresh-mowed grass and farmyards whisking over the topless car, her mind reflected on Sunday drives with her father in his beloved Sprite. He'd persuade or entice her with offers of ice cream at their destination or the chance to drive the Austin-Healey in her teenage years, but deep down, she'd always wanted to spend the time with him. Something she'd give anything for the opportunity to do once more.

Llangollen was a small rural town situated along the banks of the river Dee, with two roads in from the east, a narrowboat canal, and a stop on a historic railway line. After Bamford Manor, Charlie was unsure what to expect from the abode of Edmund Metcalfe. Although he was an ex-con, he was still the son of an earl. Pulling up to the address, she found the answer was still unclear. The home was an unassuming pre-war terraced cottage at the end of the row, but parked alongside it was a newer-model Mercedes SUV.

The home overlooked the river but was still only worth about twice what the car would have cost. Of course, flashy wristwatches, name-brand suits, and expensive wheels were too often the front for people living outside their means on credit cards and loans. There was nowhere in the narrow street for a guest to park, so she turned around and drove back to the main road, cursing herself for revealing her presence. Not that Edmund had any reason she knew of to avoid her, but if he did, the Sprite making a three-point turn outside the man's house was a giveaway.

Finding a spot outside a cemetery, Charlie parked. Grabbing her phone, which she muted, she walked beside the old stone wall lining the graveyard, returning to the cottage. She rapped on the front door. Traveling all this way had been a gamble. She had no way of knowing whether Edmund Metcalfe would be home, at work, or living in Australia, so she was buoyed when the door opened. She stared at a man she recognized from her internet search.

"Hello, Mr. Metcalfe. I'm Charlotte Greene," she said, choosing her full given name in an attempt to sound more polished and professional. "I'm with a security company looking to take over the systems at Bamford Manor and would really appreciate any insights you can share about the place."

Edmund looked Charlie over with what she perceived to be a mixture of distrust and annoyance.

"How the hell should I know?" he replied. "I've never lived there."

"I understand that, sir," Charlie pressed, knowing her window —or, more accurately, the front door—was about to close. "But you have a unique perspective, as you've spent your life on the periphery of the family."

Despite rehearsing her spiel all the way from Radclive, it sounded horribly weak now that Charlie heard it coming from her own lips. She was shocked when Edmund took a step back and invited her inside.

"Tea?" he asked as he indicated for her to sit on a worn leather sofa in the modest living area.

"Coffee, if you have it," she replied, ignoring his direction and following him to the even smaller kitchen.

She noticed the lovely view down the hillside, then over the railway tracks to the river at the bottom of the valley. A church spire reached for the clouds amongst the old buildings on the far bank.

"Beautiful cottage," she exaggerated, taking in the décor that was so old, it may well have been cool again.

Edmund scoffed as he plugged the kettle in and pulled cups from a kitchen cabinet. "The old man told my mother he'd buy her a house wherever she wanted. This is what she chose. Mother grew up in Llangollen."

"Lovely town," Charlie said, playing along, although it did seem like a nice place.

Edmund shook his head in dismay. "If she'd said a flat in London, he'd have bought it, and it'd be worth a bloody fortune in today's market. But no. Mother wanted to raise me in her home-town, so here we lived, and here she died."

"I'm sorry to hear that," Charlie said, wishing she'd had more time to take a deeper dive into the man's background.

He shrugged.

"You don't have a Welsh accent," she noted, edging closer to look at three photographs pinned to a small corkboard.

"No," he replied. "Tried my best not to, and lost any I had once I moved out and went to university."

"Why did you return here if you were so keen to be elsewhere?" Charlie asked, trying to sound engaged while squinting at the photographs across the kitchen.

Two shots were of Edmund with an older lady who Charlie guessed to be his mother.

He turned towards her, and his brow creased. She pulled herself away from the pictures and met his gaze.

"If you're in security work," he said. "I'd have thought you'd already know."

"If you're referring to your troubles with the law, then of course I'm aware," Charlie responded, hoping she sounded as though she was leaving a thick file of information unsaid.

Edmund just nodded and returned his attention to making their drinks. "Milk? Sugar?" he asked.

"Both," she replied, and stole another look at the photos.

The third one was of Edmund with his arm around a woman. She looked oddly familiar, but Charlie couldn't recall where from. The snapshot appeared to be from a night out somewhere, as they were both dressed up. The woman had clearly taken some time styling her hair and applying makeup.

"Mother passed around that time, so it made sense for me to come here," he continued. "I planned to sell the house and move, but as you can see, I haven't got around to it yet."

The kettle boiled with an escalating whistle, so he removed it from the base and poured steaming water into the mugs. Charlie wondered what had changed from his frosty initial reception. She'd hardly given him a solid reason to continue the conversation, yet he'd invited her inside, and now they were chatting away like school chums catching up on old times. *Maybe he's just lonely*, she thought.

"Let's sit down," he said, passing her the coffee cup as he walked back to the living room.

Charlie followed and sat on the sofa while he took a recliner chair with faded and frayed upholstery.

He took a sip of his tea before speaking. "What did you want to ask me?"

That was a good question—the one thing she didn't have too many of. In what she now realized was poor planning, Charlie hadn't gotten too far past conjuring up the bullshit she'd hoped would get her through the door.

"What do you know about the security company who put the system in place at the manor?" she asked, thinking on the fly.

"Nothing," he responded.

If this had been a motor race, Charlie would have made a brilliant start, shot into the lead, then sailed off the track and crashed at the first turn. She suddenly felt as though the police badge being removed from her pocket had disconnected her brain from every process, skill, and trick she'd learned on the job. She'd approached this meeting like a bumbling rookie, and she was disappointed in herself. Which, in turn, made her really pissed off.

"How many times have you been to the manor?" she asked, determined to right the ship.

"Not many," he replied. "My mother worked until her pregnancy couldn't be hidden, and then she moved here. My father would come and see me on occasion, or we'd meet him somewhere. But I was an adult before I ever set foot in the manor."

"Interesting," Charlie commented, making her next question sound like a curious sidebar. "What prompted your visits?"

"Countess Bamford died," he replied with no sign of emotion.

Charlie nodded knowingly. "Of course. Do you have much interaction with your stepbrother, Cecil?"

Edmund scoffed. "No. And we're both fine with that."

"No bonding there," Charlie followed up with humor in her voice, encouraging a response.

Edmund tensed and went to speak but held back. "What company are you with again?" he asked instead.

"GW Security Systems," Charlie lied, using the Greene and Wolfe initials to invent the name. "We're new in the market."

"How did you meet Cecil?" he asked, and Charlie began to realize why Edmund had changed his tune at the door. He was hoping to learn more from her, and perhaps even knew who she really was.

"Referral," Charlie replied. "So, sir, when was the last time you visited Bamford Manor?"

She sensed her time was running thin, so if there was anything to be learned, she'd better get to the point.

"Why don't you quit the bullshit?" he responded. "Why are you really here?"

Apparently, running thin had turned into breaking through the ice into the frigid waters below.

"To see if you were involved in stealing an item from the manor," Charlie retorted. "History says you're not opposed to breaking the law, and you just admitted to hating Cecil." Charlie looked around the room. "I'm guessing Daddy's handouts have dried up, so maybe you figured you'd help yourself to an easy picking rather than wait to see what the earl throws your way in the will."

Anger visibly rose inside the man, and his fingers clutched the arms of the recliner. He took a few moments to breathe and calm himself.

"I'd be looking at your employer, if I were you," he said, rising from the chair. "And you can leave now."

Charlie stood, but didn't move toward the door. "Why would Cecil steal his own stuff?"

"Insurance. Quick cash. Hide it from the will so he gets to keep it all. I don't know, but he's a conniving bastard so he's bound to be behind it!"

"Who else is in the will?" Charlie asked.

"You need to leave," he said, pointing to the door.

"You obviously think *someone else* will get money, or Cecil wouldn't need to hide anything," Charlie persisted, moving slowly across the room. "Is that you?"

"I have no idea!" Edmund shouted. "But they'll be charities and trusts and all sorts of other bullshit, so Cecil's probably grabbing assets for himself before the old man croaks."

He swung the front door open and held it for Charlie.

She paused on the doorstep. "You never told me the last time you were in Radclive, Edmund."

"You're wasting your time bothering me," he said. "I didn't steal anything from the Bamfords. Now bugger off and look for the damn necklace somewhere else."

Charlie whisked her foot clear a moment before the door slammed closed. "Bloody hell," she muttered to herself, and slowly walked away.

She'd driven all the way to Wales to see what she could learn, but was leaving with more questions than answers. *How did he know what was stolen?*

Following the cemetery wall, she took a moment to look back over her shoulder. The midday sun glinted off the living room window, but she caught movement and saw Edmund's face pressed to the glass. He was watching her with a mobile phone to his ear.

Hurrying to the Sprite, with a long drive ahead and London traffic to deal with, she wondered who Edmund would be calling the moment she'd left. It wasn't Cecil Bamford; she was certain of that. Reaching the car, Charlie unmuted her phone and noticed she'd missed two calls from Grant in the US. It was mid-morning in Florida. She started to call him back, then decided to wait until she was on the road or stopped for a coffee.

Instead, she typed Bamford Manor into her maps app. The software selected the best route and informed her it would take two hours and forty-eight minutes via the A41. The slower way was now the faster way due to closures on the M54.

Charlie swore to herself as she turned the car around. Her phone chimed from the passenger seat, and she juggled it in her left hand as she shifted to third gear before checking the screen. It was an alert informing her that the battery was low and she should charge it right away. She swore again. Unsurprisingly, USB phone chargers weren't standard equipment on the 1961 model. That option wouldn't be around for another 35 years.

Driving through the old town, Charlie considered stopping and buying a power bank, but the idea made her even more irritated. She had a perfectly good one at home. Her original plan hadn't included switching to the Austin-Healey, so the thought hadn't crossed her mind. Speeding into the Welsh countryside, Charlie decided she'd stop and top up with fuel in Whitchurch, where she'd have to suck it up and buy a power bank in the gas station.

Horn honks from behind caught her attention, and she scanned the tiny rearview mirror mounted on the top of the dash. Whatever had taken place appeared to be over with, and a rather forlorn-looking Vauxhall Astra, with what sounded like a hole in the exhaust, closed to a hundred feet behind her. Charlie laughed, the faded red paint reminding her of Grant's Honda Del Sol in the Florida Keys. The memory nagged her once more to call her brother so they could compare notes.

Six miles out of town, the road came to a T-junction, where Charlie came to a stop, waiting for a car to pass by. She glanced in the mirror again and saw the red Astra behind her. The man behind the wheel drummed his fingers on the steering wheel, and two things converged in Charlie's memory at exactly the same moment.

The first was that the woman in the picture with Edmund Metcalfe was Heather Cartwright. She was all dolled up with makeup and nice clothes, but now that the penny had dropped, Charlie knew it was the Bamfords' maid. Which explained how Edmund knew about the necklace.

Her second spark of recognition was from her walk from the pub to the flat just the previous evening. The man she'd spotted in the cloth cap, who she'd briefly thought was following her shortly before she'd been attacked, was behind the wheel of the car now sitting right behind her at the intersection.

Charlie looked right, and the road was clear. She checked left, then waited a few moments until an oncoming van was only a hundred yards away. Dropping the clutch, she launched the little sports car across the road to the accompaniment of a raucous horn from the protesting van driver. Grabbing second gear and flooring the gas pedal, she checked the mirror to catch a two-finger salute from the van driver in case she was unsure whom the horn was intended for. And behind him, the red Astra had lurched into a gap smaller than the one Charlie had chosen, causing further chaos and confirming her suspicion. She was being tailed.

11

The sun cast a glare across the laptop screen. Grant moved the mouse around until he found the brightness factor in the computer's settings. As the LCDs on the screen intensified, the words became clearer.

Under the patio table at Grant's feet, Wrench curled up next to a bowl of water that Tracy had brought out to the dog. It never failed. The staff at Sharkey's Sharkbite Grill almost always brought out Wrench's water before Grant ever got the chance to order a beer, and today was no different. Tracy had come scuttling out of the bar, ignoring Grant and dropping on her haunches to scratch Wrench behind the ear. The dog had stretched his lips back, exposing his teeth in a smile that might be mistaken for an angry snarl by someone not familiar with the dog's idiosyncratic grin.

Now, Grant worked on a pint of Blue Dolphin Beer as he studied the information on the computer. Grant had arrived back from Miami an hour ago. The confrontation at Sunshine Gourmet Import's office had left him wary and a little hungry. He glanced at his phone. He'd tried calling Charlie to give her an update but had reached her voicemail. Which was full. She should have seen the missed calls, but still hadn't called back.

"Hey there," Angie greeted as she walked across the patio. Like all other women, she bent first to greet Wrench before straightening and pecking Grant on the cheek with a kiss.

Grant slid half a plate of conch fritters across the high-top table. Angie plucked one of the fried balls of dough from the plate and dipped it into Sharkey's signature Kickin' Bayou Sauce.

"Not hungry?" she questioned, gesturing at the plate.

"Distracted," he admitted. "We went to this Sunshine Gourmet up in Miami. Guess who I ran into."

"I don't know," she replied with a shrug.

"Angie!" Tracy called as she came out onto the patio. "How was London?"

"It was fine, considering," she told the waitress.

"Oh, right," Tracy retorted with a rush of pink in her cheeks. "Sorry about your father, Grant."

He gave her a conciliatory wave.

"What can I get you, Ang?" Tracy asked.

"I'm done for the day, so make it a Tanqueray and tonic."

Grant curled his lip.

"Whatever," Angie commented to his look of disgust. "I got the taste for gin in London."

"Couldn't have found something like scotch," Grant noted. "At least it doesn't taste like glass cleaner."

"No, I tried that one you had after the funeral. It tasted like dirt. What do they call that?"

"Peat."

"More like mildew," Angie joked as she flashed a smile at Tracy. "Can I get the Fish Melt?"

"You got it, Ang." Tracy jotted the order down on a pad as she walked back into the bar.

"What were you saying?" Angie asked Grant.

"I was going to tell you who I ran into," he explained. "The man from the plane."

Angie's eyes widened. "The guy from first class?"

Grant nodded. "I told you he was watching us."

"What did he do?"

"He confirmed he was involved."

Angie pulled her head back in shock. "You got him to admit it?"

"Not so much, but he pulled a gun on me. That certainly qualifies as something, don't you think?"

She didn't say anything for a full thirty seconds. Finally, Angie asked, "Are you alright, though?"

Grant didn't point out what a stupid question that was. The confrontation with the man had been hours ago, and now Grant was two beers and half a platter of fritters into his next step. Instead, he answered, "Yeah, thanks to Wrench here. While he's not great at keeping an eye out, he certainly had my back when it counted."

As if aware that he was being praised, Wrench stood up, spun in a counter-clockwise circle, and plopped onto his hind legs so that his head rested on Angie's right knee. At his cue, she scratched behind his ears.

"Good boy," she told him. Angie's eyes lifted to Grant. "Was it worthwhile?"

He cocked an eyebrow at her.

"The trouble at the office," she remarked as if the man with the gun had been nothing more than a misdelivered package.

"Maybe. The place hits all the earmarks of a front. There was nothing much in the building. I found a couple of names, though. I'm trying to research them now."

"What have you got?" she asked, turning the computer to face her.

"I think there's a parent company called Uhuru Global Exports."

"Uhuru like on Star Trek?" Angie questioned.

"Your inner nerd is showing," Grant teased.

Angie rolled her eyes.

He added, "But yeah, like Uhuru from Star Trek. When I googled it, I found *uhuru* is a Swahili word for 'freedom.' The emails I found were also in Swahili."

Angie furrowed her brow. She dragged the laptop across the table.

"What are you doing?" he asked.

"Shut up and give me a second," she ordered.

Grant lifted his hands in a faux surrender. "All yours," he announced.

Angie typed on the keyboard. "Let me see if I can access the state database," she explained.

"Are you going to get in trouble?" Grant asked.

"No, this is all public information." Her typing didn't slow as she talked. "It's not privileged."

Angie clerked at the county court while she studied law at night. Grant had used her position to weasel small bits of information out of her, but he didn't want to get her into trouble, either. Since meeting Charlie, he'd reevaluated his life. Cutting the pills out wasn't the only thing he needed to do. Grant thought he might be too much of a taker—most addicts were. He was determined to be more self-aware of such things.

"Here it is. Uhuru Global Exports doesn't have an office in Florida itself, but it lists a child company, Sunshine Gourmet."

"In Miami," Grant said.

"Yup, and that's Sunshine Gourmet's only US location."

Grant nodded.

"There's nothing else about it." She tapped the keyboard some more. "But Uhuru Global has a profile here with customs."

"Angie, is that still legit?" he asked warily.

She cut her eyes up at him with her patented "shut-up" face. Grant obeyed the silent command.

"They are based in Tanzania," Angie told him.

"Where's that?" Grant questioned.

"Africa. I think it's on the east side of the continent, but I've never been there."

Grant lifted one eyebrow at her, and she shrugged. "You can take me any time you want."

"I don't even want to go," he pointed out.

Angie curled her nose in disgust. "You'd stick to the Keys forever."

"Can't beat the fishing."

"Well, this is interesting."

Grant leaned forward.

"Want a bit of history?" she asked.

"Not especially, but shoot."

"Have you heard of Turath Zanjibah?"

Grant shook his head. "Have you?" he inquired sardonically.

Angie smiled. "No."

After she sat silent for half a minute, Grant motioned with his hand for her to continue.

"Turath Zanjibah is a political group in the area."

"Tanzania?" Grant asked.

"Yes," Angie muttered. "But specifically Zanzibar, I guess."

"I've heard of Zanzibar," Grant acknowledged.

"It's part of Tanzania," Angie told him.

"Are you saying politicians own this company?"

Angie shook her head. "Not exactly. But there is a flag in the computer. The State Department warns that Uhuru Global Exports is connected to Turath Zanjibah."

"Are they terrorists?"

"Doesn't say that. More like political activists, I think. The name means 'the heritage of Zanzibar,'" Angie continued to read. "They are an Omani organization."

"Omani?"

Angie's head bobbed as she read. "From the country of Oman. Apparently, at one time, Zanzibar was ruled by that country."

"This feels like a lot of history," Grant noted.

"I'm giving you the Cliff's Notes version."

"Right. Zanzibar is part of Tanzania."

"An island," Angie corrected.

"An island off Tanzania. And it once belonged to Oman?"

Angie nodded, and Grant continued, "And this Talath Zanzibar is a group of political activists doing what?"

"It's Turath Zanjibah."

"Okay," Grant admitted. "So, what does this group want?"

Tracy appeared with Angie's Fish Melt. "Want another beer, Grant?" she asked.

Grant responded by tilting his empty bottle toward him and judging the quantity in it. "Yeah, I'll have another."

"Oh." Angie lifted her head and straightened her back. Grant perked up as well at her expression.

"Turath Zanjibah has their own website," she declared.

"Modern times, indeed," Grant mused. "Even a banana republic activism group deserves a website. What are they campaigning for? Do they want to be free from Tanzania?"

"Seems so. They claim the British stole Zanzibar from them."

"The British stole lots of places from lots of people, from the little I paid attention in history class," Grant scoffed.

"It also talks about recovering stolen artifacts and valuables," Angie continued. "They claim the British took some of the sultan's treasures. Turath Zanjibah are pursuing the return of these treasures they feel belong to the Omani decedents."

"Treasures?" Now Grant fully perked up. "Like a big fucking jewel?"

"I'd classify a necklace like that as a treasure," Angie agreed. "There's a bunch more about how the sultan's family was divided, and the British backed one side as a puppet government. But that's way too much history stuff for you."

"I agree," Grant chuckled.

Angie turned the computer around for him to see. An image of a large ruby set in gold floated over a picture of a desert landscape. The crappy Photoshop job on the website looked amateurish. Angie clicked on the menu across the top of the screen, which was set to the English translation. She selected "About Us."

Grant froze, leaning forward. He pointed to a photo of a group of men standing in the arched doorway of an ornate building.

"Can you make that bigger?" he asked.

Angie moved the mouse around until the picture enlarged on the laptop.

"It's him," Grant stated, tapping his index finger on the picture.

"The guy from the plane?" Angie asked. She held down a few keys and took a screenshot of the man's face.

"And the warehouse in Miami," Grant replied. "I think I already know it, but we need to verify his name."

Angie started a reverse image search on the man's face. While the internet scanned through millions of images, she attached the screenshot to an email.

"Who are you sending it to?" Grant asked.

"Guy with the Bureau of State Investigations. He wants to take me out to dinner."

"Whoa!" Grant raised a hand in protest. "That's unnecessary."

She narrowed her eyes at him. "Anything I want to do is necessary. We aren't anything yet."

"But—"

"No buts. You're doing great, Grant, but we've been down this road before."

His chin drooped as he pulled his eyes away from hers. She was correct, and the fact stung Grant. He'd been wallowing in his own self-doubt and self-destruction for over a year now. Angie had been there for him the whole time, even if she'd told him he had to clean his shit up before they could pursue anything more serious.

Grant wished that had been the wake-up call he had needed, but it wasn't. Somehow, it was the brutal, scathing assault from his newly discovered sister that had cut him to the quick. While she didn't say it, Grant realized how much it hurt Angie that she hadn't been able to get through to him. He loved Angie. Hell, he'd loved her as far back as he could remember. Perhaps that was why it hadn't been enough. There was this knowledge that Angie was always around. Had always been around. Would always be around. It was a comfort that didn't allow him to feel the pressure to change.

"Besides Grant Wolfe, I know exactly how to get what I want out of a man without giving him exactly what he wants."

Grant wanted to respond with something pithy like John Wayne might say in *Rio Bravo*. But nothing came to mind, and he doubted that quoting the Duke was a great way to actually win over a woman. Even John Wayne might struggle to make those lines work nowadays.

Angie smiled. "See, that was fast."

She spun the computer around for him to see the screen. An email from Gary Dunker with a state of Florida seal on the letterhead appeared. She opened the attachment, revealing an FBI file. The picture was a grainy but clear enough photo of the man who'd pointed a gun at Grant that morning. Saleh Al-Maawali.

"Figured," Grant blurted. "That's the name Charlie found for the rental car in England. And it mentions here about him being a member of that Turath Zanjibah bunch," Grant read from the screen.

"According to this, Interpol flagged him as a person potentially associated with a burglary in Berlin two years ago. A golden scepter encrusted in rubies disappeared from a banker's collection."

"Damn. He might have the necklace with him," Grant muttered.

"This could be your lead!" Angie exclaimed. "If the necklace that Bamford had was from Zanzibar, it might make sense he'd come after it."

"I wish Charlie would call back," he groused, checking his phone again. "If she can get with Bamford, we might learn a bit more about the provenance of the jewels."

"Or not," Angie pointed out. "Kinda weird that he didn't offer any insights up when we were there."

"Good point," he agreed.

"Here's your beer, Grant," Tracy interrupted as she set a cold bottle down on the table.

"Thanks, Trace," he replied, setting his phone aside to take a swig.

Grant looked at the computer screen again, where the face of Saleh Al-Maawali stared back. He now wished he'd stuck around in Miami and followed the guy, but he'd been more concerned with getting him and Wrench away unscathed.

"Tanzania..." he muttered, wondering if the man indeed had the necklace with him.

Grant snatched up his phone again and scrolled through the list of contacts before finding the one he was looking for.

The phone on the other end rang twice before it clicked, indicating someone had answered.

"Rat, it's Grant Wolfe. I have something I need you to do."

12

Charlie berated herself for not noticing someone following her all the way from London. *Or had it only been from Bamford Manor?* Regardless, she'd allowed herself to become preoccupied with hopeless reminiscing about her father and missed the tail. Quite how, she wasn't sure, as the man was equally inept at covertly following as he was at jumping her the night before.

A handful of options presented themselves, and she mulled them over while keeping to the speed limit. The Astra was still behind the van and had remained there despite having several opportunities to pass, so Charlie knew she had time. Her first option was to lose him. The little Sprite was woefully underpowered by modern standards, but it was nimble with well-balanced handling, and she was a skillful driver. On the other hand, she doubted Flat Cap had much prowess behind the controls. And he was driving a knackered Vauxhall Astra, which issued a plume of oily smoke every time he lifted off the throttle.

The alternative, which hung in her mind, was to create a situation where she could confront the man and turn the tables. If Charlie pulled into a gas station or store, she could sneak up on him wherever he chose to observe from and see if he'd talk. Flat

Cap had surprised her last night, but she fancied her odds if he was the unsuspecting prey. She touched the back of her head where the bump was tender to the touch, reminding her of how stiff and sore she still felt. Her phone flashing another low battery warning tipped the scales on her decision.

Risking the phone dying altogether, she zoomed into the map and searched along the route she was taking. Whitchurch was only five miles away, and traffic would get busier when she turned onto the A41 to skirt the town. About every mile along the route until then, narrow lanes branched off into the countryside like a spider's web linking cottages and farms to small hamlets.

Charlie watched the dot on the map near one of those lanes, and she quickly studied where it led. Glancing up, she saw the turn, and by the time she looked down at the phone again, it had died. Tossing the useless device to the passenger seat, Charlie braked hard, downshifting the Austin-Healey from fourth to third to second, blipping the throttle between each shift to match the engine RPMs to the lower gear. With the tires fighting for grip, she eased off the brake as she turned hard into the lane.

From behind, she heard the startled van driver slam on his brakes, followed by the obligatory blast of the horn. Charlie sped away from the turn and was in third gear, eyeing the curve ahead before she stole a glance in the rearview mirror. Flat Cap was veering back onto the asphalt with a cloud of dirt and black engine smoke in his wake. Charlie grinned. It would have been too easy to lose the guy at the first turn. Now she'd have some fun.

Typical of English country lanes, the road was only wide enough for one vehicle. If someone came the opposite way, both vehicles would need to put half the car over the grass verge on their side in order to pass by. Which meant for Charlie, as the lead vehicle, every blind curve was a game of roulette. *How fast dare she drive?* There'd be no time to stop if she met an oncoming car mid-corner. Her adrenaline surged and her nerves tingled as she pushed her luck around the first few turns, accelerating hard between them.

Charlie quickly realized the flaw in her plan. Flat Cap didn't have to gamble. If he didn't see or hear a massive accident in front, then Charlie had made the corner and he would know that nothing was coming. He was soon gaining on her by taking the corners faster, despite his lack of skill.

Any ruse her pursuer had intended to maintain was out the window. He was no longer tailing her. They were in a full-blown high-speed chase, and Charlie was upping the stakes with every new turn. Faster and faster, she pressed her luck, praying she wouldn't meet a tractor in the middle of the corner. Tall hedges lining the fields blocked any view of what lay ahead, and loose gravel and mud made the surface unpredictable and treacherous. Throwing caution to the wind, the little Sprite was now four-wheel drifting through every turn.

Charlie stayed in third gear and braked lightly for a left curve, which led quickly into a right. She held her breath, knowing any vehicle she met would mean the end of her father's beloved Sprite, not to mention her own neck. Breathing a sigh of relief, she accelerated down the following stretch unscathed and could see the next corner was tighter than the others. In the mirror, Flat Cap was fighting the wheel, his hands flailing like he was conducting an orchestra. The Astra fishtailed off the prior corner, flinging dirt and grass from where he ran down the verge, and had now fallen back from the speeding Sprite.

By either instinct or luck, Charlie cautiously braked hard and downshifted to second gear for the next turn, slowing just a little more than she judged necessary. Ahead, a metal gate guarded the entry to a hayfield, and the hedgerow loomed like a wall, indicating the corner turned sharply by ninety degrees. She continued braking firmly, and just as she was about to turn into the bend, an old man on an even older bicycle appeared from the opposite direction. Their eyes met, and a look of shock coated his face.

Charlie maintained light pressure on the brake pedal, forced to turn a few feet later to miss the startled fellow. Coaxing the steering wheel into the corner, she prayed she wouldn't overburden the front tires. If they locked, she'd be in the outside hedge. If she let off the brake, the car would need more road than was now available to make the corner, and she'd be in the hedge, anyway.

Forcing her eyes around the turn, Charlie eased completely off the brake pedal as she pointed the front wheels at the bicycle, which was now exactly at the apex of the turn. The Sprite reacted like a gem, sliding through the turn and drifting a few feet away from the inside verge where Grandpa wobbled by.

The left tires of the Sprite ran perfectly along the muddy base of the left side verge, and Charlie straightened the wheel while letting out a whoop of relief. Behind her came an almighty crashing sound. Her eyes darted to the mirror just in time to see a flash of red disappearing behind the hedgerow out of sight.

Braking to a stop, Charlie ground the gears, trying hurriedly to select reverse. Spinning the tires, she shot backwards and stopped again where the metal gate used to guard the hayfield. The bent and scarred frame now hung open, dangling from one remaining hinge. The Astra had come to a rest fifty feet into the field, having parted the tall grass like a dull red mower. Steam billowed from the front, where Charlie assumed the radiator had succumbed to its confrontation with the gate. Terror rose in her heart as she imagined the old man pinned between the two. She switched off the ignition and gingerly stepped from the car.

"Scared the bloody life outta me," came a voice with a rural Welsh accent.

Charlie whirled around to see the old man standing next to the back of the Sprite, steadying himself against his bicycle.

"Are you okay? Did he hit you?" she asked.

"I dare say I lost a year or two off the ticker," he replied, scratching his head. "Don't suppose I have too many to give no more, either."

"I'm so sorry," Charlie said, feeling awful.

Pulling over at a gas station and banging on Flat Cap's window seemed like a much better option now.

"Think he's alright?" the old man asked, nodding towards the Astra.

"I'll see," Charlie replied. "Do you have a phone?"

"I do."

"Mine's dead, so can you call the police?" she said, wondering if she could slip away before they got there.

"Take me a bit," the old man said.

"Okay," Charlie said, unsure why dialing 9-9-9 would be so difficult. "Hand it to me, and I'll call them."

"Hand you what?" he replied. "I don't have one of them newfangled mobile phone things. I'll have to cycle home. Got a phone there."

Charlie couldn't help but laugh. "Tell you what. I'll check on this idiot, and you pedal home, call from there."

The old man nodded and shakily threw a leg over his bike. As Charlie watched him weave down the lane, she heard a groan from the Astra. She jogged over to the car and trod the knee-length grass down to reach the driver's side. Upon inspection, she realized the damage was even worse than she'd imagined. The hood was buckled, and the car appeared to be several feet shorter than it had looked in the mirror. The driver's airbag had been deployed and now laid limply in Flat Cap's lap, although his hat was now nowhere to be seen.

Charlie tried the door, but it wouldn't budge. The side window was down, and she peered inside. From what she could see in the footwell, the impact had smashed the engine and transmission backwards, crumpling the firewall and trapping the man's feet. His head rolled from side to side as he groaned. Blood trickled from his broken nose, courtesy of the airbag.

"Hey. Who are you, and why were you chasing me?" Charlie asked, pushing any sympathy she had aside as her own sore head reminded her of what this guy was capable of.

"Ambulance," the man muttered. "Call the bloody ambulance."

Charlie thought she detected a Welsh accent, but it was hard to tell in his mumbling state.

"Not until you tell me who sent you."

The man sounded like he was swearing at her. She stepped back and looked the car over.

"I bet a fuel line might have come loose under the hood. What do you think? Be bad if that got on the hot exhaust, right?"

The man tilted his head and forced an eye open. "What? Get me out!"

"Nah. I think you're buggered, mate," she replied, pointing at his feet. "You're pinned like a donkey's arse. Hate to see this piece of shit light up with all this dry grass around. Ugly way to go, that."

"You gotta help me! Get me out!" he spat, both his eyes open and reflecting his terror.

"I'm not helping you. You were just chasing me until you ran out of talent. I help you, and you'll probably turn on me."

"I wasn't going to hurt you," he whimpered.

"Oh?" she said, "Like last night? You smacked me in the bloody head!"

Charlie reached in through the window and shoved his knee. The man screamed in pain as his mangled foot ground against the twisted metal pinning him in the car. He weakly slapped her hand away.

"I didn't mean to hurt you!" he cried. "I'm just doing this for a few extra quid. I've never done anything like this before."

"That's obvious," she commented unsympathetically.

"I was supposed to follow you. Find out where you went and who you met with."

"Working for who?" she asked again. "Who the hell is interested in what I'm doing?"

Flat Cap took a few deep breaths. "Edmund."

"Edmund?" Charlie echoed incredulously. "He knows where I was. His bloody house!"

"He called me when you left," he muttered, and at least Charlie felt better about not missing a tail all the way to Llangollen. There hadn't been one.

"Why's he interested in me?"

Flat Cap slowly shook his head, which made him wince. "I don't know. Something about his half-brother stealing something and screwing him over."

"That makes no sense," Charlie thought aloud.

"I just needed the money, alright? Now, will you get me out before this thing catches light?"

"Oh, that was all bullshit. I think you're fine," Charlie replied. "Well, relatively fine. There's no fire I can see, and I don't smell petrol. Sit tight, and the police will be here soon. I'm sure they'll send an ambulance, too."

"What? You can't leave me!"

"Doesn't look like you're leaking all that bad, but I wouldn't wriggle around too much. You never know, you might pull the plug on an artery down there," she said, pointing to the footwell.

As she walked back to the Sprite, Flat Cap wailed a string of profanity from the Astra.

13

"You have to be kidding me," Grant complained, returning to the kitchen counter from the bathroom.

"What?" Angie asked.

"She still hasn't called back," Grant said irritably.

He called his sister's phone again, which went straight to a message once more. Grant dropped the phone on the table and groaned.

"Still no answer?" Angie asked.

"No," he replied.

"It's nearly ten o'clock over there," Angie realized, looking at her watch. "She's probably in bed. You could have left a message," she reminded him.

Grant's face scrunched up in disgust. "Her stupid voicemail is full."

Angie shrugged off his statement. "You're pacing."

Grant froze in front of the kitchen sink. He turned toward her with the realization that he had, in fact, been pacing.

"It just means you're preoccupied," Angie pointed out. "You always do it."

"I'm thinking," he admitted.

"Wanna talk it out?"

Grant cocked his head to the side. He discovered he did want to discuss it. The facts had been rolling around his brain like dice. Maybe if he verbalized them, he could piece together the clues.

"We have a stolen necklace from this Bamford Estate. And Bamford doesn't have the money, it seems."

"We know it?" Angie asked.

"Well, we suspect it," he clarified. "Although Bamford implied as much."

"If you can trust what he said," Angie suggested.

"True. He may have reasons for keeping things close to his chest."

"He also showed us the cash in the safe, but continue. What else do you know?" Angie asked.

Grant thought for a moment before responding. "We have a connection from Bamford to Sunshine Gourmet, which is part of this Uhuru Global Exports. There's a connection to an Omani activist group in Tanzania, who are international thieves."

"We don't know that, either," Angie corrected, and Grant cut his eyes over at her. She was going to make a phenomenal lawyer one day.

"Right," he agreed. "Alleged," he added, "though the cop in him considered "alleged" to be the same as "guilty." Angie, on the other hand, subscribed to the notion of "innocent until proven guilty."

Grant's phone buzzed on the table, and he took two long strides across his kitchen to grab it. His face dropped slightly when he realized it wasn't Charlie.

"Rat, my man. That was fast."

The soft, mousy voice on the other end replied, "When you're good at something, it doesn't take you long to do it."

"*Touché.*"

"I got a hit on your man. Saleh Al-Maawali is booked on a Qatar Airlines flight out of Miami to Dar es Salaam."

Grant covered the phone's microphone and stared at Angie. "Where is Dar es Salaam?"

"Tanzania," Angie answered without looking up from her phone.

"When's the flight, Rat?"

"7:40 this evening."

Grant glanced at the clock on the microwave. "Shit. That's in three hours."

"I don't schedule the planes, Grant," Rat informed him.

"Anything else on him?"

"Not much. He used a Visa for the airline. Same card used for a rental car in the UK, a hotel over there, and a flight to Miami, but that's all. Must be a new card."

"Sounds like it," Grant acknowledged. "Look. If you get anything else, leave it in a message. I'll touch back with you later."

"You owe me," Rat warned him.

"Of course, man. I've got you," Grant promised.

Rat hung up without a goodbye.

"He's flying to Tanzania?" Angie clarified.

"I have to follow him."

Angie's eyes widened. "Follow him?"

"Yeah, can you watch Wrench?"

The dog, who'd curled up on the sofa since they'd arrived home, heard his name and lifted his head to assure himself that he wasn't missing anything important. No one had any treats out, so Wrench let his head drop back between his front paws. No point in getting excited over nothing.

"Of course," Angie answered. "But what are you going to do?"

"He's the only lead so far. Everything indicates he must be the guy who stole the necklace, or at least orchestrated it."

"Grant, he already pulled a gun on you," she pointed out.

"But at least at the airport, I'll know he's unarmed. Plus, I don't plan on him seeing me. The idea is to follow him at first."

Angie nodded, and Grant suspected the gesture was actually laden with sarcasm. He ignored it.

"What about Charlie?" Angie asked.

"I'll try her again before I board. Or maybe send a text so she gets it in the morning. Hopefully, she can find out more about where the necklace came from."

Grant hurried out of the room, and Angie stared after him. Wrench lifted his head again at the commotion. Still no treats, so he resigned himself to a longer nap.

"Can you try to book me on that flight?" Grant called from the other room.

"Do you want a hotel, too?" she asked as she opened the laptop. Under her breath, she muttered, "Going to law school just so I can book your travel like I'm the Priceline girl."

"Did you say something?" Grant shouted back.

Wrench lifted his head again. Angie gave the dog a wink and answered Grant with, "No, just talking to Wrench."

"Good," Grant said, sticking his head through the hall door leading to the bedrooms.

"Your card just got declined," Angie announced after a few minutes.

"Dammit," Grant cursed. "I got an invoice out for that last case, but she hasn't paid yet."

"I just footed the bill for London because you didn't have any money," Angie reminded him.

"Don't worry, I'll pay you back. Charlie has to wire me my share of Bamford's fee."

She rolled her eyes. "I'm not concerned, but this is a $3500 ticket. I doubt you can swing that even if your client paid you."

"Hold on," he announced as he marched out of the room. Two minutes later, Grant returned to the kitchen with a green American Express card.

"Where did you get that?"

"It's Mom's."

"Grant, you can't do that. She's dead."

"But the bank doesn't know that yet."

"I think that's fraud," Angie stated.

"Only if I don't pay it back," he countered.

She shook her head in defeat before reaching up and grabbing the card. "I'm not breaking any laws here," she suggested loudly.

"We don't see anything. Do we, Wrench?"

Uninterested, Wrench let out a huff through his nostrils.

"There, you're booked on the 7:40 pm flight," Angie said. "Gets into Tanzania Saturday night. You didn't get a lot of choice for seats."

"Thanks," Grant told her as he took the credit card back. "I'll save this for another emergency."

"Don't forget your passport," she called as he moved to the back of the house.

It took him less than ten minutes to throw a few changes of clothes into a small carry-on bag. Angie watched him scurry around the house.

"Don't forget some Aleve or Advil for your leg," she reminded him.

"Right," he replied as he hurried to the bathroom. Angie heard the rattle of a pill bottle as he ran back to the bedroom.

"I think Al-Maawali might have the necklace on him," Grant suggested as he came into the den with the hard-case rolling suitcase.

"Why would he bring it to the States just to fly back to Tanzania with it?" Angie wondered.

Grant twisted his face. "Okay, it's a maybe," he replied as if agreeing with Angie's question. "Perhaps he had something else to collect here?"

"He's up to something," she conceded. "What exactly is your plan if he does have the jewelry? If Bamford didn't report it stolen, you can't exactly have this Al-Maawali arrested for a crime no one reported."

"Guess we'll have to take it back," Grant decided. "You know, one wrong turn deserves another."

"I don't think that's how the saying goes."

Grant shrugged. "Can you drive me to the airport?"

Angie nodded.

Grant gave her a smile. "I love you, Ang."

Wrench, now sensing something more was amiss, popped up on his feet. His body tensed when he saw the suitcase, and the dog trotted toward Grant and sniffed at the bag.

"All right, buddy," Grant said as he kneeled down to scratch the dog's head. "Angie will take care of you until I get back."

Wrench rubbed his muzzle against Grant's neck. The man stood up, giving the dog another pet behind his ears.

Friday afternoon traffic clogged the Ronald Reagan Turnpike, turning the trip to Miami International Airport into a slow-moving ordeal. Despite trying to get off the highway, Angie still found bumper-to-bumper traffic on the side streets. Eventually, she got back on the turnpike simply because it was moving a fraction of a second faster.

Grant tried Charlie again, but the phone wasn't even ringing now. Instead, it went straight to the message explaining the recipient's voicemail was still full. He texted instead.

"Charlie, I'm flying to Tanzania. Following Saleh Al-Maawali. Find out where Bamford and his family got the thing. There's a connection to Tanzania. Call me ASAP. Otherwise, I'll try you again when I land."

"Who lets their voicemail get full?" he complained after hitting send. "You think it's a British thing? Too posh to deal with such trivial matters," he added in a terrible highbrow English accent.

Angie just shook her head and gave him a coy smile as she followed the exit sign for the airport. Sending the text jogged a thought loose in Grant's mind, and he logged into his cellular account, adding an international plan. The idea of being in a strange country, alone, without a way to communicate, didn't seem smart.

"You're going to have to hurry through security," she warned him as she pulled up to the departures gate for Qatar Airways. "You only have an hour till take off."

Grant leaned over and kissed her on the cheek. "Thanks, Ang. I'll message you when I land."

"Be careful," she urged.

"Want me to bring anything back from Africa?" he asked.

"Can you pick up a gorilla?" Angie suggested.

Grant chuckled. "I'm the closest thing to a primate you'll get."

"Dumbass, you are a primate," she called as he slammed the door.

Grant turned back and gave her a wave, blowing a kiss with his right index and middle fingers. He turned and ran into the airport, heading straight for security, where a line stretched past the stanchions.

With growing impatience, Grant took his position at the back and waited. His feet shuffled a few inches as the woman in front of him moved forward.

14

———————

After leaving the crash scene, Charlie decided her best bet was to get as far away as possible, as quickly as possible. Figuring the old man would mention her presence, she hoped her involvement would be limited to being a witness after the fact and the police wouldn't care that she left, but there was no guarantee. The best place for the Sprite was tucked away in the garage at Bamford Manor.

Arriving without incident or stops for phone chargers, she switched cars at the manor house. Charlie tried calling Cecil, but he didn't answer, and she didn't bother going inside the house. She left the Sprite in the garage, with the little car looking forlorn, all covered in road grime. Her dad would have had a coronary if he could see his precious Austin-Healey put away in such a sorry state, but she didn't have time to dwell on the matter.

As much fun as the Sprite had been, she was glad to be back in the luxurious Jaguar SUV as the evening cooled. Plugging her phone in to charge, she realized how much she'd missed that simple modern convenience. Charlie drove into Buckingham and parked in the marketplace off the high street. A small castle-like building, signed as "The Old Gaol," sat opposite a row of shops, including a fish and chip takeaway. She was starving after an eventful day.

Five minutes later, with a paper bag of greasy food covered in salt and vinegar resting in her lap, Charlie pondered her next move. It was 6:30 p.m., and traffic back into London meant a long, boring drive. One she couldn't face. Recalling a hotel on the edge of Buckingham she'd noticed on the drive up, Charlie set her dinner on the passenger seat and drove through town.

Her choice was between a Travelodge and a Premier Inn, and the former won, as it was the first she came to. And it had a coffee shop next door. Grabbing her backpack and her fish and chips, she trudged inside. With relief that her credit card was working once again thanks to the money that had "appeared" in her bank account after the Florida disaster, she bought a room and sat on the bed, eating her now lukewarm dinner.

It was five in the morning when she came to, her half-eaten fish and chips scattered over the bedspread. Charlie, still fully clothed, hadn't even managed to pull the covers back. More mentally exhausted since the funeral than physically tired, she'd crashed out and slept for ten hours straight. Swiping the mess away from her legs, she reached for her phone on the bedside table, but it wasn't there.

"Bugger," she muttered, realizing she'd left it charging in the Jag.

Stumbling from the bed, she used the bathroom, then wandered out to the car, retrieving her phone. Turning it on, the device buzzed and beeped with a series of missed calls and texts from her brother. Which, she realized in dismay, added to the missed calls she hadn't returned from Grant the day before. Charlie wondered why he hadn't left a voicemail. Walking towards the coffee shop, she read the text.

"Bugger," she repeated with a groan, rereading his words several times. It was thin, but she'd learned a little more about the history of the necklace, so there was only one thing left to do. "But how the hell do I get to Tanzania?"

Aborting the coffee run, she ran back to her room and quickly showered. While toweling dry, Charlie checked her backpack. For once, her lethargy had paid off, as her passport was still in the zippered interior compartment, untouched since returning from Florida. She wondered what weather she'd encounter in Tanzania and doubted her overnight bag choices aligned. But that was the least of her worries. She had to get there first. Using her phone's travel app, she searched for flights.

"Bloody hell," she muttered, looking at the prices, which were all in the multi-thousands of pounds.

She wondered what Grant had found, or if he'd thrown caution to the wind and spent a third of his portion of the front money on his ticket. Maybe the flights from Miami were cheaper—which, of course, made zero sense as they required an additional intercontinental leg—but airlines' pricing never made sense. *How could a flight with a stopover, creating more airport fees and extra fuel, be cheaper than a direct flight?* Because the airline could, she knew was the answer.

An idea sprang into her mind, and although it felt like a major long shot, she hurriedly looked up the number, anyway. Charlie's Scotland Yard career may have been cut prematurely short by twenty years or so, but she'd made a few good contacts during her abbreviated tenure.

"Is dis Charlie Greene?" came a delighted man's voice after two rings. He had a thick Eastern European accent. "Dis very early for you, no?"

Roman Ponomarenko ran a freight business from Stansted Airport north of London. A few years back, Scotland Yard had busted a group importing drugs from South America. He was caught up in the mess when they chartered one of Roman's planes after their own had mechanical issues just as the task force was closing in. The Ukrainian had claimed he had no knowledge of the contents, which Charlie hadn't completely believed. But she was confident he hadn't been part of the drug ring, just a cargo operator turning a blind eye, and Charlie had helped him steer clear of the prosecutor's gunsight. He owed her.

"How's the international cargo world treating you?" she asked.

"Terrible!" the man claimed. "More tariffs and restrictions every day, too much competition, and everybody want me pay more. I barely stay with face above water."

Charlie laughed. "And your new house in Spain is coming along, okay?"

Now Roman laughed, too. "Wife keep adding things. Every time cost me more money. I hate dis house, and I never sleep one night there yet. But yes, is okay. Thank you for asking. But I'm guessing you not call just to ask about very expensive house?"

"I need to get to Tanzania in a hurry," Charlie said.

"Heathrow have planes go every day," he replied.

"Yeah, I'm on a budget."

"You want me to smuggle Scotland Yard police lady to Tanzania?" he asked in surprise. "I get much trouble for dis."

"I'm not with Scotland Yard anymore. And I'm not asking to be smuggled. I have a passport, Roman. I just need a ride."

"Which police you with now?" he asked.

"I'm a private investigator."

"Really? Dis cool. Like guy on TV... what his name? Shitty office, cute secretary. You know dis?"

"Cormoran Strike?"

"Dat him!" Roman enthused. "I love dis show."

"Tanzania, Roman?" she reiterated.

"Cargo plane not have lady bring drinks and shit like dat, Charlie. Seat fold down from wall and hurt arse."

"I don't care. I just need to get there as soon as I can."

"Tanzania?" he questioned as she heard tapping on a keyboard. "I no have plane to Tanzania."

"Shit. Anything close?"

"Barcelona," he replied.

"That's not close," she pointed out.

"No, but I have plane go there," he said, and typed some more. "When you need?"

"As early as two hours from now, until as soon after that as possible."

"Ten in morning work?"

"This morning?"

"*Tak.*"

"Yeah, that's mega," Charlie replied, amazed her long-shot idea might actually pan out. "Where does it land?"

"Nairobi, Kenya," he replied. "But…" he stammered, "maybe dis not work."

Charlie put the call on speaker and scrambled for a map to see how far Nairobi was from Dar es Salaam in Tanzania rather than relying on her rusty high school-level geography knowledge.

"Nairobi would be perfect," she reacted, seeing the two countries bordered each other. "What's the problem?"

"Not best flight for you. Have plane to Morocco on Sunday. Dis better."

"That's not even close, Roman. Put me on the Kenya flight."

"Not possible."

"Make it possible. You owe me," she added, in case he'd forgotten.

She heard a long sigh, then Roman must have covered the phone as his voice became muffled while he conversed with someone else in the room. Why he felt the need to hide their chatter, she had no idea. They were speaking Ukrainian, from what she could tell, and it quickly became heated, going by the increasing volume. Finally, Roman barked something at his employee, then uncovered the phone.

"Be at warehouse at Stansted by nine. I make dis happen for you."

"Thank you, Roman," she replied. "I really appreciate the help."

"Not thank me," he said. "And do what pilot on plane say, okay? Very important."

"No problem. He won't even know I'm aboard," Charlie replied.

She hung up and quickly gathered her things before putting directions into her phone. An hour and a half drive. She even had time for breakfast. As she walked out of the hotel, she called Grant's phone, which went straight to voicemail.

"I'll meet you in Tanzania. Leave your flight info on my voicemail. I'm on a cargo plane to Kenya. When I get there, I'll get the first flight into Tanzania."

Hanging up, she realized she hadn't said a word about Edmund or the man who'd chased her, but if Grant was correct, then none of that mattered. Edmund was paranoid and mistakenly chasing after her while the real thief was flying all over the world. He was guilty of being jealous of his stepbrother and having an affair with a maid from the manor—which was ironic, based on his parentage—but Charlie doubted he'd stolen the necklace.

The other thing that stood out in her mind was how hopelessly vague her travel plans sounded in the message she'd just left. Charlie hadn't even asked Roman when her flight would land. But then again, she was flying in the back of a cargo plane while Grant sat in a comfortable seat on a commercial flight, so the least he could do was figure out a way to meet her at the other end. Where she'd wring his neck if she found out he'd flown business class.

***

"Sir, you aren't allowed in this area," the five foot-tall flight attendant declared much louder than Grant would have liked.

"I'm sorry," he offered demurely. There was no point in causing a scene when there were still too many hours to count in this flying aluminum can.

Air travel as a concept didn't bother Grant, but once he was on the plane with a few hundred strangers, his anxiety started climbing. He couldn't remember if he'd always felt that nervous energy in the pit of his stomach before the shooting, or since. So much of his life revolved around whether something was before or after he took a bullet to the leg.

Now, he wondered if he could refer to things in the future as BC or AC—Before Charlie or After Charlie. It seemed like her appearance in his life might be a threshold to remember. After all, for a man who had flown nowhere in over a decade, he was back on another transatlantic flight.

He was curious how far this PI business with Charlie could last when there was an ocean between them. Charlie didn't seem inclined to leave London, but it would be nice if she came to the Keys to live. After all, he hoped he was rebuilding something with Angie. Then there was Wrench. The poor mutt was a Florida dog. He'd shrivel up in the damp, wet climate of London. Grant thought the same might happen to him, too.

"Please take your seat. The captain still has the fasten seat belt light illuminated."

"I'm sorry," Grant offered as he turned back toward his row. Despite his attempt, he hadn't put eyes on Saleh Al-Maawali. The man wasn't in coach, and since Angie had put Grant in the very last row, he'd had plenty of chance to see everyone from the back of the plane. Business class was separated by a curtain and a service area for the flight attendants to prep meals and drinks. He'd only slipped through the first curtain before the flight attendant working in the small galley had stopped him.

As he trudged back to his seat, Grant waited in the aisle as the line for the lavatory streamed past his seat.

"Excuse me," he pleaded as he tried to push through the crowd.

"Wait your turn, sir," a middle-aged white woman demanded. She turned her head up to stare at him with righteous indignation.

"I'm just trying to get to my seat," he told her in defense.

"Why are you out of it?" the woman inquired with a harsh voice that screeched up a few decibels at the end of the question.

"Why are you?" he countered, letting his voice lower to the police officer tone he'd used when confronting a dangerous suspect.

"Hrmph," she grunted back, and Grant muttered a curse under his breath as he pushed past her.

"My seat," he announced, pointing at the empty space in the back row. The woman in the middle seat held her two-year-old child Grant thought might be a boy, but the child was wearing a frilly smock.

"Ugh!" a man grunted as Grant squeezed past him.

He plopped into his seat, only to feel the hands of the two-year-old grab his arm.

"Nicky, stop that," the mother declared in a thick British accent.

Still unclear about the child's gender, Grant shifted in his seat, trying to turn away from the kid. Instead, he faced the crotch of the grumpy woman in line. She glared at him.

"Do you mind?" she growled.

Grant bit his tongue, folded his arms across his chest, and leaned back. This flight was only fourteen hours long. He needed to pass the next twelve in relative peace.

He checked his watch. It was almost ten in Florida. He didn't know what time zone he was currently in. It seemed like there must be a time change as they crossed the ocean. How many little islands were out in the Atlantic? Surely there were a few. Bermuda for sure.

He closed his eyes and tried to drift to sleep. The constant movement beside his head as more passengers joined the line made relaxing difficult. If he'd realized what a shitty seat he would have, he might have opted for some Xanax or a small relapse on the morphine to get through the next twelve hours.

That won't do.

He scolded himself for the thought. Getting off the pills had proven to be an arduous task, and so far, Grant felt proud that he'd succeeded. The last thing he needed was to relapse simply because he was stuck on a flight to hell.

Suddenly, a hand slapped his face.

"Nicky, don't!"

Grant opened his eyes to see the mother trying to pull Nicky back into her lap.

"I'm so sorry," she muttered.

Grant only nodded. What else could he do? He let his head drop back again. The droning din of aircraft engines vibrated through the floor. He focused on the hum as he tried to hypnotize himself to sleep.

When he opened his eyes again, the lights were dimmed. He glanced to his side to see Nicky resting his head on his sleeping mother's shoulder.

Grant checked the time. It was one in the morning in the Keys. He wondered if Charlie ever tried to call back. Should he be worried? He didn't think so. After all, the pair of them had gotten along quite well independently almost all their lives without a sibling checking up on them. Still, it was nice to know that someone besides Angie might miss him if he were gone. Well, besides Angie and Wrench. Wrench would be the one to care the most, he thought.

A prepubescent kid strolled past him and yanked open the lavatory door. The bright light inside spilled out into the darkened cabin. Quickly, Grant shielded his eyes from what seemed like a spotlight gleaming out at him.

As soon as the door shut, his eyes adjusted back to the low light. He closed his eyes again. The door flew open as the kid came out only a few seconds after going in.

"Didn't wash your hands, huh?" Grant murmured.

The boy turned to stare at Grant, who returned the glare with a certain stoic countenance he hoped scared the boy into using the forward bathrooms.

Flying commercial sucks.

15

At ten to nine, Charlie handed her passport over to a woman in Roman's warehouse at Stansted Airport's cargo area on the north-west side of the runway. The woman appeared to be expecting her, so Charlie waited in the reception area as directed. Fifteen minutes later, the receptionist reappeared and handed the passport back.

"You're good," she said in what Charlie presumed to be a Ukrainian accent. "Plane leave at ten. Wait here. Don't go outside. Somebody get you when time. Okay?"

Charlie shrugged and nodded. It didn't sound particularly like standard Department for Transport security protocol, but she'd never been a freight passenger before, so she didn't have a relevant yardstick. Or a right to complain, as she was getting a free ride. While waiting, she checked for voicemails or messages, but had yet to hear a word back from her brother. She tried figuring out what time zone he was in, but as he was most likely in flight, he would have crossed multiple time zones, making it impossible to guess.

It would be nice to know exactly where he was heading. Tanzania was a big country, with Dodoma as the modern capital, but Dar es Salaam on the coast was both larger and more heavily visited. She thought about calling Angie, but it was four in the morning in Florida, and it didn't seem fair to wake her up. She decided to quit worrying about it. As long as he left her a voicemail with details while she was in the air, it would all work out.

Charlie relaxed in the cushioned reception chair. She had a long flight ahead, and it wouldn't be until she landed in Kenya that she'd need to choose a final destination. Short-hop commuter and small aircraft flights took off regularly to all the major cities in the area from Nairobi, so she'd have options.

At 9:45 am, a man wearing a pair of jeans, a distressed leather jacket over a black T-shirt, cowboy boots, and a captain's cap opened the office door.

"You the cop?" he asked in a laid-back Texan accent.

"Former detective," Charlie corrected.

He grinned. "I like that better. Come with me, darlin'"

Charlie picked up her backpack and followed the man into the warehouse, wondering whether she'd fallen into an Indiana Jones movie or if the pilot just thought he had.

"Jump in here, and we'll have you on your way in no time," he said, pointing to an airplane cargo container shaped to fit in the hold of the plane.

"I'm not flying in there!" she protested.

"Wanna go to Kenya, darlin'?"

"Yeah."

"Then get in the box. We'll get you out once we're airborne."

"No way is this aboveboard," Charlie muttered.

"Wanna go to Kenya?" he repeated.

"Yeah, yeah, yeah," she grumbled.

She squinted at the dark interior of the container. It looked to be about five feet square, with one upper quadrant angled to fit against the side of the curved fuselage. The lower half was full of wooden crates with a couple of packing blankets thrown on top.

"Stretch out, relax, and enjoy the ride," the captain joked as Charlie reluctantly climbed inside the open hatch at one end.

"What about light...?" she tried asking, but he closed the door, and Charlie heard a forklift truck rumble towards her. In no time, she was bouncing along on her way to the plane.

Her container must have been the last one loaded, as shortly after, she felt the aluminum crate shove up against something solid. Tie-down straps ratcheted, then all went quiet until the sound of jet engines reverberated through the fuselage. Pulling her cell phone from her pocket, she turned on the flashlight function. The space seemed even smaller with the door closed, and she cursed herself for going along with this nonsense.

She called Roman's number, but it quickly went to voicemail, leading her to believe he was blowing her off. She pressed against the door—which, of course, didn't budge—then checked around for a way of opening the latch from the inside but found none.

After a few minutes, the plane began moving, and Charlie resigned herself to the fact she'd be leaving England in what felt like a metal coffin. All she could do now was hope someone remembered to let her out once they were airborne.

Grant woke up a few times during the night, but each time, he dropped back off to sleep with ease. When the cabin crew brought the lights up, he straightened up to check the time. It was about eight in the morning back home.

"We have crossed into European air space," the captain announced over the PA. "If you look out the window, you can make out the southern coast of Spain and the Mediterranean Sea."

Grant stretched his neck to peek past the two people across the aisle in his row. All he could see through the small Plexiglass window was blue skies with a few large puffy clouds. He would trust that the pilot knew where he was going, and if he didn't, then there was little Grant could do about it.

"We will be landing in Istanbul in just over two hours. The seatbelt sign has been turned off, so feel free to roam about the cabin."

Grant took the opportunity to get into the bathroom before the line formed. He splashed some water on his face before running his wet fingers through his hair. Even though he hadn't done anything except sit for the last ten hours, he felt desperate for a shower. There was something about air travel that did that to him.

When he came out, he found another queue had formed alongside his seat. He pushed through and sat back down just as a man in his row decided that now was a good time to stretch his own legs. Grant got up again, letting the young mother and Nicky out before the older man in a sports coat and polo shirt sidled past.

While he was on his feet, Grant moved forward. If he could slip into business class, he might spot Al-Maawali. He walked forward, pausing at the lavatory at the front of the coach section.

Casually, Grant leaned through the curtain to look into the galley. Empty. He let out a breath of relief as he stepped into the nook and pulled back the curtain on the other side. The cabin crew was doling out plated breakfasts to the first-class passengers. Grant saw a woman working her fork through scrambled eggs, a sausage link, and a piece of buttered toast. Somehow, the toast appealed to him the most, and he wondered if the coach passengers would be fed, too. Probably not; they were expected to bring something from the terminal. At those prices, Grant thought he could have upgraded to the upper echelon.

He spied the back of Al-Maawali, who sat in the third row from the front. He'd be off the plane long before Grant, but they both had to go through customs after getting their luggage. In the end, both of them were on the same flight out of Istanbul to Dar es Salaam. In fact, that plane would only be intercontinental and might be a smaller aircraft.

"Sir, can I help you?" a male crew member asked with a German accent.

"No, sir, I was just waiting to use the bathroom."

"Do you mind waiting in the rear section?"

Grant smiled congenially. "Of course not."

Saleh Al-Maawali turned his head toward Grant, and Grant quickly tried to pull the curtain closed.

Did he see me?

Grant wasn't sure, but he didn't want to test the theory by glancing again. Besides, the German crewman waited impatiently for him to return to his section.

After getting back to his seat, Grant flopped down. The attendants in the back were pushing the beverage cart toward him, and when they arrived, he got a small cup of coffee. It would hopefully sustain him until he landed. He was only going to be in Turkey for about two hours before the next plane took off. Enough time to call Charlie and maybe find a Turkish coffee, if there was a place in the airport.

By the time he finished his drink, the crew began taking up the trash and empty cups. Then it was time to put up the tray tables and buckle up for the landing. Nicky began poking his shoulder, and Grant kept his head facing forward under the assumption that if he didn't give him the satisfaction of looking at the little shithead, the kid might grow bored.

By the time the jet touched down, he was ready to sprint off the plane. His leg was throbbing again, and if Nicky touched him one more time, Grant thought he might break the boy's fingers off. As the plane taxied across the tarmac, Grant decided his best plan was to avoid Al-Maawali in the airport. It was stupid to try to get a look at him. If Al-Maawali spotted him, the man might change his flight plans.

All the passengers rose to their feet as soon as the plane stopped rolling. Grant waited a few seconds before getting out of his seat. A throng of people clogged the aisles as the crew opened the forward door. He pulled his carry-on luggage out of the overhead bin and shuffled along with the mass of people. How humans could make something as easy as getting off the plane an ordeal, Grant would never understand.

He already missed being home. The Keys felt crowded during the tourist season, but even then, he could escape onto the water with no one around for miles, provided he avoided the sand bars and party spots. Right now, he felt like a Twinkie on an anthill.

Finally, he moved forward. The old man and Nicky's mom were the only people behind him. It still took ten minutes to meander to the front and escape the aircraft. When he reached the gangway, he took out his phone. He'd turned it off to conserve the battery, and now, as the lights cycled on, he stepped into the Istanbul airport terminal. The screen finally came on, asking for his passcode.

"Sir, we need you to come with us."

Grant lifted his head from the phone to see three officers. He couldn't tell if they were security or police.

"What's going on?" he inquired.

"We need you to come with us," the one in the middle repeated. His hand was touching the sidearm at his waist.

"What?" Grant muttered as the one on the right stepped forward, grabbing him by the arm and turning him around. He felt the cold metal of handcuffs snap around his wrists, and the officer snatched his phone from his hand.

Grant asked, "Why? What did I do?"

Across the terminal, Grant saw the sly face of Saleh Al-Maalawi watching intently as the officers took Grant by the arms and guided him away from the gate.

16

———

"How you doin', darlin'?" came the pilot's voice, accompanied by the rattling of the container's door opening.

Charlie startled awake, sitting up and banging her head on the metal ceiling.

"Easy, girl," the pilot drawled. "Don't hurt that pretty head of yours."

She glared at the man, but shuffled out, stretched her legs, and rolled her shoulders, which already ached. Charlie couldn't believe she'd actually fallen asleep inside the container.

"How long have we been airborne?" she asked.

"'Bout an hour," he replied, turning and pulling aside a heavy curtain. "Coffee?"

Charlie followed, her eyes adjusting to the dim lighting of the cargo bay after the pitch-black inside the box.

"What are you carrying?" she asked, looking back at the cargo containers.

She could only see the first two, as their shaped design filled the interior perfectly. Charlie realized if her box had been placed anywhere farther back, she would have been trapped until they'd unloaded.

"Pet food," the pilot replied.

"I don't think that was pet food I was sleeping on," Charlie commented, thinking about the wooden crates.

The man paused and let the curtain drop. "Says pet food on my manifest, darlin'. I don't ask beyond that, and you shouldn't, either." He eyed her up and down. "Roman told me you'd be no trouble. He right about that?"

Charlie was fed up with the "darlings" and flirtatious looks but reminded herself she needed to get to Tanzania. And it wasn't like she could get off at the next station.

"No trouble at all," she replied. "I was just curious."

He nodded and lowered his voice. "Got another fella riding shotgun this trip. Best not be curious around him, I reckon." His face broke into a smile. "I'm Tex, by the way. Don't think I said so before with the hurry to get goin' and all."

He extended a hand, which Charlie shook, noting his firm but respectful grip.

"Tex? Really?" she questioned with a laugh, thinking he must be pulling her leg.

The man seemed like a caricature from a movie, and she pictured him whooping as he buzzed treetops over a South American jungle with guerrilla fighters taking shots at him from the ground.

"Since first day in boot camp. Air Force-trained," he said. "Charlotte, right?"

"Charlie," she replied. "Since Dad said I acted more like a boy." She left out the "police-trained" part.

"Like a boy, huh? No mistakin' you now," he responded with a wink.

Charlie resisted the urge to punch him in the nose. He seemed harmlessly flirty, matching his 1980s movie persona, but she was used to punching men on the nose for making sexist comments, and the habit was hard to shake. He swung the curtain aside once more and led her through an area with a pair of jump seats next to a lavatory and into a small galley. He poured her a coffee into a plastic mug while she looked at the man asleep in one of the fold-down seats. His head bobbed with the light movement of the plane, and she didn't envy him the neckache he'd have when he woke up.

"Here you go," Tex said, handing her the mug. "Creamer and sugar around here somewhere, if you're so inclined."

"This is good," she replied, and followed him again when he opened the door to the flight deck.

The co-pilot looked over his shoulder as they entered. He was younger than Tex and wore a USAF sweatshirt. He slipped off his headset and stepped from the cramped seat.

"I gotta pee," he said, walking past them.

"That's Mayday," Tex said, sliding into the left seat.

"He's the touchy one?" Charlie asked.

Tex laughed. "Nah. He's a pussycat. The bobblehead character in the back is the guy I was talking about. Just stay outta his way."

Charlie wondered how that would be possible for the next eight hours while the four of them occupied the same crowded area, but if the man stayed asleep, it would help. She wasn't that lucky, though. The door opened again, and Bobblehead stood, staring at her.

"You policewoman?" he snapped in an Eastern European accent.

"Former," Charlie replied.

"What is former?"

"Means I'm not anymore."

He frowned at her. "You are police, or no?"

"No," she responded, figuring his English skills weren't up to a more detailed explanation.

He rubbed the back of his neck, and Charlie smiled inside. They'd only been acquainted for thirty seconds, and she was already convinced her prior empathy had been misplaced. She wished he'd stayed asleep. The man was in his thirties, with short-cropped black hair and several days' worth of unshaved stubble. He was close to six feet tall, and appeared muscular and lean from the way his collared shirt fell on his frame.

Mayday returned, so Bobblehead stepped aside to let him in. The co-pilot gave her a brief nod as he went by, and Charlie hoped no one would be urgently repeating his nickname over the radio on this trip. Which raised the notion of how and why he'd come to be called Mayday, but she kept her concern to herself.

"Where you go?" Bobblehead asked, and Charlie turned to see he'd filled the doorway again.

"Kenya," she replied, damned if she'd give him anything more.

"Why?" he asked suspiciously.

"Want to tell me why you're going to Kenya?" she rebutted.

"Not your business," he snarled.

"Exactly," she said, and walked toward him.

Behind her, she heard Tex getting out of his seat. "Now, now, you kids need to play nice on my airplane."

Charlie stopped two feet from Bobblehead. "I need to use the loo. You can move and I'll use the one over there, or you can stand in the way while I spray your legs. One way or another, I'm going to be peeing in about thirty seconds."

Bobblehead's brow creased in confusion until Tex rattled off something in what Charlie could only guess was Ukrainian. Bobblehead's expression turned to surprise, and he stepped back. Charlie continued to the lavatory. While she relieved herself, she heard the two men talking outside, but couldn't understand a word. When she was done and had returned to the cabin, Bobblehead was back in the jump seat and Tex was leaning against the flight deck doorway.

"Got a bottle of water?" Charlie asked.

"Sure," he replied, and pulled one from a carton in a galley cabinet, handing it to her.

"I think I'll retire to my cabin if that's okay?" she said.

Tex laughed. "Door open or closed, ma'am?"

Charlie looked at Bobblehead, who already had his eyes closed, then turned back to Tex and raised her eyebrows.

"He won't mess with you," Tex said, correctly guessing her concern.

"Open, in that case."

"Sleep tight," Tex said, grinning as he returned to the flight deck.

Charlie moved through the heavy curtain and climbed into the container. Out of curiosity, she folded the shipping blanket back and looked at one of the long wooden crates below. She couldn't see any markings. Smoothing out the blanket, she set the water bottle aside and laid down to rest.

For the second time on the flight, Charlie awoke with a start. From the rattling, shaking, and roar of the engines, she quickly figured out they were landing. The rapid deceleration had her body sliding down the blanket, and she shoved a foot against the edge of the door opening to hold herself in place. Once the plane had slowed and Tex turned off the runway, Charlie dropped from the container and yawned.

The curtain was suddenly thrust aside, and Mayday looked at her with wide eyes.

"Come with me, quick," he hissed. "Stay quiet."

She wondered why the man wasn't up front when they were taxiing, but sleepily followed.

"What happening?" Bobblehead barked from his seat.

"We'll be at the cargo terminal in a couple of minutes," Mayday replied, but Charlie could tell from his nervous tone that something was up.

Apparently, Bobblehead could too as he lurched to his feet and reached for the flight deck door. Before his fingers found the handle, Mayday had a Heckler & Koch VP9 pressed to the man's ribs. Where he'd produced it from, Charlie could only guess, but she was wide awake now. Bobblehead froze and muttered something in Ukrainian.

Mayday nodded toward the cargo hold. "Nice and slow. Put your hands on your head, buddy. We're going that way."

Bobblehead looked at him, but didn't move. Charlie lifted her hands and placed them on her head. "Hands on head, mate," she repeated.

Bobblehead scowled at her, but did as ordered. With his hands raised, he began moving toward the back.

"Hey, wait up," Mayday said. "You need to frisk him."

Charlie wasn't sure what was going on or how she fit into the puzzle, but figured siding with the two men who'd been pleasant was better than the one dickhead who had a gun pointed at him. She stopped Bobblehead with a hand on his shoulder and patted him down. Raising her concern another level, she relieved him of a Margolin 22 caliber pistol and a vicious-looking switchblade knife.

"The container," Mayday ordered, and all three of them swayed as the plane ran over an unusually large seam in the taxiway.

Bobblehead lunged, pushing Mayday's gun hand up and away while swinging at the man's jaw with his other fist. Charlie brought the butt of the gun she'd taken from Bobblehead down on its former owner's skull. The punch landed at the same time as her strike, filling the galley with groans and crunching noises. Both men dropped to the deck, out cold.

"Bugger me," Charlie said, grimacing.

She swung the flight deck door open to a sea of flashing lights out the windows, illuminating the night sky in greens and reds.

"What the bloody hell is going on?" she shouted, and Tex pivoted around.

"Where's Mayday?"

"The wanker bloke knocked him out."

"Fuck!" Tex exclaimed. "Where's Alexei?"

"If Alexei is the Bobblehead wanker, then he's knocked out, too."

Tex frowned, his head swiveling as he slowed the plane to a stop, reaching the emergency vehicles. Armed men in military fatigues and red berets poured from the back of a pair of personnel trucks. Tex's hands flew around the controls as he came out of the seat.

"We have to move fast!" he exclaimed, rushing past her.

In the galley, Mayday was coming to, but Bobblehead was still unconscious.

"Grab his legs," Tex ordered, and the two of them lifted the Ukrainian and struggled through the curtain to the cargo hold.

With very little finesse or care for the man's well-being, Tex swung Bobblehead's upper body into the open container, wrenching the man's ankles from Charlie's grip. The body teetered in the open hatch before slumping with a thud to the deck.

"Fuck," Tex growled.

This time, the two of them took an armpit each and shoved Bobblehead's limp form into Charlie's private cabin, heaving his legs inside so the door would close. A loud thumping came from the big cargo door beside the container.

"Quick, we need to sort Mayday out," Tex spat.

Charlie stopped him before he disappeared through the curtain. She still had no idea exactly what was going on, but instinct urged her to help as best she could.

"I'll get Mayday," she said. "You answer the door."

Tex gritted his teeth. "There's a spare cap upfront. Mayday knows where. Put it on. You're crew now."

With that, Charlie left Tex to deal with the authorities, then raced to the galley, where she found Mayday struggling to his feet.

"What happened?" he muttered, rubbing his jaw and using his other hand to steady himself against the doorway.

"No time," Charlie urged. "You need to do co-pilot things, and Tex said there's an extra cap somewhere?"

Mayday winced as he nodded, but staggered onto the flight deck. Charlie closed the door behind them as she heard Tex opening the big cargo access in the back.

"Up there," Mayday said, pointing to a narrow cabinet as he slid into the right seat and donned the headset.

He quickly began communicating with the tower, so Charlie pulled out the cap and slipped it on her head. It was at least two sizes too big, but she figured that was a minor problem compared to the lack of pilot credentials and the body in the container.

Urgent voices echoed from beyond the flight deck door. Unsure what else to do, Charlie slid into the left seat and put the headset on. Her ears were soon filled with all kinds of instructions and confirmations between the tower and various aircraft, but it appeared Mayday had smoothed over that side of things as he didn't respond to any of it. Out front in the glow of the taxiway lights, men carrying M16s formed a semicircle around the front of the plane.

"Look to the left of your leg," Mayday said over the intercom. "Pass me the black pouch."

Happy to look somewhere other than out the window, Charlie spotted what he was talking about sticking out of a mesh pocket against the fuselage. She took the pouch and handed it to Mayday. She could tell from the shape and weight of the contents that it held a wad of cash.

The flight deck door swung open, and Tex strode in, followed by a large, dark-skinned man in uniform. Tex nodded to Mayday, who returned the gesture.

"Well, well, well," the Kenyan man said jovially in a heavy accent. "Who do we have here?"

"Training," Tex answered, and threw Charlie a glance, which she took to mean "be quiet."

"I'd prefer seeing your trainee more often than you," the military man said with a laugh.

"She don't bring you gifts," Tex replied, and Mayday held up an envelope.

Charlie could tell from the thickness that it contained only a portion of the money that had been in the pouch. The Kenyan smoothly took the envelope, and it disappeared inside his jacket.

"This was quite the surprise," Tex said, looking out the windows at the light show on the tarmac. "A heads-up woulda been nice."

The big man shrugged his shoulders. "Sometimes, I have to

appease men further up the food chain, my friend. It's out of my hands."

"Yet we still placed that gift *in your hand*," Tex pointed out.

The Kenyan smiled. "Yes, you did. Because you're a smart man, Tex."

The pilot shook his head and sighed. "Take that first container. I'm betting you'll find what you need and the man responsible."

"Perhaps my men should examine more of the cargo," the Kenyan said, his expression turning serious.

Tex looked at Mayday, who was still rubbing his jaw, then back at the Kenyan. The big man burst out laughing and slapped Tex on the back.

"You worry too much, my friend! Enjoy your stay. I'll see you next month." He winked at Charlie. "You too, I hope," he added before turning and leaving the flight deck, barking orders the moment he reached the cargo hold.

Tex blew out his cheeks. "Son of a bitch."

"What was that all about?" Charlie asked, slumping in the seat.

"Extortion, that's what that's about," Tex groaned. "A fella can't make a dishonest living these days without The Man taking his fucking cut."

17

———

"What the hell is going on?" Grant demanded as the airport police escorted him to a holding cell.

"Place your belongings in here," a dour matron in her sixties ordered from behind a large wooden desk. She extended her hand with a clear plastic bag. Her English was impeccable, and Grant thought he recognized a hint of a British accent. However, he wouldn't suggest that if Charlie had been there. Now that he thought about it, maybe the accent wasn't British. Hell, it might have been South African for all he knew.

"Can I know what's going on?" he asked her.

The desk officer rolled her eyes up so that her pupils stared at him over the tops of her half-frame glasses perched on the bridge of her nose. A gold-plated chain connected one temple tip to the other so that she could pull the reading spectacles off her face without losing them.

"I cannot say," she replied after a second.

Grant considered arguing that he had certain rights, but this wasn't America. Whatever rights he had back home didn't hold up here. Besides, Grant had been a cop long enough to know the number-one mistake criminals made that ended up putting them in prison. They almost always talked too much. If Grant could go back and count the cases where he'd gotten a warrant and often a conviction when he didn't have enough evidence, all because the perp didn't know to shut up, he guessed it would push the three digits.

"Fine," Grant conceded. He pulled his wallet and passport out of his pocket before depositing them in the plastic bag. "I'll wait then. The officer took my phone. Can I get it back?"

"No," she snapped, sealing the bag with his belongings.

"Will you at least make sure it's with my stuff?"

She ignored his request, instead motioning for an officer at her side to take him away. Grant groaned as the man stepped forward, talking in Turkish.

"I don't know what you said," Grant told him in long, slow words.

The matron rambled something to the officer in Turkish, then she told Grant, "He doesn't speak English, so don't cause a problem for him." Her tone was firm, leaving no doubt in Grant's mind that it was an order.

The officer motioned for Grant to move through a door on the left. When he entered, Grant found a white, sterile hallway. Most of the walls and ceiling tile had yellowed over the years. The airport's security department hadn't seen any upgrades since the '90s.

"*Dur!*" the officer snapped, stopping in front of a large wooden door.

Based on the man's tone, Grant assumed he meant for him to go into the room. The Turkish policeman fumbled with the keys as he unlocked the door. Grant wondered what the hell was going on. Their treatment was confusing. While they were going through the motions of arresting him—or at least holding him—they weren't taking the precautions Grant would have done when detaining a suspect. The guard wasn't on high alert. Even now, as he tried to unlock the door, he left himself open to an attack by Grant. It almost seemed comical.

Where would he go, though? Grant could easily knock the cop down. Maybe even disarm him. But he was stranded in Istanbul. Before he could get out of the airport, the police would have plenty of time to mobilize and recapture him. He decided that doing anything rash would be an exercise in futility. In fact, it would likely make the situation worse.

But he didn't have enough time to wait it out. He only had a two-hour layover. If he did anything to delay them, he might miss his next flight.

Grant stepped into the small cell that could have been mistaken for a closet. It had to have been the worst interrogation room Grant had ever seen. If someone were designing sets for a Cold War spy film, this hole would fit the bill. The walls of the room were bare cinderblock, and the ceiling was covered in solid wood paneling. Grant wondered what was on the other side of the veneer. Most likely more concrete. At least, that was his guess after seeing the rest of the building. They might have installed the ceiling panel to dampen the echo in there.

Or, as Grant's eyes examined the room, he realized they'd used the panels to hide the wires that ran to the single camera above the door. It was by far the newest addition to the cell.

"Burada bekle." The guard gestured at a single metal folding chair in the middle of the room. Above the seat, a fluorescent tube light fixture dangled on two thin aluminum chains. The ballast's hum intensified when the cop pulled the thick door closed.

Grant stared up at the ceiling and wondered again what was going on. He paced around the room, dragging his fingers over the surface of the cement walls and the hefty door. While it was made of wood, the thing was solid. It would take more than a shoulder to break through it, certainly from the inside. Hell, it might take a battering ram just to bust it open.

Grant stared up at the camera. If he wanted to disable it, he could do that with ease, but he knew it still wouldn't help his cause. He pulled the chair to the back of the ten-by-ten-foot cell. When he sat down, Grant rocked the chair back to teeter on its rear legs. The backrest bumped up against the cinderblock, which Grant rested his head against.

After half an hour with no contact, Grant got up from the chair, stretching his legs and back.

"Hey, can I see someone?" he shouted as he locked his eyes on the camera lens above the door. *Did the camera even have a microphone?* He continued regardless. "Come on. I need to get to my plane?"

So far, he hadn't resorted to the "I'm an American, I have rights" defense. Grant knew the pointlessness of that. Nothing mucked up a bureaucratic nightmare like entitlement. Still, he couldn't stay here forever. While he didn't want to piss off his captors, he needed something to happen. His fist banged on the door. "I have a flight to catch!" he shouted.

He paced around some more. The buildup of nervous energy began to take its toll. His hand moved down to his thigh, subconsciously rubbing the dull ache.

After another half hour, the throb stretched into a gnawing, pulling sensation. His Advil was in his carry-on luggage, which the matron officer now had. Unless they let him out right now, there was little chance he could make his flight.

Grant returned to his seat, but the position only exacerbated the pain. He straightened his left leg, hoping to relieve the discomfort. Finally, after what felt like another thirty minutes, he stood up again and paced the room. Without a phone or a watch, he was guessing at the time, but his internal clock was close.

He tried walking quickly in circles to work the muscle. He knew most of the pain was subliminal, but that didn't help the feeling subside. Eventually, he tired of the pacing. The poor sleep on the plane—thanks in part to little Nicky—and the stress of his predicament were wearing him down.

He shoved the chair over in frustration. When the metal crashed against the concrete wall, he reflected on a story he recalled his mother telling him. When he was about ten, he'd complained about having to wait somewhere with nothing to do. Now, he couldn't remember what the exact circumstances were, but as a boy, he only knew that the experience was interminable. But his mother told him that spies often endured long periods of isolation so that they could combat any fears or anxiety of confinement. She encouraged him to use the opportunity to build up his resilience.

In retrospect, he was now curious how much truth she'd put into that story. After Grant learned that his mother was an American agent, it changed some of his perspective about her and the tales he heard growing up.

He plopped down on the floor, stretching his body out prone. He stared at the humming light. It had a flicker at one end of the bulb that occurred every twenty-three seconds. He began counting the flashes, but somewhere around forty-two, he lost count and drifted to sleep.

When the doorknob rattled, Grant sprang up. He had rolled to his right side, tucking his arm under his head like a pillow. The inside of his mouth felt like someone had stuffed it with cotton balls, and his lips had the dried residue of drool streaking from the right corner of his mouth. He pushed up to his feet, dragging the back of his hand across his face to clean off the spittle.

A burly man in a cheap gray suit entered. Where most people might add a spark of color with a bright tie, this man maintained the colorless theme by choosing charcoal.

"Mr. Wolfe?" he read from a file folder in his right hand. After finding the name and pronouncing it aloud, he lifted his eyes in a silent question of, "Are you him?"

"Yes," Grant muttered as he tried blinking himself awake. *How long had he been asleep?* It had been more than a few minutes, but still groggy, Grant felt out of place. "What is going on here?"

"We are releasing you." The statement came out almost like a question.

"What is going on?" Grant asked again.

"It was a case of mistaken identity," the man told him. Each word came out slow and meticulous as he tried to get his English and diction correct.

"What does that mean?"

Grant's bureaucratic warden stared at him as he tried to work out what his prisoner was asking.

"Mistake," he finally repeated to Grant.

"What time is it?"

The man glared at Grant without answering. After realizing he wasn't getting an answer, Grant said, "Can I get my stuff?"

The gray-suited fellow stepped back out of the doorway. Grant watched his face. There was nothing but a blank expression on it. Grant moved into the corridor, and the gray man fell into step behind him. The matronly officer in the front was gone. A white-haired officer reclined in the same office chair. Grant bet that the woman would never allow herself to be so relaxed.

The clear bag filled with his belongings was on the desk. His hard-sided rolling carry-on stood at attention on the floor with its handle raised.

Grant froze when he saw the clock on the wall. The hands indicated it was twenty minutes till nine. He'd been asleep for almost four hours—give or take a few minutes. His flight had left three hours ago.

He cursed under his breath, and the officer at the desk stared up at him.

"What is all this about?" he asked again. "I've missed my flight."

The man at the desk shrugged and looked over at the gray man. He lifted his shoulders as if confused.

Grant grabbed the clear bag. "Can I go?"

Both men nodded with an expression that implied that was a given. Grant grabbed the handle on his luggage and dragged the bag out the door.

Once clear of the security office, he fumbled in the clear plastic pouch for his phone. He needed to message Angie and Charlie to let them know he'd lost Saleh Al-Maalawi.

"Dammit," he blurted out loud.

The phone screen was black, and a spiderweb of cracks spread out from the top right corner. When he tried to turn it on, nothing happened. The battery was dead. He thought back, realizing he'd just turned it on when the cops had grabbed him. The bastards hadn't turned it off. He stared at it a little more before trudging back to the terminal.

While there were still flights coming and going through Istanbul, the traffic had diminished from when he'd first landed. He found a table next to a Starbucks, which was unfortunately closed. He was reaching to unzip his bag to find his phone charger when he eyed the electrical outlet.

"Dammit!" he growled as he stared at the receptacle, a European type for which he hadn't thought to bring an adapter.

No chance of finding a flight online, then. He grabbed the bag and pulled it along until he found an attendant at the desk for Oman Air and Qatar Air.

"I need some help," he confessed.

When the Turkish woman behind the counter answered him in English, he felt some relief. "How may I help you?" she asked in careful syllables.

"I need to get to Dar es Salaam, ASAP!"

Her forehead wrinkled.

"As soon as possible," he clarified. "The police held me up, and I missed my flight."

She nodded as she typed into the computer. "What is your name?"

Grant told her.

"Oh, yes. Your flight was at 18:40," she announced.

"Yes, what can you get me on that will get me there the quickest?"

The airline employee leaned in to study her screen. "We have a flight leaving here at 1:55 am with a stop in Kilimanjaro. The flight from Kilimanjaro leaves at 9:05 and arrives Dar es Salaam at 10:15."

Grant stifled a yawn. "Please. That will work."

When she told him the price, he balked.

"We can't refund the other airfare. You missed the flight."

"That wasn't my fault," he argued.

She gave him a sympathetic expression. "There is nothing I can do."

He grunted in frustration as he fished into his wallet for his mother's American Express card. Grant was grateful he'd brought it along.

The Oman Air employee took the card without reading the name on it. She swiped it and handed it back. Five minutes later, Grant was heading toward Terminal B. His stomach grumbled. Initially, he'd hoped to get a bite between flights, but now most of the food vendors were closed for the night.

He found a stand still open and purchased a Çokonat, a Turkish candy bar, and a Gazoz, a local carbonated lemonade that Grant found much better-tasting than the candy bar. After settling into a chair at the gate, he waited for his flight to board.

At 1:15 am, the crew began boarding the Airbus A330. Grant was delighted to find that the young woman who'd helped him had upgraded him to business class. She hadn't mentioned it to him, and he worried he'd been grumpy with her. Now, he stretched out in his seat and soon fell asleep. If nothing else went wrong, he should arrive in Dar es Salaam by mid-morning. Where he'd face the daunting task of tracking down Saleh Al-Maawali again.

18

After Tex had shepherded Charlie through immigration in the commercial section of Nairobi's airport, she'd been left to figure out the rest for herself. A taxi ride to the almost deserted passenger terminal netted a flight booking to Dar es Salaam for the following morning. Tired, hungry, and starting to worry about Grant, she'd found a hotel nearby and crashed out.

Turning on her phone when the plane touched down Sunday morning at 10:05 am, Charlie was disappointed to discover no new calls, texts, or voicemails. As she disembarked at the terminal, she logged on to the airport Wi-Fi and called her voicemail, wondering if the system was failing to alert her as she was out of the UK.

"Your voicemail box is full and cannot accept any new messages," came a digitized voice.

Charlie groaned. She listened to the most recent message, which was two months old. From her father. Standing in the hallway with passengers flooding by either side of her, Charlie listened to Keith Greene's voice, casually asking whether she'd prefer he bring home Thai food or Mexican for dinner. A message she'd never heard before, and the last one he'd ever leave for her.

If Charlie allowed herself to ponder on that moment at the

funeral services, which she tried not to do, her certainty of the man in the trees being her father was rapidly receding. Grant was probably right; it had been a mixture of denial and wishful thinking.

She let out a long sigh and closed her eyes as she selected "erase all." There was no time to sort through dozens of old voicemails and choose what to keep. Walking on, Charlie called Grant's phone, which went straight to his voicemail.

"I'm in Dar Es Salaam Airport. Call me."

Reaching the immigration section, Charlie groaned one more time. The area was a sea of humanity. The line wound back and forth in a zigzag of stanchions and ribbons, guiding the passengers like cattle to the slaughterhouse. Her delay in the hallway had lost her about fifty spots in the queue.

After twenty-five minutes of watching the uniformed immigration agents steadily leave their booths until only one remained, she was still ten people away. Behind her, only a handful of passengers had been slower than her to reach the checkpoint. They must have been the last plane of a wave, as the room was now almost empty. As she was about to turn back, a new group of passengers began filing in, indicating another arrival. Charlie squinted and did a double-take.

"Grant!" she yelped, and shuffled backwards in the line, which was greeted with frowns and grumbles from the other passengers. "You're moving up a spot," she muttered to them. "Don't whine about it."

"What are you doing here?" Grant asked as he wound back and forth down the empty rows.

Charlie began unclipping ribbons from stanchions to make a straight path to the new arrivals until they met and quickly joined the back of the line.

"I got your message about coming to Tanzania," she replied as though it were obvious.

"Right, but I didn't mean that you had to come here."

"Bloody hell. Nice to see you, too."

"I didn't mean it like that," he responded. "I just mean I'm chasing a lead that could come to nothing, that's all."

"Well, you could have left your flight details for me," Charlie complained. "I can't believe we arrived about the same time."

"They killed my phone," Grant replied. "Besides, your voice-mail is full, so how could I leave you a message?"

"No, it's not," Charlie argued.

"Yes, it is! I tried a dozen times."

"Okay, well, it was," Charlie admitted. "I cleared it out."

Grant shook his head and shuffled along with the line.

"You broke your phone?" she asked.

"No. The immigration, or police, or whoever they were in Istanbul did. They detained me there. Otherwise, I would have been here last night."

"You were arrested at the airport?"

"Detained," he emphasized, then lowered his voice. "Saleh Al-Maawali spotted me. I think he had me held so I missed the flight."

"Blimey. That's some pull, if the bloke can have Turkish police jump at his wishes."

Grant nodded. "That's what I thought, too."

"What's our first move?" Charlie whispered.

Grant looked around them, but everyone appeared to be consumed with their own travel concerns.

"We have to find Saleh Al-Maawali."

"No shit," Charlie hissed. "I meant, where will he be?"

Grant scowled at her. "If he hadn't had me detained in Istanbul, I would have followed him and I'd know that, wouldn't I? Now, I guess all we can do is check out the address for Uhuru Global Exports."

"Who are they?" Charlie asked.

Grant frowned, and then a light bulb appeared to come on. "Shit, sorry. I forgot you don't know any of this."

As they edged forward in line, he explained his confrontation with Saleh Al-Maawali and how he'd tracked him to a company in Tanzania. They finally reached the desk, and Charlie held her breath. *If the thief could pull strings in Istanbul, surely he'd have influence in Tanzania?* But apart from the man asking how long they intended on staying, he seemed generally uninterested, stamped their passports, and waved them through. They'd told him a week, so Charlie quickly checked the date on the entry stamp and was relieved to see it was for thirty days. She hoped they'd be long gone by then.

"Okay, where's this export company, then?" Charlie asked as they walked through baggage claim.

"Don't we need to grab your luggage?" Grant asked.

Charlie raised the strap of her backpack. "Traveling light. A possible overnight in Wales has turned into an international trip, so I should pick up a few things or I'll be a bit whiffy if we're here more than a day."

"Whiffy?" Grant laughed. "You have a funny way of saying things, Greene."

"I speak English, Wolfe," she replied with a broad grin. "The original kind."

They walked past customs, who showed no interest in them, then Charlie used her credit card to take out one million Tanzanian shillings at an ATM—the equivalent of four hundred US dollars.

Continuing outside, they discovered a chaotic mass of vehicles and people. Taxi drivers, each claiming to be the best tour guides in the city, vied for their business. Grant pushed past them to a quiet middle-aged man with dark skin leaning against the hood of his white sedan. The car sported the green stripe of the local taxis down the side.

"English?" Grant asked him.

"Either proper or American will do," Charlie added.

"I speak both," the man replied with an accent. He grinned, and his eyes twinkled with humor. "Where do you need to go?"

"Uhuru Global Exports," Grant said. "They're on Nelson Mandela Road. Do you know where that is?"

The taxi driver's expression tightened, and his brow furrowed. "Near the docks. Are you sure this is where you want to go?"

Grant paused by the rear door. "Why do you ask?"

The man looked at Charlie before turning his attention back to Grant. "This is not the best place for a nice young lady. Is better I take you to your hotel. We have very nice hotels and excellent beaches. I think this would be better."

"That sounds great, but our business is with these people on Nelson Mandela Road," Grant responded, then grinned at his sister. "And don't worry, she's not that nice."

Charlie punched his arm.

The taxi driver shrugged his shoulders. "Very well. I take you to your place of business. My name is Juma. Welcome to Dar es Salaam."

Traffic was busy, but steadily moved along Julius K. Nyerere Road, the main drag heading east toward the ocean. The temperature sat in the mid-eighties, and the taxi had all the windows down, so a dusty breeze blew through the car, combatting the bright sunshine and heat from all the vehicles. Toyotas appeared to be the locals' favorite mode of transport, and they varied greatly in age and condition. Small buses and vans were also prevalent, and scooters zipped in and out of lanes as though the riders were determined to be knocked from their machines. Juma seemed unfazed by any of the chaos, and the Bob Marley sticker on his dashboard reflected his laid-back demeanor.

"Hey," Grant said quietly, nudging Charlie. "Did you notice anyone watching us at the airport?"

"No. Which seems odd if our guy knew you'd chase him here once you were released, right?"

"I was half-expecting to be detained again," Grant admitted, focusing on something ahead of them.

Charlie realized he was looking in the side mirror. "See something?"

"I'm not sure. There's a beige car with a broken headlight about three cars back. I see one guy in the front. I've noticed him back there since we left the airport."

Charlie resisted the urge to turn and look out the back window. Juma must have overheard Grant as he now peered in his mirrors.

"Are you two in some kind of trouble?" he asked, although his tone sounded like one of interest rather than concern.

"My sister is a big deal in the UK," Grant replied, keeping a straight face. "The paparazzi hassle us sometimes."

Charlie rolled her eyes. "I look nothing like Adele," she mumbled. "Even the skinny version."

"Then pick someone else you look like," Grant chuckled, amused by his sister's reference to a mistaken identity incident they'd experienced in the Florida Keys.

"You are very pretty lady, if is okay to say?" Juma said, looking in the rearview mirror. "You are an actress?"

"Yes," she replied, trying to think of someone famous she resembled in even the slightest way.

"What movies?" the driver asked. "I watch lots of Hollywood movies."

He seemed to have forgotten the possible tail, but Charlie noticed Grant remained vigilant, even turning around for a better look.

"Have you seen any of the *Star Wars* movies?" Charlie asked, more concerned about the beige car than the complicated excuse Grant had invented.

"Of course!" Juma enthused. "You are in *Star Wars* movies? Wait, wait, I know. You are Daisy lady, right?"

Charlie shrugged. "Please don't spread the word, Juma. We'll have no peace whatsoever if word gets out."

Grant shook his head. "Swing for the fences, why don't you?" he whispered. "*Star Wars*, seriously? You couldn't go with some shitty subtitled film he wouldn't know?"

"You started it," Charlie groaned. "Are we being followed or what?"

Grant relaxed in the seat. "He just turned. I think we're okay."

The drive took another five minutes, and Juma was right. As they approached the industrial area near the docks, the traffic thinned, and tall wire fences surrounded businesses whose yards were full of trucks, containers, and junk. Juma pulled over in front of one such entity, where a small sign above an office door read "Uhuru Global Exports."

"I don't think your friends are here today," the driver commented. "It is Sunday. Not many work on Sunday. I wait while you check."

"That's okay, but do you have a card?" Grant responded. "I'll call you when we're done."

Juma looked at the chain and padlock securing the gate to the compound, then over his shoulder at Grant. If he thought to question their rationale any further, he apparently decided against it and took a card from the chest pocket of his shirt.

"Here. Call me, and I will return. I take my lunch now, so I won't be far away."

"Thanks, Juma," Grant replied. "Keep my suitcase safe, okay?"

The taxi driver touched his hand to his chest. "You have my word."

Once they'd settled the fare, Grant and Charlie exited the taxi and waited for the driver to leave. Charlie eyed the faded and dusty paint of the building and the nine-foot fence protecting it.

"I think it's safe to say Saleh Al-Maawali isn't here, Grant. No one is here. Shouldn't we come back tomorrow?"

"I'd rather look around now," Grant replied, holding the padlock to the gate in his hand so he could examine it.

"You want to break in?" Charlie asked, scanning the exterior of the building for cameras.

Grant pulled his lock pick set from his back pocket.

"Like the man said," he replied. "This isn't the safest area."

19

"Is this what the police in Florida learn to do?" Charlie asked her brother as he kneeled in front of the door.

"Ha, not so much," Grant admitted. "However, it might surprise you to learn that our mother taught me to pick a lock."

"Really?" Charlie gasped. "That's hardly your average mother-son activity."

Grant slipped the point of the hook into the keyhole, allowing the tool to move the springs in the cylinder. "I was about ten, I guess. She locked the keys in the house. Mom gave me the picks and talked me through the process."

"You didn't think that was weird?" Charlie asked.

"I was ten," Grant pointed out. "I thought it was the coolest thing in the world. The first time took me half an hour. The next time, I did it in ten minutes."

"There was a next time?" Charlie asked.

"A few. After all, it made me the coolest kid in school."

Charlie lifted her eyebrow as Grant turned the knob. "Did you time that one?" he asked.

His sister shook her head in disbelief.

"Come on," he pleaded. "That was like forty-five seconds, tops."

"Yes, very good," Charlie remarked as if he'd brought a finger painting for her to admire.

Grant rolled his eyes as he replaced his pick set. "Fine, don't marvel. Let's go inside."

"You don't think they have an alarm?" she asked.

Grant made a production of looking around. "In this shitty neighborhood? I doubt it."

When they stepped through the door, Charlie pulled it closed. The Tanzanian sun that had beamed through the opening vanished, plunging the pair into darkness.

"Find a light," Grant commanded.

The two moved, fumbling along the wall for a switch. Something clattered to the floor on Charlie's side of the room.

"Careful, we don't want to leave a mess," Grant warned.

"Oh, hush," Charlie complained when Grant cursed.

The crash of shattered glass sounded, punctuated by "Fuck!" coming from Grant.

Charlie chuckled. "Careful, Grant. We don't want to leave a mess."

Grant groaned. The lights came on as he found the switch on the opposite side of the room.

"Why wouldn't they put that by the door?" Charlie asked.

Grant nodded toward the door, where another panel of switches sat. Charlie had missed them in the dark.

"I couldn't see it," she said defensively.

Grant waved off the remark with a smile. "Let's take a look around."

They found themselves in an office, or what seemed to pass for an office. A wooden table sat on one side of the room. The bits of glass on the floor had once been a pitcher that had rested on the edge of the table. A puddle of water surrounded the broken shards.

Stacks of papers loomed six to eight inches off the table and covered half the surface. Grant started flipping through them. On the opposite wall was a row of filing cabinets. Charlie grabbed the handle on the top drawer and tugged.

Locked.

"I'm going to need your lock-picking skills," she informed Grant.

"Okay, let's swap then," he said as he moved across the room to the cabinets.

Charlie switched places and began rifling through the paperwork on the table. "It's all in another language," she moaned.

"Take pictures with your phone," he suggested. "We can translate it later."

Across the room, the top drawer screeched like an attacking owl as Grant pulled it open. "What have we got here?" Grant mused as he lifted a magazine out of the cabinet.

Charlie turned to see Grant holding up the open magazine to inspect the centerfold.

"What the hell?" she barked.

"It's a vintage issue," Grant noted. "1987. That's Jessica Hahn."

"Who?" she asked.

"No one you'd know," he informed her as he turned the magazine at an angle and let his head copy the motion.

"You want to take that back to the hotel with you?" Charlie growled.

"Don't be a prude," Grant scolded.

"Alright, Spanky. Can we get on with this before the police show up?"

Grant tossed the magazine back into the file drawer and slammed it shut. He pulled open the next three, finding a hidden stash of booze and a box of receipts. Most of the small bits of paper were nothing more than the slips that came out of a cash register and only listed numbers.

"Here's a credit card statement," Charlie stated. "In bloody Swahili, of course."

"What did you expect?" Grant asked.

"It would make it a lot easier if everyone just spoke English."

"That's mighty empirical of you," Grant said.

"I believe you mispronounced 'efficient.'" Charlie held the paper up to read it. "There's a charge for an airline."

"Get a picture of it. Let's see if we can find anything that connects us to our thief."

"Al-Maalawi," Charlie offered. She let her eyes roll around the office. "If someone had the power to get you detained in Turkey, why would they work out of this dump?"

"I've seen drug lords working from diners before. When people are doing shady shit, they like to spread around the evidence."

"These look like shipping manifests," Charlie said as she flashed a stack of pages to Grant. "Can't read them, but they look like it."

"Pictures," Grant reminded her. "I'm going to check in the back. Keep an eye out."

Charlie nodded as she snapped a few pictures of the pages. Grant opened a door leading deeper into the building. He found himself in a dark corridor. His fingers dragged along the plastered wall as he proceeded into the abyss.

Thud.

Grant smacked into a wooden door. He grasped around until he found the knob. When he opened the door, he found a warehouse. Sunlight streamed through windows along the roofline. He blinked twice as he stared at a collection of vehicles. It was an odd assortment of cars, trucks, and motorbikes. Grant walked up to a Mercedes Benz GLE 450. There was a gash down the passenger side of the car, where it had either hit something or been hit.

He checked the driver's door. It was unlocked, so he slipped behind the wheel. Inside, the car smelled brand new, and he shifted his ass in the leather seat. Reaching across to the passenger side, Grant opened the glove compartment. The service manual and registration were the only things in the box.

Grant unfolded the turquoise-colored paper. Surprised, he found it to be in English. Across the top, he noted the words

"Motor Vehicle/Registration Card." He scanned down the page, reading the make, model, and vehicle control number. The paperwork stated it belonged to Uhuru Global Exports, and under that was the name Omar Al-Shomari.

Grant took the registration with him after replacing the service manual back in the car. He closed the door and walked around the rest of the vehicle. *Maybe they were exporting cars?* Nothing else in the warehouse reminded Grant of something a company might sell. There were plenty of reasons a warehouse might be empty, but Grant didn't buy any legitimate one. He guessed that Uhuru Global Exports only functioned when it needed to.

"Grant!" Charlie called from the office.

He folded the registration into a tight square and placed it in his pocket before heading back down the dark hallway to the office.

"Find anything?" he asked.

Charlie was peering out the window when he came into the office. Her stance stopped him in his tracks.

"What's wrong?" he asked.

"Remember the beige car you spotted earlier?"

"The one with the broken headlight?" he clarified. "What about it?"

"It's here."

Grant cut across the office in three swift strides. The beige car, an old Toyota Cami, sat on the street in the exact location where Juma had dropped them off earlier.

"Can you see his face?" Grant asked.

"There's too much glare. I can only make out his shape."

Grant nodded. "Me too. He's on the phone."

Charlie turned to stare at her brother. "He's calling for help."

"That's my guess. Or maybe he's getting instructions on how to deal with us."

"Great," she muttered. "We need more time to search this dump."

"Well, I found a name," Grant offered like a conciliatory prize.

Charlie turned to watch the Toyota out the window. "I've got bugger all that looks useful."

"I found a vehicle registration listing an—" Grant removed the paper from his pocket to read, "Omar Al-Shomari. I'm going to have a hell of a time remembering all these hyphenated names."

"I'm not sure now is the time to worry about how anyone spells their name," Charlie scolded.

The Toyota driver had turned the engine off. Despite the sunlight reflecting off the windshield, Grant could still distinguish the silhouette enough to see the man was no longer on the phone. But he hadn't gotten out of the car, either.

"He's waiting for backup," Grant considered. "If he'd gotten instructions to come in, he'd be out of the car by now."

"I'm not sure if you're being optimistic or not," Charlie said. "He could be loading his gun as we speak."

"Why would he keep an unloaded gun on him?" he asked.

"So he doesn't shoot his own foot off."

Grant frowned at her. "That's ridiculous."

Charlie narrowed her eyes. "Only an American would think that."

"No, this guy isn't concerned with gun safety. He's a fucking criminal."

"Fair point," she conceded. "But right now, we have to worry whether he called for friends or is going to kill us himself."

"We could be jumping the gun," he said, groaning at his accidental pun. "The guy could be here to help."

"Now who is being ridiculous?" Charlie scoffed. "The only people who know we're here are Saleh Al-Maalawi and the people he works for."

Her point was hard to argue.

"Thoughts?" he asked her.

"Call Juma," she suggested. "He can come get us."

Grant nodded. "You think this guy is going to let us stroll out of here and get into the cab without lifting a finger? Not to mention, we would endanger our new friend Juma."

"Whatever we are going to do needs to happen soon."

Grant grabbed the wooden table and dragged it across the floor, scattering papers everywhere. Its legs squealed as they scraped over the bare concrete. He rammed it up against the door.

"That won't stop them," Charlie stated.

"It's better than trying to call an Uber. Even if the guy out there lets us get to the car, he could still follow us."

"You want us to just wait in here and hope the table stops them?"

Grant's face contorted into a half-smile. "No, follow me." He was already dashing through the back door and down the dark hallway.

"Shit!" Charlie shouted when she stepped into the warehouse.

"We need one with keys," he told her.

"Might want to make sure it starts, too," she advised.

"Look at you. Thinking and everything."

Charlie rolled her eyes. "Someone has to."

Grant started with the Mercedes. No keys. He tried three more —a Daihatsu truck, a Toyota Corolla, and a Bajaj Boxer motorcycle. No luck, although all but the motorcycle were blocked in by the Mercedes.

He looked over at his sister. "Wait, didn't you hot-wire the minivan in Key West?"

"Yeah, but turning a key is much faster," she pointed out.

"That's great, but none of the keys are here, and we don't have time to hunt for them. Here," he continued, opening the door to the GLE 450. "Hot-wire this thing."

Charlie shook her head from across the warehouse. "Mercedes' are a bugger to nick. Besides, I've got one," she announced.

Grant hurried over to his sister, who held aloft a set of keys. He stopped in front of her.

"Isn't there anything else?" he asked.

She shrugged. "Have you found anything? This is all I've seen so far."

Grant stared at the vehicle. The Honda scooter had been hand-painted bright pink with what resembled house paint. The dull finish on the plastic molding had rubbed off in chalky streaks.

"You've got to be kidding me," he grumbled. "I'll start it up if you can open the door." He pointed to the back of the warehouse at a roll-up door.

"Bugger that," she told him. "You get the door. I'm driving."

20

Bright sunlight streamed into the warehouse as Grant lifted the roll-up door. Charlie twisted the Honda's throttle and waited for the centrifugal clutch to engage and send the scooter on its way. Instead, the motorcycle coughed, spluttered, and stalled.

"What are you doing?" Grant yelled. "We gotta go!"

"Piece of rubbish," she groaned, hitting the starter button again.

Anticipating the misfire, she eased into the gas more gently. The scooter belched smoke, but stumbled forward and cleared the door.

"Get the gate!" Charlie shouted, pointing to the entrance in the fence they'd come through.

Grant looked at her in confusion before following her finger. He took off across the parking area and flung the gate open. Charlie spluttered the scooter along behind him and wiggled the handlebars through the opening.

"Shit," Grant cussed as Charlie felt his weight settle on the seat behind her. "He's out of the car."

"Still think he's here to help?" she teased, and tried revving the engine higher to speed away.

Grant smacked into her back as the Honda coughed and misfired a few more times.

"He's coming, Charlie!" Grant warned, swaying back and forth as the scooter bucked its way forward.

"I'm trying!" she yelled. "This stupid thing won't go!"

"Gun!" Grant screamed. "He's got a gun!"

Charlie stole a glance over her shoulder and saw the dark-skinned man in his thirties or forties running down the dusty paved road as the motorcycle barely moved faster than their pursuer. Turning back to see where she was going, she swerved to avoid a chicken who chose the wrong moment to cross the road.

"Go, go, go!" Grant yelled. "He's aiming at us!"

Charlie ducked, despite her brother making a nice shield behind her, and eased back on the twist throttle, hoping the engine would cooperate. She held her breath, waiting for the gunshot. But nothing came.

"He's running back to the car," Grant announced, the relief palpable in his voice.

The scooter's engine finally cleared out, and the motorcycle accelerated down the road, albeit at an unimpressive pace.

"I have no idea where to go!" she said, realizing they were heading in the opposite direction from the way they'd arrived.

"Stay off the bigger roads with this piece of shit," Grant advised. "We're sitting ducks if this thing won't go any faster."

Nelson Mandela Road was a principal thoroughfare for trucks and tankers, running between petroleum tanks, grain silos, and sprawling warehouses. Charlie took the first road she found on the left, turning away from the water. Worried she'd lock the front brake on the dirt and dust covering the road, she searched with her right foot for the rear brake like most motorcycles had. Finding nothing but the floorboard of the scooter, she squeezed the right lever and slowed enough to turn.

The front tire slipped before finding a clear patch of asphalt and gripping again, causing the motorcycle to buck. Grant hung on to his sister's waist for dear life.

"Have you ever ridden a motorcycle before?" he shouted in her ear.

"Of course!" she replied. "You can ride a bike a year before you can get your car license in England."

"Really?" Grant questioned. "They let you loose on a motorcycle first?"

"Yeah," Charlie said. "But they have to be 50cc or less," she added with less vigor.

"What?" Grant yelped. "That's not a motorcycle!"

"Neither's this!" Charlie pointed out, noticing the scooter didn't have any mirrors attached to the handlebars. "Is he chasing us?"

She felt Grant twisting around behind her. "Yup!"

Charlie figured they were now traveling close to fifty miles per hour, but she knew it wouldn't be enough to keep the Toyota at bay on an open road. After a left kink, she could see a major road up ahead, which would be even worse for them.

"Hang on," Charlie warned. She braked, trying the left lever where a clutch would normally be.

She'd guessed right; it was the rear brake. The scooter slowed, but not enough. Charlie carefully applied the front brake, and Grant pushed against her as they decelerated harder.

"What are you doing?" he yelled. "We need to go faster, not slower!"

Anticipating the motorcycle sliding, Charlie put her right foot to the ground as she eased off the brakes and leaned into a right turn.

"Lean with me!" she screamed at her brother, who seemed determined to remain upright.

"You're going to kill us before that guy has a chance to!" he complained, but leaned with her as the scooter shot around the turn, bouncing onto a dirt trail behind a warehouse.

From the racket behind them, she guessed the beige Toyota had attempted the turn, too. Charlie quickly glanced back to see the car emerging from a cloud of dust with its front valance dangling underneath, held on by a stubborn fastener.

"Charlie!" Grant yelled, and she turned back to see the trail ending at a building.

To their left, a wire fence blocked any access, but Charlie spotted a worn path into a stand of trees to the right and hoped it didn't lead to an outhouse. Without backing off the throttle, she aimed the scooter at the trees and felt Grant's arms clamp even more tightly around her.

"You're fucking nuts," he gasped, leafy branches whipping their shoulders as they sped into the shadows of the woods.

Charlie squinted in the sudden change of light, spotting the narrow walking trail by the lighter shade of brown against the scrub grass and weeds.

"*Hujambo wewe!*" came a voice, and a man jumped from the pathway as Charlie and Grant sped by.

"Sorry, mate!" Charlie called out without slowing.

A brighter spot in the low-hanging branches promised an exit from the woods, and she steered the Honda down the trail, which she could see more clearly now her eyes had adjusted. Emerging into the bright sunshine, she squinted again, trying to pick out the details ahead. Something large blocked the way.

"Oh, shit!" Charlie squealed, and grabbed both brakes.

The tractor-trailer was stopped at the main road on their left, with its rear still inside a container yard on their right. For a split second, Charlie wondered whether they could ride underneath the trailer and estimated that she might fit. But there was no way Grant would.

Releasing the front brake, she steered right and pulled hard on the rear brake. The back tire instantly locked.

"Charlie!" Grant screamed as the scooter crashed to the ground and skidded underneath the trailer.

"Argh," Charlie groaned as her shoulder and arm hit the dirt before skating along the trail on her hip.

A shadow fell over her as she slid under the trailer with the scooter rattling alongside and her brother grunting and cussing close by. She came to a stop and whooped.

"That was bloody close!"

The diesel engine revved, and the truck began moving when Charlie realized she wasn't quite clear of the big rear tires. Rolling to her side, she cleared them in plenty of time, but looked back to see Grant still underneath the trailer.

"Grant, get out!" she screamed, then, unable to reach him, switched to frantically waving at the truck. "Stop! Stop!"

But it was too late. Oblivious, the driver kept going, swinging out into the road as Charlie turned away, closing her eyes and covering her ears to avoid the sight and sound of her brother being crushed to death.

After a few moments, she dropped her hands and heard the truck shifting gears as it drove down the road. She peeked from one eye and saw the scooter had survived, although the pink paint had taken a further beating. Next to the Honda stood her brother.

"You are the worst rider ever," he spat, dusting himself off.

Charlie ran over and banged him playfully in the chest with both fists. "I thought you were a goner," she said with a ridiculous grin on her face.

He grabbed her wrists. "Well, you failed. I'm still alive."

"How?" she asked.

"I laid flat between the tires, but the differential housing nearly took the back of my head off," he replied, rubbing his dusty hair where he'd been scratched.

Charlie couldn't take the smile off her face. She was beside herself with relief.

"Help me pick this thing up," she said, taking hold of the handlebars.

"I'm not getting back on that thing with you," Grant responded, but he helped her, anyway.

"What do you mean?" she gasped. "That was bloody brilliant skills right there."

"You crashed!"

"No, I didn't," she said defensively. "I strategically laid it down to save our bacon. I could have ridden underneath, but it would have knocked your block off, so I chose the next best option."

"Did you just make it sound like it was my fault we skidded under a trailer?"

"Only because it was," she said, trying the starter button. Miraculously, the engine fired up. "Get on," she told her brother.

"No chance," he replied, holding up both hands and stepping back.

Behind them, tire squealing came from the road, and they both turned. The beige Toyota had its brakes locked up as it skidded to a stop, having spotted them.

"Go, go, go!" Grant shouted, jumping on the back of the seat.

Charlie opened the throttle, and the scooter lurched forward, veering to the right of where she was steering.

"What the bloody hell…" she muttered before realizing the front forks and handlebars were twisted from the fall. Driving straight ahead now required steering to the left.

Continuing down the trail with the handlebars oddly angled toward the road, the Honda bounced along the rutted path.

"He's trying to follow us!" Grant shouted, and Charlie heard the Toyota's engine complain as the car hit the bumps behind them.

Ahead, she could see another exit from a yard on the right, and beyond, the trail seemed to end at another building. Her choices were the main road or risk going into the yard, which was protected by a tall wire fence covered with tattered dark green sheeting. Apart from spotting the roof of a warehouse, she had no idea whether it housed a dead end or another exit.

"Take the road!" Grant yelled as Charlie cranked the scooter in the opposite direction through the gate into the yard.

A long warehouse stretched into the distance, with trucks backed up to loading bays as far as she could see. Charlie was about to tear along the road in front of the trucks when she noticed one pulling out and heading their way, blocking her path. She braked hard and swerved right, trying to figure out the wacky bent steering.

"I told you to take the damn road!" Grant complained, then pointed to a roll-up door at the end of the warehouse. "Go in there!"

"Inside the building?" Charlie questioned as she heard the Toyota skidding into the yard behind.

"You brought us in here!" Grant pointed out.

"Fine," Charlie conceded. She raced towards the door, one of the few at ground level.

Once inside, she squinted again, adapting to the dimmer light, and noticed a glistening off the smooth concrete floor. She figured it would be treacherously slippery. A forklift appeared from behind the towering rack on their right, and Charlie whipped the scooter left, ducking under the raised forks. As Grant was still on the seat, she guessed he'd ducked, too. She heard him swearing under his breath.

Several men waved their arms, focusing on the scooter until their gaze shifted beyond it.

"He's still coming, isn't he?" Charlie asked.

"Yup!" Grant replied. "And he's hauling ass!"

The men ahead chose to scatter, clearing a path between palettes of cardboard boxes Charlie steered her way through, hoping the dogleg would hinder the car more than them. But the sound of squealing tires in their wake was closer than she'd expected, and the end of the building wasn't too far away. And with no obvious exits. Light flashed in her eyes from each loading door on their left, with drivers and workers staring at the crazy white people invading their warehouse on a beaten-up pink scooter. Charlie had to find a way out.

"Hold on tight!" she warned Grant.

"What are you going to do?" he asked nervously, and she felt him lean over her shoulder as she veered left. "No, Char…"

If he finished his sentence, she didn't hear it. Spotting two unoccupied loading bays with the doors rolled up, Charlie exited the building through the only option she'd seen so far. With the throttle pegged, the scooter left the building four feet above the concrete pad below.

Reminding herself to keep the handlebars turned slightly to the left, she kept the throttle wide open with the Honda's engine screaming through the air. When they hit the ground, the suspension immediately bottomed out, sending a shock wave through her body and launching her butt out of the seat. Charlie hung on for dear life as the scooter fishtailed beneath her, and she peered at the ground racing by just beyond the front tire. Two firm hands yanked her back down, and she finally let off the throttle and grabbed the brakes.

As the Honda skidded to a stop, they both turned as they heard more rubber squealing and echoing from inside the warehouse. The Toyota appeared with all four tires locked up as the driver tried to stop on the shiny concrete. He almost did.

The front tires slid beyond the drop, and the underside scraped along the edge, making an ear-splitting sound like nails on a chalkboard. Just as it appeared the Toyota would be stuck hanging out the doorway, the nose tipped, and it crashed into the ground below.

"Ouch," Grant muttered, then shook his sister's shoulders. "We'd better go."

Charlie opened the throttle, and the scooter limped away, the front wheel wobbling badly.

"I think we need a new ride," she commented.

"You're tough on equipment," Grant said, shaking his head.

"So I've been told."

Charlie found a large open gate, which led them back onto Nelson Mandela Road, where she turned right, back toward where they'd started.

"You're also a fucking maniac," Grant added.

"Yeah, that's been mentioned a few times, too."

21

———

"I think I like that guy," Grant said when he saw Juma's taxi parked across the road from Uhuru Global Exports.

"I don't see anyone else, so maybe One Headlight didn't call in the cavalry after all," Charlie commented, pulling the scooter up behind the white taxi.

They both got off. Charlie looked for the center stand peg, but couldn't find it.

"Probably wiped it off in one of your hare-brained maneuvers," Grant pointed out.

Charlie let go of the handlebars, and the Honda fell to the ground with a thud, its pink paint further destroyed by the beating it had taken in the past fifteen minutes.

"Juma, you're a gem," Charlie said as they walked to the driver's door. "Thanks for coming back for us."

The door swung open, and a man, decidedly not Juma, beamed. "I am Mo. It is my pleasure to meet you."

"Where's Juma?" Grant asked suspiciously.

They'd only ridden with the man from the airport, but Grant had felt good about the guy from the beginning. This was a curveball they didn't need.

"I'm Juma's cousin," Mo replied. "We share the taxi. His son has a football game, but he tell me to take best care of you two."

Grant peered inside the taxi and noted the Bob Marley sticker on the dashboard. The taxi license in a holder was also Juma's.

"Get in, get in," Mo urged, looking around. "This is not the best area to be standing around."

Grant nodded to Charlie, and they climbed in the back.

"Is my bag still in the trunk?" Grant asked.

"Yes, sir," Mo said, closing the driver's door. "Where to?"

"Anywhere but here, for starters," Charlie said, checking out the back window in case One Headlight had decided to pursue them on foot. Although she suspected he'd be limping along after the spill the Toyota took.

"We need internet," Grant remarked.

"I know a place," Mo told him.

"Where is it, Mo?" Charlie asked somewhat warily.

"Café over in Sea View," he stated as if that was all the information she needed.

"Where is that?" she demanded, the harshness escalating in her words.

"Mo, that'll be perfect," Grant acknowledged. He turned to Charlie. "You wouldn't know the area, anyway," he reminded her.

She pursed her lips without another argument. Grant guessed she was saving it for another time, so he leaned back in his seat as Mo navigated the busy streets. A thought entered his mind that these streets didn't look much different from some in Miami, though he realized that was a narrow-minded American way of thinking. While he'd traveled some, most of his life had existed in the Florida Keys. His mother had never traveled much, either, and as a kid, he assumed it was because she worked as a hairdresser and never had the money. Now, as he thought back on his childhood, he wondered if it was simply because she was hiding.

Although, based on what he'd learned about Keith Greene, that hadn't stopped their father from going where he pleased. He found himself nursing a feeling of regret and envy for his sister, which he knew was stupid. He'd had a great childhood. After all, how many people get to grow up on an island? The Keys had all the feel of the Caribbean, with only a few hours' drive to Miami if he wanted to experience an urban existence.

Honestly, he admitted that wasn't something he cared about. Grant had loved growing up on the ocean. He could walk out to the dock, and within half an hour, be on the water. Sure, Charlie had gotten the benefits of growing up in London and all that a metropolis offered, but he'd had the vast Atlantic to play on.

Not that knowing Keith and Charlie wouldn't have been nice. He felt like his parents had run into hiding without considering any other options that might have kept their family together.

Charlie twisted around in her seat again. She let out a huff of relief. "No one back there," she commented.

Grant opened his eyes to see Mo staring at him in the mirror before the taxi driver's eyes returned to the road ahead.

It took another fifteen minutes to reach Mo's destination. He pulled up in front of a square building with a wooden panel facade and a round logo that read "Central Park Café."

"You'll find best internet here," Mo said as he turned around in his seat to face them. "They have good food, too."

"Awesome, I'm starving," Grant confessed. "How much for the ride?"

Mo grinned, exposing a yellow smile. "Only ten thousand shillings."

"Where's that cash you took out?" Grant asked Charlie.

She dug into her pocket and pulled out a wad of bills.

Mo's eyes lit up like a Christmas tree as she figured out the note with an elephant was the correct amount.

"What about a tip?" she whispered to Grant.

"Later," Grant replied, loud enough for Mo to hear.

"I drive you more?" the driver asked as he took the money.

"Later," Charlie told him. "Can you meet us back here in about an hour? We need to find a place to sleep tonight."

"You don't have a hotel?" Mo asked.

"Not yet," Grant admitted.

"I have the place for you," Mo informed them. "Perfect for you two." He gave Charlie a wink in the rearview mirror.

"Thanks, Mo," Grant said as he got out of the car. "I'll carry my bag with me. In case you get busy and we don't see you again."

"I'll make it back, sir," Mo promised.

"Good," Grant said, removing his luggage from the trunk.

"Bit stingy, not tipping him," Charlie pointed out after Mo pulled away from the curb.

"Figured the lure of accumulated gratuity might be an incentive for him to actually come back," Grant replied.

"I think overpaying generally gets people to come back," Charlie commented.

"I bet you he'll be here in an hour."

Charlie pursed her lips again. But instead of arguing or taking the bet, she walked toward the entrance of the Central Park Café.

"Why did they have to make it so American?" she wondered aloud as they entered the building.

The interior was bright, with white-washed walls and butcher-block counters. Strands of flowers like leis hung from the ceiling. A girl behind a lighted podium lifted her face to see the pair as they came into the entrance.

"Table for two, please," Grant told the hostess.

The girl gave a broad smile as she lifted two menus and motioned for them to follow her.

"Do you have Wi-Fi?" Grant asked as he pulled his laptop out of his luggage.

"Yes, the password is 'Friends,'" the girl told him.

When she walked away, Charlie scoffed, "Friends? Bit bloody corny, isn't it?"

"Next time you're in America, I'll take you to what we consider to be an English pub and you can marvel at the stereotypes there, too."

"There's avocado bloody toast on this menu," she muttered.

"And a burger," Grant noted with some satisfaction.

He started typing on the computer.

"What are you searching?" she asked.

"Omar Al-Shomari," he told her. "I want to know who he is and how he's connected."

"It could be the man just owns the car you got the registration from."

"Probably, but the paperwork showed Uhuru Global, too. I'm thinking Omar has something to do with them."

The same hostess came back to the table to take their order. Grant ordered the burger, and Charlie opted to try one of the rice dishes. Both ordered coffee, which the waitress quickly brought to the table.

"Listen to this," Grant said as he sipped the black coffee. "Uhuru Global Exports is owned by Omar."

"Maybe it is a lead. So, who is he?" Charlie asked.

Grant spun the computer around for her to see the picture of Omar Al-Shomari at a festival called Eid El-Fitr in Zanzibar. The image showed a man in his late fifties laughing with a young girl at the post-Ramadan festivities.

"There are a few more articles about him. Most are about his charitable efforts in restoring historical monuments and buildings in Zanzibar," Grant explained. "The local news deems him a phil-anthropic citizen with a love of the island's history. Look, he's got a plaque at this museum here."

The picture Grant showed had the same man. This time, he wasn't caught mid-guffaw. He sported what Grant had heard his captain once refer to as a "press smile."

"Grant," Charlie said as she stared at the computer screen, "take a good look at that photo."

He turned the computer back around, and his eyes narrowed to slits as he studied the picture. "Shit!" he blurted out. "That's our other friend."

Behind Omar Al-Shomari stood a figure in the background. While the face was out of focus, the features matched those of Saleh Al-Maalawi.

"The connections are getting tighter," Charlie remarked. "At least we know we're on the right path."

"Omar has a mansion in Zanzibar," Grant told her as a picture of a white block house appeared. "Looks like it's in a swanky part of Zanzibar City. Right on the beach."

"What do we really know?" Charlie asked. "Al-Shomari owns Uhuru Global Exports, for which Sunshine Gourmet Imports is a subsidiary, and employs Saleh Al-Maalawi, who we think nicked the necklace. So why would a rich guy in Zanzibar send someone to steal it? I mean, it's probably priceless, but if Omar has all this good standing in the community, he'd be risking everything." She took a drink of coffee. "Besides, we have no actual evidence. None of this would hold up in a court."

Grant furrowed his brow. "No one is paying us to prosecute anyone. All Bamford wants is his jewels back. That's what he's paying us for."

"I suppose," she agreed.

"Listen, it's getting late," Grant pointed out. "Let's find a place to crash for the night. I haven't slept in a bed since Thursday. Even this coffee is only pushing back my exhaustion."

"We sleep and go tomorrow to Zanzibar?" she questioned.

"It seems like we need to meet Omar. Let's get Mo to pick us up. He said he had a place we could stay."

"I don't want to stay with him," Charlie clarified. "He's weird. Where did Juma go, anyway?"

"Don't be silly. He said they share the cab. It makes sense."

"Fine," she relented. "But he's still weird."

Grant pulled out the card that Mo had given him and dialed the taxi driver's number. "Pay the bill while I get him," Grant told her before speaking into the phone. "Mo, can you pick us up?"

Charlie flagged down the server and asked for the bill, which the woman produced from her pocket. Charlie counted out more notes from her wad of cash, giving the waitress a decent tip.

"We'll need more shillings if we start buying hotel rooms.

Unless we use a card," she whispered at her brother, who gave her a silent nod.

"Yeah, we'll be ready in five minutes," Grant told the driver. "Can you take us by a Western Union to exchange some money?" A pause. Then, Grant said "thanks" and hung up.

"He's on his way," he told his sister. "Let's get outside and wait for him."

Three minutes later, the taxi pulled up in front of the Central Park Café. Grant and Charlie climbed in the back, and he set his bag between them.

"You said you had a hotel?" Grant asked Mo.

"Yes, sir," came the response as the car pulled onto the street.

"Can we get a flight tomorrow?" Charlie asked Grant.

"Where are you going?" Mo asked.

"To Zanzibar," Charlie answered.

Grant nudged his sister. "Our friend in the Toyota might be looking for us at the airport again."

"You have people after you?" Mo asked, interrupting again.

Charlie gave Grant a cautious look.

"We don't want to advertise our destination," Grant responded, then remembered their prior story. "You can't say anything, but my sister here is an actress, and we get followed all the time," he told Mo. "Best we stay away from the airport and the fancy hotels."

It sounded like a BS story even as he spoke the words, but he figured Juma had bought it, so maybe his cousin would, too. Mo stared at Charlie.

"You very pretty."

"Okay, now you *are* making it weird," Grant intervened.

Mo seemed to snap out of his trance. "You don't need to take a plane," he pointed out excitedly.

"How do we get there, then?" Charlie asked.

"I get you to man with boat."

"A boat?" Charlie questioned. "How far is it to Zanzibar?"

"Fifty kilometers."

"Not too far," Charlie acknowledged.

"Wait. How far is fifty kilometers?" Grant asked. "We don't use that newfangled metric crap."

"The Romans invented the metric system, Grant."

"I don't care if Keith Richards came up with it during a jam session with the pope in the 1800s. Tell me how far it is in miles."

"Bloody Americans. You can't possibly use the same system the rest of the world uses, can you?"

"It's not like it's my doing," Grant protested. "I have nothing against the metric system, but it wasn't what I was taught. Besides, it was you imperialists that brought your system over to the States."

Mo grinned in the front seat. "I really don't know how long a mile is."

"Fifty K is about thirty miles," Charlie moaned.

"Thank you," Grant responded, throwing his hands up. "And you're right. That's not too far."

"Okay, Mo. Let's go see your guy with a boat in the morning," Charlie told the driver.

"Absolutely," Mo beamed, happy to help.

"Does he take American Express?" Grant asked.

Mo shook his head slowly. "Best if you have cash."

"Then we definitely need a bank with an ATM or a Western Union," Grant stated.

Mo drove half a block, weaving through the honking traffic until he bumped the taxi over a driveway into a small strip mall. The familiar Western Union decal on the window was the only English in the place.

"Wait here," Grant told Charlie as he ran into the shop. Five minutes later, he emerged with two million more shillings, which he hoped, along with Charlie's cash, would be enough to cover a hotel and the boat ride. He'd been worried that getting too much off the Amex card might signal an alert. Eventually, the fine folks at American Express were going to figure out Fiona Wolfe had passed away.

"Okay, that's done. Let's get to the hotel." Grant said, slamming the door and subconsciously patting his pocket. "We need a cheap, out-of-the-way place, okay?"

Mo nodded cheerfully as he pulled out onto the street. It only took ten minutes to navigate through Dar es Salaam before he stopped in front of a white building about six stories tall.

"I will call my man and see how early he can take you on the boat," Mo promised.

"Thank you," Charlie said, giving the street a nervous glance.

Construction along the opposite side left half the businesses closed. She looked at Grant, but he shrugged. He figured they didn't have too many options.

The pair got out onto the street and studied the building. Grant noticed the sign reading "Jangwani Inn" in English. It appeared to be translated into other languages as there was a script below the English words.

"I'll be here in the morning," Mo offered. "Seven, okay?"

"Thanks," Grant replied. "Sure. Get us on that boat as early as your guy can leave."

Mo nodded, then pulled away, leaving the brother and sister on the street. They walked into the lobby of the Jangwani Inn.

"What the bloody hell?" Charlie muttered when she saw the interior.

A toothless woman stood behind the front desk, which looked like it had been a grocery counter in a former life. As they neared her, Grant curled his nose. The room had a moldy aroma. His feet shuffled through the shag carpet that had lost more shag than it still had. Tufts of fabric balled up where feet had worn the pile down. A mirrored disco ball hung from the ceiling over the middle of the room. Several of the glass panes on it were missing or broken.

"Are you Mo's friends?" the woman asked in passable English.

"Yes," Grant answered.

"He say take good care of you," she spoke while gumming a piece of bread. When Charlie saw the plate holding the crusty loaf, she recoiled as a roach scampered off the plate. As if the bug hadn't been there, the woman grabbed the bread and used the one front tooth she still had to cut through a chunk and tear off enough to fill her mouth. Bits of white and spittle fell out of the woman's face.

"I have you in room 324. On floor three." The woman slid a brass key on a plastic key ring across the Formica countertop.

"Thank you," Grant said, picking up the keys.

"It's fifty-thousand shillings for tonight."

Grant peeled the bills off what he'd gotten from the Western Union. The clerk wiped her mouth with the back of her hand before grabbing the cash with her slobbery fingers.

"Is there a lift?" Charlie asked.

The woman stared at her as if she didn't understand the question.

"Elevator?" Grant tried to explain, making a rising motion with his hand.

The woman took a few seconds to announce, "No. Stairs over there." She pointed toward the end of a hallway.

As they walked down the corridor, Charlie muttered, "This is a shithole. Next time, we book our own rooms."

"It won't be that bad," Grant assured her as they started up the steps.

On the second floor, a man stretched out on the top step. They both paused to examine him.

"Is he dead?" Grant asked.

Charlie shook her head and twisted to glare at her brother. "No, he's asleep. Or passed out."

They stepped over him and found the room. When Grant turned the key and opened the door, a rat that stretched about fifteen inches from nose to tail sat up on the bed and stared at the pair in the doorway. He made no move to scurry away.

"Look at that bugger!" Charlie moaned. "I'm not staying here."

"We already paid," Grant pointed out.

Charlie lowered her chin to peer over the bridge of her nose at Grant. "I'm not staying here," she repeated. "I don't care if I sleep on the street. It's better than here."

"Fine, let's go find a Holiday Inn."

22

Charlie stood by the edge of the dusty road and looked around. Even the brightly colored signs atop the local businesses had a layer of dirt, along with anything that remained stationary for more than a few minutes. Cars seemed to go in all directions, and people meandered the sidewalks, which were little more than baked dirt on the other side of the concrete curbs.

"I don't think we'll find a Holiday Inn anywhere near here," she commented.

"Let's get back to the main road Mo turned off of to get here," Grant suggested, heading across the street toward a road heading east. "Maybe they have the non-rat-infested accommodations that way."

Charlie laughed as she followed along. "We're now entering Mafia Street."

"Hopefully, it's named after a glamorized Hollywood ideal rather than the real thing," Grant commented, but they both quickened their pace regardless.

At Msimbazi Street, they slowed and looked both ways. Buses ran along a center lane, with busy traffic on either side of the wide road. A concrete sidewalk extended as far as Charlie could see, and the businesses and office buildings appeared to be of significantly better quality than Jangwani.

"I see a hotel sign," she said, pointing to a glass-faced building a few hundred yards away.

Grant began walking, and after a few minutes, they stood before the AAA Travellers Hotel.

"Looks like the Ritz compared to the last place," Grant joked, although the hotel was probably a two-star back in America.

"We should use cash again," Charlie pointed out. "I know we've used cards at a few places to get money, but Saleh Al-Maawali and Omar Al-Shomari already know we're here in Tanzania. We just need to avoid giving them a location we're staying at for any period of time."

"Agreed," Grant said, and pushed the door open to walk inside.

A man looked up and smiled at them from behind a proper check-in counter, which Charlie considered a promising start. He even wore a gray business suit.

"Do you have a room available for tonight?" Charlie asked.

"Certainly, we do," the man replied in perfect English. "We have top-floor suite with king bed, special for you."

"Ew!" Charlie exclaimed. "That's my brother, and we're not from Louisiana or the royal family, so we sleep in separate beds, mate."

The man looked slightly confused but pressed on, undeterred.

"Two beds, then?"

"Two beds," Charlie confirmed.

"How much?" Grant asked, getting straight to the point.

"Special price for tonight," the man replied, holding his hands together as though in prayer. "Two hundred thousand shillings."

"Bollocks," Charlie blurted, then double-checked the math in her head. "Yeah, bollocks. We'll find someplace else, Grant."

"This money's got me all fucked up," he whispered as they turned to leave. "How much is that in real money?"

"In pounds?" Charlie grinned.

He frowned at her. "Dollars, sis. The world works in dollars."

"About seventy."

"Wait, wait, wait!" the man shouted. "I'm sure I can find a room to make you happy."

Charlie and Grant stopped and turned around, but didn't walk back.

"Happy is no rats, no bugs, and eighty-thousand shillings. Cash." Charlie said firmly.

The man made an expression like they'd just dragged his grandmother from his home and beaten her to a pulp using her pet dog as a club.

"You are trying to shut my business down. I will be on the streets at this price."

"Okay," Charlie rebutted, shrugging her shoulders. "See how much you make with no one in that room."

They began turning once more.

"One hundred thousand is best I can do, and I lose money at this crazy price. My wife will be very angry with me."

"Eighty thousand or we leave," Charlie shouted over her shoulder, hand on the door.

"Fine, fine, fine!"

The manager quickly recovered once they handed over the cash. They gave their names as Daisy Ridley and Henry Jones.

"I thought you are related?" the manager questioned.

"Her married name," Grant replied. "Ugly divorce. I wouldn't bring it up if I were you."

Leaving the front desk, they waited until they were inside the elevator before they burst out laughing.

"Who on earth is Henry Jones?" Charlie hooted.

"Indiana Jones!" Grant replied.

"Really? That's bloody perfect."

"I'm still trying to figure out how much eighty-thousand shillings is," Grant admitted. "How come that amount?"

"I think it's about thirty dollars," Charlie replied, double-checking her math again. "He had a slip on the counter from another customer, and I saw that number on it."

"Nicely done," Grant said, and offered her a high-five.

"Yeah, we English don't do that," she said, leaving him hanging.

"Seriously?" Grant grunted, clearly offended.

Charlie's face slid into a big grin, and she slapped his hand, still held in the air.

"Nah, we do. But it's a bit unfair," Charlie continued as they walked down a hall to their room. "We give you the Beatles and Led Zeppelin, and you give us high-fives and Justin Bieber."

"He's Canadian!" Grant rebutted, opening the door with the key card.

"Fine. Kanye West, then," Charlie said smugly as she walked inside.

"Yeah. Fair play. You got me there," Grant conceded. "But hey, how about Michael Jackson, Elvis, the Eagles?"

Charlie shook her head. "They help, but still tough to overcome Kanye West."

The room was clean, rat and bug-free, and they both crashed out for a good night's sleep. Setting an alarm on her phone, Charlie was up earlier than she liked, but was ready to get on with their mission.

Downstairs, the same manager was behind the front counter.

"Anywhere to get a decent cup of coffee around here?" Grant asked.

"Best place in Dar es Salaam, sir," the man enthused. "Turn left and left again at the first street. One hundred meters up. The Brotherhood Café. Very fine coffee and breakfast."

"Okay, thank you," Grant responded.

"Tell my cousin I sent you," the manager called out as they left.

His directions were good, and Charlie hoped the coffee wasn't the best in Dar es Salaam as it was average in her mind, but the breakfast wrap she ate on their way back to the Jangwani Hotel was tasty.

"What's our strategy when we get to Zanzibar?" Charlie asked as they left Mafia Street.

"I was thinking about that last night," Grant replied. "We have no idea whether this Omar guy is even on the island. We should run a little surveillance on this mansion of his and see what's going on. Hopefully, we'll be able to tell if he's home."

"He might have security, too," Charlie pointed out. "A big money guy in this part of the world probably has a few bodyguards."

"True," Grant agreed, looking at his watch. "We're a few minutes early."

As they approached the rundown hotel, a young boy stared at them from the doorway, then ran inside. Charlie figured he wasn't used to seeing two white people wandering around this neighborhood until the snaggle-toothed woman appeared and started yelling something in Swahili.

"Whoa, whoa, whoa. Calm down, lady," Grant urged, looking around at a sea of curious faces staring back. "What's your problem?"

The woman switched to broken English. "You owe me for damage! Very bad men. Bad for business. You owe me money!"

"We don't owe you bugger all, lady," Charlie jumped in. "We paid you upfront for a shithole room we didn't use."

"Bash in door and break things!" she yelled.

A younger man came out of the hotel and put his arm around the woman. They rattled off a conversation in Swahili before the man turned to Grant and pointed a finger.

"You rented room from my grandmother?"

"Yeah," Grant replied. "But we didn't use it. She's been paid already. We gave her cash last night."

"Then you're responsible for the room," the man said, his face turning fierce. "You have to pay for damage."

"What the bloody hell are you rabbiting about?" Charlie shouted. "The room was a total flea-bite dump full of rats and bugs, but the door was on the hinges when we left."

The woman continued ranting in Swahili despite her grandson's attempts to quieten her.

"Two men came looking for you last night," he explained. "They smashed the door in, so you have to pay."

Grant and Charlie looked at each other in disbelief.

"How would anyone know we were here?" Charlie muttered.

"The taxi driver," Grant replied, shaking his head. "He brought us to this dump."

Charlie turned as she heard a car pull up behind them. "You bastard!" she yelled, seeing Mo behind the wheel of the taxi.

Mo got out and stood by the driver's door. "What's going on?"

"You sold us out, that's what's going on!" Grant growled.

Mo looked baffled, but his expression quickly changed to horror. "We go now! Get in!"

"I'm not getting back in with…" Charlie began, but hearing the front door of the hotel fly open made her spin around.

A large, muscular man wielding a machete stood in the entrance. Grandma pointed at Grant and Charlie.

"Oh, fuck!" Grant groaned. "Get in the car!"

They both scrambled for the door handle while Charlie heard heavy footfalls behind them. Grant flung the back door open and shoved his sister headfirst inside, then jumped back as the blade sliced down on the top of the door, crunching the metal frame.

"Go!" Grant screamed, but Mo was already on the gas, and the taxi lurched forward.

Charlie pushed herself up and watched out the back window as the cab accelerated away. Grant was running after them as fast as he could, dragging his wheeled carry-on, with the lumbering giant swirling the machete in the air in pursuit.

"Slow down so Grant can jump in!" Charlie ordered.

Mo eased off the throttle, but not nearly enough for Grant to catch them.

"Slow down, Mo!" she screamed, and the driver tentatively backed off more.

Grant was stretching away from his crazed pursuer, but his suitcase was bouncing in the air as he clung to the handle, slowing his progress. She knew he wasn't far enough ahead to allow him time to get in the car without the giant reaching them. And Charlie had no doubt the man could cut open the taxi like a tin of sardines.

"Open the boot!" she yelled. "Open the boot, Mo!"

The driver reached down and pulled the lever, releasing the catch on the trunk, which flipped up and blocked Charlie's view. She shuffled across the back seat and hung her head out the side window.

"Jump in, Grant!" she screamed.

Grant reached out and grabbed the lip of the trunk with one hand while his other trailed with the roller bag skipping, twisting, and bouncing in his wake.

"Sod the bag, Grant!" Charlie yelled.

Grant launched the case forward, and Charlie heard a thump against the underside of the trunk as the bag ricocheted into the compartment.

"He's in!" Mo shouted triumphantly and hit the gas.

"No!" Charlie cried out, but it was too late. Her brother was windmilling his arms, trying to stay on his feet, and the giant gritted his teeth with renewed vigor.

"He didn't make it, Mo! Slow the hell down!"

Mo looked in his side mirrors and let out a string of what Charlie could only imagine was profanities. She turned to face the front, and her eyes went wide.

"Mo!"

The driver looked up, staring at the petrified faces of the first few vendors at the beginning of a street market. Mo cranked the wheel left, and the taxi's tires screeched in complaint as the car skidded into a side street. Charlie was crammed against the door, clinging onto the handle to stop herself from flying out the side window.

"Slow down!" she heard Grant scream from behind.

"Oh, dear," Mo groaned once he gathered the car back up and aimed it straight.

Charlie swung around to see the junction ahead, with the main road packed with morning traffic. And a red light. Mo had no choice but to brake, and the trunk lid flung up on its hinges. Charlie felt a beefy thud into the back of the car, and as the taxi came to a stop, the trunk lid slammed closed.

"Mo! We gotta go!" Charlie shouted as the enormous man reached the back of the car and swung the machete down like an axe.

The blade tore into the sheet metal, and the man's bicep muscles bulged and glistened as he struggled to wrench the blade back out.

Mo laid on the horn and accelerated forward, scraping along the front bumper of a van and the rear bumper of the next car as he wiggled his way across traffic. The giant lumbered along behind, growling like a grizzly bear as he finally pulled his blade from the twisted metal. He immediately raised the machete to bring another crushing blow down on the tin above Grant's body. Mo surged ahead through a tiny gap, and horrible scraping noises emanated from both sides of the taxi.

The giant swung, the tip of his blade grazing down the back of the trunk and wedging into the sheet metal above the rear bumper.

Mo screamed in terror and floored the gas pedal. As the taxi lurched forward, all Charlie saw out the back was a bright turquoise flash filling her view. She cringed at the awful thud as the city bus swatted the giant away, leaving his machete sticking in the air like a tail.

23

———————

"What the hell!" Grant shouted from the dark confines of the trunk.

"We're trying!" came Charlie's muffled voice from outside.

"It smells like a dead possum in here."

"Open the damned trunk, Mo!" Charlie shouted.

"I am trying, miss," the taxi driver insisted, and Grant heard the key wiggling in the lock. "The knife—it jammed something."

"Open the fucking trunk!" Grant shouted, banging on the lid.

"Grant, it's the machete," Charlie explained.

"I know that. The damned point is poking me."

A loud screech echoed around the claustrophobic trunk, then a thin beam of sunlight streaked through the slot left by the blade.

"Try it now!" Charlie ordered the taxi driver.

There was more scratching as Mo wiggled the key again. The trunk lid didn't budge. Grant shifted to roll around.

"Do you have a wheel brace?" Charlie asked.

"I don't know," Mo stammered.

"What?" Grant asked, trying to hear them through the metal and insulation.

"What do you call it?" Charlie stammered. "The thing to change the tire. Tire iron?"

"Lug wrench," Grant offered, wiping his forehead as he squinted through the machete hole.

"Oh, lug wrench," Mo repeated. "It's probably in the trunk."

"Yes. It's in here," Grant announced, finding the steel rod.

"Why did someone come after us at the hotel?" he heard Charlie ask.

"I didn't tell anyone," Mo denied.

"No one else knew we were there." Charlie persisted, raising her voice.

"Charlie!" Grant shouted.

"What?"

"Can we figure all that out after I'm out of the trunk?"

"Right, sorry."

The slit of light allowed Grant to see a little more inside his metal cell. Sweat bubbled on his forehead, and he noticed the beads forming on his chest. If he didn't get out soon, he'd drench his shirt with perspiration.

"Wait!" Grant called as he heard the keys scraping once more. "I think the latch is broken. I'm going to jam the lug wrench into the crack. When you are ready, I'll pull down."

He twisted around. Using his fingers, he found the seam near the latch and shoved the prying end of the bar into the crack.

"Okay, let's try it," Grant said.

He heard the key again and started pulling down on the tool. Nothing moved.

"Keep trying!" he demanded as he attempted to use his weight against the lid.

There was a tiny crack that emanated from the metal. Grant eased back and relaxed. "One more time," he announced. Grant didn't say that if this didn't work, he was about to hack his way through the back seat to get out of what now felt like an oven.

Again, the key turned. Grant pushed his weight down and used his legs to press up against the trunk. A loud pop sounded, and something hit Grant as the lid sprang open. Fresh air filled the space as he took in a deep breath. Sunlight blinded him, and he raised his hand to shield his face.

"You're bleeding," Charlie pointed out. "Did he get you with the machete?"

After several blinks to allow his pupils to adjust, Grant reached up to touch his face, where a single stream of blood dribbled down his cheek.

"No, it was the latch," Grant told her. He sat up and picked up a piece of metal that had snapped off the lock when they'd opened the trunk. He smeared the blood away with a swipe of his hand.

"What happened to that ogre?" Grant asked.

"He took the bus," Charlie replied.

Grant looked at her in confusion but moved on. "Okay, so what the hell happened at the hotel last night?"

Charlie turned to Mo. "Someone grassed on us."

"It wasn't me," Mo stammered.

"No one else knew we were at that hotel," Charlie said to Mo, her voice raised an octave.

"Hold up, Charlie," Grant said as he climbed out of the trunk. He faced Mo. "There is some explaining that needs to be done."

"I didn't do anything," the cabbie argued. "What happened?"

"Someone thought we were staying at that dump you took us to," Grant explained as he leaned against the car. "Since it was your suggestion to go to that shithole, it puts the spotlight on you."

Mo shook his head. "I wouldn't do that to you."

"We don't know you," Charlie blurted out. "How can we trust you?"

"We're friends," Mo told them.

Grant shook his head. "Where is Juma?"

"Juma?" Mo repeated.

"Yeah, your cousin," Charlie said.

"He's at home. I work Mondays."

"I'm not buying it, Mo," Charlie snapped. "You just showed up in Juma's taxi. It's too convenient."

"Mister, it's not true. Juma is my cousin. We work together," he pleaded with Grant, perhaps thinking he might be more reasonable than his sister.

"Hold on, Mo," Grant told him. "Charlie, a word?" He motioned for her to follow him a few feet away.

"We can't trust him," she reiterated.

"No, but we also need him right now."

"Why? We can't find another taxi driver?"

"That we could, but he's supposed to arrange a boat for us. Do you know anyone with a boat around here?"

"No," she relented. "But are we going to let him take us out on the ocean, where we could easily be shot and fed to the sharks?"

"I agree we need to be careful, but I don't have any better ideas. Do you?"

She curled her lip. "No."

"Then I don't see that we have too many options. Okay?"

"Fine," she agreed. "But if he screws us over, I'm going to rip his spleen out."

Grant shook his head. "His spleen? That's mighty specific."

"It'll hurt more."

His hands lifted in surrender. "Remind me to stay on your good side."

"Bloody right."

"Alright, Mo." Grant marched up to the cab driver. "Who did you tell about us staying at that hotel?"

The man's head twisted back and forth. "No one. Well, I told Juma I was taking care of you."

"Where was Juma?" Charlie demanded again.

"Charlie," Grant said in a calming voice.

She responded with a glare, but backed off.

Grant turned to Mo. "What about the boat?"

"It's waiting for you at the dock," Mo replied nervously.

"Look, we're going to give you the benefit of the doubt," Grant said, pointing at Mo's chest. "However, if I suspect there's been a hint of a double-cross—well, I'll let her have a go at you."

Charlie pinched her eyes tight as she stared at Mo. He shrank back from her, and Grant suspected the cabbie may have overheard their conversation. He now feared for his spleen.

"I promise you," Mo stammered. "I am your friend."

"Then let's go to the boat," Grant suggested.

The ride to the bay took half an hour. They drove without a word. Every bump on the road sent the trunk lid flopping up and back down.

"He said he'd meet us at the ferry terminal," Mo finally offered with a hint of anxiety.

"How long is the ride?" Grant asked.

"He said it's about two hours."

The ferry pier was located on the north side of the harbor among the towering skyscrapers that overlooked the bay. Mo pulled up in front of a building with a sign in English and Swahili. The English version read "Karimjee Foundation." Next door, the building advertised that it was the marine police headquarters.

Grant eyed the police building with some relief. *Would Mo bring them this close to any cops if he was trying to kill them?*

Mo parked in the small parking lot. "Follow me," he said as he got out of the cab. "It's down here."

Grant and Charlie trailed behind the driver, each giving the other a wary glance. Grant mouthed the words, "Don't worry." To which Charlie rolled her eyes.

The path between the towering buildings was a narrow side-walk. When it opened up on the bay side of the building, the pair found a small dock with five boats moored side-by-side. A man in a White Shark runabout with a blue Bimini top saw Mo and waved.

"This is Amani," Mo introduced the brother and sister to the man in the boat. "He can take us to Zanzibar. Very discreet."

"What do you mean 'us?'" Grant asked.

"I feel bad about the hotel business, and Juma told me to help you all I can. I feel I must go with you, to make sure you have no more trouble."

"Grant?" Charlie murmured.

"Maybe it's not a bad idea."

Her hands moved to her hips. "Really?"

"Do you know anything about Zanzibar?"

She raised an eyebrow.

"Better the enemy you know," he offered.

She gave a curt nod. "Isn't that a ferry over there, Grant?" Charlie asked, pointing at the large vessel that read "Zanzibar Ferry."

Grant turned to see the boat. "Yeah, but if I was old Omar, that's exactly where I'd be looking for us if he thinks we may try to reach the island."

"I don't like any of this," Charlie warned.

"Can't disagree with you there," Grant admitted. He gave Amani an appraising stare. The man was probably a fisherman. His skinny figure had lean muscles from working on the water every day. "It's still smarter to get there covertly, don't you think?"

"Probably, but I still don't like it," she repeated.

Grant turned to Mo. "Does Amani speak English?" he asked.

Mo shook his head. "No, I'm sorry. But I can translate for you."

Grant gave a nod as he scanned the mostly clear blue skies. The only clouds were the same type he saw every day over Key Largo.

Mo began talking to Amani in Swahili. The boat driver responded with a few nods and a string of words Grant had no way of understanding, but the tone of the conversation struck him as casual. Amani showed no surprise at whatever Mo told him.

"Amani says he can take you," Mo said. "Two-hundred-thousand shillings."

Grant sensed Charlie was doing the math in her head, and she nodded. "That's not bad," she said, pulling the bills from her pocket.

After counting out the fare, Grant, Charlie, and Mo joined Amani on the White Shark, bringing their meager luggage.

Charlie gave the taxi driver a begrudging stare, then whispered to Grant. "I still say he's up to something. Didn't it bother you that he's not upset someone hacked his taxi up?"

"Perhaps he has insurance," Grant countered. "Or he felt terrible that someone tried to kill us."

"I don't know," she murmured as she settled into the seat at the stern of the boat.

Amani steered the runabout into the bay, Mo seated alongside him. The two 150-hp outboards rumbled louder as he increased speed into the channel. Grant leaned back in the seat and watched the traffic on the water. By the time the White Shark cleared the inlet, Grant dozed off.

When he awoke, he knew it had been more than a few minutes.

"Grant!" Charlie hissed as she slapped his arm.

"What?" he groaned, straightening up on the rear seat, wondering why she'd ruined his nap.

"Someone's coming."

Grant's head turned to see a speedboat heading towards them at a rapid pace. "Who are they?" he asked.

"How would I know?" Charlie snapped. "But for some reason, we're slowing down for them."

Grant realized Charlie was right. Amani had subtly backed off the throttle. A green coastline loomed two miles ahead. The speedboat was still a mile away, but would soon catch up.

"Don't slow down!" Grant rose to his feet and moved toward the center helm.

Amani turned to look at him and said something in Swahili. Mo stood up as if he hadn't been paying any attention, spinning around in surprise.

Grant moved toward the pair. "Go! We need to lose them."

Amani didn't respond, and Mo barked something in Swahili. Amani shook his head.

"Grant, he doesn't understand English," Charlie reminded him.

"Shit!" Grant muttered.

Amani pulled the throttle back, letting the boat slip into neutral.

"No!" Both Grant and Charlie yelled together.

Amani moved from the helm, his eyes wide and panicked.

"Grant!" Charlie screamed.

Spurred by Charlie's cry, Grant shoved Amani away and slid onto the captain's seat. He slammed the throttle down. Both outboards roared as their RPMs spiked and the propellers spun to full speed. The White Shark lurched forward, slamming across the peak of a wave.

Mo lost his balance and fell off the seat, plopping onto the deck of the boat. He clambered around until he got his feet back under him.

Grant had grown up on the water, and he'd been driving a boat since he was six years old. He'd outrun summer storms, gales, and even a hurricane on one occasion. While the water wasn't rough, he maneuvered the 23-foot hull into the troughs of the waves. The speedboat was now behind them, and their target was unmistakable.

Amani shouted at Grant. His gestures indicated he wanted the helm back. Grant glared at him, and the man shrank back.

"What are you doing?" Charlie shouted in Grant's ear. She stood behind him, her hands gripping the back of his chair.

"We can't outrun them," Grant admitted, stealing another look at the pursuing boat.

It was a cigarette boat of some kind, but Grant couldn't tell which brand. That wouldn't matter because whichever make the boat was, it could outrun the White Shark with ease.

"What then?" Charlie shouted into the roaring wind.

Grant focused on the shoreline. They'd closed the distance to a mile and a half. It would take another couple of minutes to cover that distance. The turquoise water surrounding the island indicated the ocean became quite shallow as they neared land. The White Shark had a sharp V-shaped hull, but he guessed it should be beachable. Although the same was probably true of the cigarette boat, he hoped their draft was deeper in comparison.

"We hit the shore and run for it," Grant advised.

"Are you bloody nuts? Can we make it?" she asked.

Over his shoulder, Grant saw the cigarette boat squeezing down the gap between the two crafts.

"I hope so," he prayed as he swung the runabout to starboard to ride the crest of the next wave.

Amani gathered his courage and started for the wheel. Grant wondered if the boat driver now realized he intended to beach the fisherman's vessel. The American stiff-armed him aside, and Amani rushed toward a compartment in the bow.

"Charlie, stop him!" Grant ordered.

He watched her dash forward and catch Amani by the scruff of his shirt. Charlie jerked him back, and the man lost his footing when Grant turned sharply. Amani tumbled into Charlie.

Scrambling to his feet, the driver lunged for Grant once again, but Charlie came off the floor like a cat, slamming into Armani. He stumbled to the side, hit the gunwale, and flipped into the sea.

"Amani!" Mo shouted. "You lost Amani!"

"Fuck him," Grant snapped. "He can swim to shore."

"You okay?" Grant hollered back at Charlie without taking his eyes off the line of sand he now saw on the shore. Silently, he prayed there were no rocks ahead. If the boat hit a jagged outcropping or coral head at this speed, all three of them could be thrown out in spectacular fashion. He squinted but couldn't see the telltale black splotches that indicated rocks amid the turquoise water.

"I'm fine," Charlie finally muttered, moving alongside her brother. Grant noticed her eyes flick toward Mo and then back to the bobbing head of Amani.

The whine of the engine behind them grew louder.

"Grant, they're right on top of us!"

He risked a look. "Hang on!" he shouted as he jerked the wheel all the way to port.

The nimble White Shark cut hard and spun around. The engines whined as the boat changed directions, and the propellers spun pointlessly. It took less than a second for the thrashing blades to work, sending the White Shark past the cigarette boat in the opposite direction. A Donzi, Grant noted as the bigger, less agile boat flew by.

Grant took advantage of the small lead he'd gained by heading parallel to shore. He didn't want to lose the distance to land, and when he was back up to full speed, he steered the White Shark toward the coastline once again. The Donzi had slowed before its driver had changed direction, but the powerful speedboat raced back up to its top speed in mere seconds.

"They're still coming!" Charlie called out.

"No kidding," Grant retorted.

"You are going to kill us!" Mo called out.

Grant didn't think he'd be the one to kill them. It was the men in the cigarette boat behind them. The Donzi could outmatch him in a straight line, but Grant could use 180-degree turns to stay just a few seconds ahead of the powerhouse vessel.

As the Donzi approached their stern, Grant warned Charlie again, "Hold on!"

With the other boat so close, he reacted differently this time. The helm spun, and Grant yanked the throttle into neutral. With the sudden loss of power and change in direction, the rear of the White Shark swept around in an arc. Grant threw the boat's motor into gear, shoving the arm all the way forward. He glimpsed the Donzi's driver as the cigarette boat zipped by less than three feet off the port side.

They were now less than a mile from shore, and figures were visibly moving along the beach. People would both help and hurt, Grant realized. It would slow him down, trying to reach the beach without hitting a swimmer, but hopefully, the people in the Donzi would think the same thing.

It took him a second to realize the absurdity of hoping villains cared about innocent bystanders.

The Donzi was behind them again. Each turn gained him a brief respite, but the other driver seemed skilled enough to now antici-pate Grant's next move. The Donzi was only overshooting the White Shark by a short distance. Grant had lost the advantage of surprise.

When the speedboat bore down this time, a passenger moved

forward as the driver tried to put the bow right onto the White Shark's stern.

"He's trying to board!" Charlie shouted.

"That ain't happening," Grant muttered under his breath. The depth gauge stated 1.2 meters, then one meter. At .8 meters, Grant turned to starboard.

A sudden jar, followed by a grinding sound, sent the White Shark into a skittering slide across the water. The boat heeled into the skid, and the propeller buried itself for a second in the sand. Swirls of powder muddied the water as the White Shark struggled forward once more.

Narrowly missing them, the Donzi shuddered to a violent stop as the hull dug firmly into the sea floor and the occupants tumbled around like bowling pins. Grant couldn't hold back a grin. He'd guessed right about the bigger boat's draft.

His smile quickly vanished when he heard a loud clunk, then a screech of metal and a waft of smoke from the stern.

"What was that?" Charlie shouted.

"I think I hit something," Grant acknowledged as the boat lost power and became sluggish. "Only one engine is working."

"Amani is going to kill me," Mo moaned.

"Can we make it to shore?" Charlie asked as she shot a death glare at Mo.

They were now a hundred yards from the beach. Grant hurriedly aimed toward an empty patch of sand, leaving the men in the Donzi staring after them as the driver attempted to free the speedboat.

A few moments later, the White Shark suddenly lurched forward as the hull dug into the seafloor, and Grant pulled the engine into neutral.

"We have to hoof it the rest of the way," Grant announced.

Mo turned to look at the motors as Charlie scooped up her backpack. Grant grabbed Mo by the collar and dragged him over the side, landing in a foot of water. Waves lapped against Grant's legs when he hit the sand. He pulled his roller bag out of the boat and rested it on his shoulder. Charlie splashed into the warm bay beside him.

Mo stared at them, unsteady on his legs.

"What about this wanker?" Charlie asked.

"Get to shore!" Grant snapped at Mo. He grabbed the taxi driver by the neck and pushed him in front of them. "I think we were right to suspect him," he muttered.

"I've been bloody telling you." Charlie snapped, coming to a stop and looking around. "Grant? Where are we?"

"I think this is the southern tip of Zanzibar," he replied with little certainty. "At least, I hope that's where we are."

A small crowd moved toward them as Charlie, Grant, and Mo made their way up the beach, Charlie shoving Mo in the back to keep him moving.

"I don't know who those people were, I swear to you," the taxi driver whimpered.

"Shut up," Charlie snapped, scanning the curious onlookers for the next threat.

"We need to keep moving," Grant urged, picking up to a jog as they reached the shade of the trees, where upturned wooden rowboats lay out of the sun.

Beyond, a dirt road led between scattered buildings, and Charlie checked over her shoulder to make sure the Donzi crew wasn't coming after them. From what she could see, they were still stuck in the sand.

On their left, an old block wall lined the road, and at the first opening, Charlie shoved Mo into an orchard with no one in sight. Spinning him around, she grabbed a fistful of the man's shirt and wound up to punch him, but Grant stepped in.

"Wait!" he yelled, and Charlie reluctantly released her prey.

"That's twice, Grant," she spat. "Twice this bastard has tipped them off."

"I didn't, I swear," Mo protested. "Juma said for me to help, so I helped."

Charlie scoffed. "Juma's either dead in a ditch somewhere or he's in on it, too."

Mo put his hands together. "I pray my cousin is well at home, and I'm telling you we're not working for anyone."

"Give me your phone," Grant demanded, holding out his hand.

Mo dug into his pocket and handed over the device.

"Unlock it."

Mo took it back and entered a code. Grant snatched the old iPhone from him while Charlie moved closer to see the screen.

"It's all in bloody Swahili," she complained as Grant scrolled through texts.

"Look up a translator app or something on your phone," Grant suggested.

"And what?" Charlie argued. "Type in all that gibberish? It'll take all day, and they won't be stuck in the sand forever, will they?" she added, throwing a thumb in the direction of the beach.

"Please, you have to believe me," Mo pleaded again. "I'm a good man. I wouldn't do this to you."

"Bollocks," Charlie muttered. "I should take out his spleen."

"You're not removing his organs," Grant said, shaking his head. "But I'm keeping his phone, and we're leaving him here," he continued, turning back to Mo. "If you try to follow us, she's coming after your body parts, and I won't stop her."

The man's mouth hung open, and Charlie stared at him coldly, flicking her eyes down to his midriff for a moment. Mo flinched, so she figured the point was well and truly made.

"What am I supposed to do now?" Mo asked as they walked away.

"Give your mates a hand getting their boat off the sandbar," Charlie called back over her shoulder.

"These people are not my friends," was the last thing Charlie heard as they left the orchard.

She didn't doubt it. If Omar Al-Shomari and Saleh Al-Maawali indeed had the reach they'd displayed so far, they could easily threaten a taxi driver to do their bidding. But in her mind, it didn't matter what means they'd used. Mo had put them in peril twice, so he'd used up any sympathy votes she may have had.

"You know what's odd?" she asked Grant as they plodded in their squishy, wet tennis shoes along the dusty road.

"That you would ask me what's odd when everything that's happened since I met you has been odd," he replied, awkwardly dragging his roller bag along behind them in the dirt.

Charlie frowned and was about to retort, but stopped herself, considering his point. "While that might be true, I do feel it's a bit uncalled for," she finally said.

Grant grunted. "Charlie, we're lost on an island off the east coast of Africa with a bunch of Omani zealots chasing after us, and you want to play twenty questions?"

"Well, that was going to be my point," she said testily.

The road became paved, and the wheels on Grant's roller bag rumbled along, accompanied by his sigh of relief.

"Fuck, that's better," he muttered. "A roller bag seemed like a normal way to go when I was still in civilization where there are planes, and cars, and asphalt." He looked at his sister. "Do you actually *have* a point?"

"Don't get all grumpy just because I planned ahead," she rebutted, lifting the shoulder straps on her backpack to demonstrate the ease of carry.

"You packed for an overnight for Wales, then ended up here," Grant pointed out. "That's not planning ahead."

"Grumpy, grumpy, grumpy," she mumbled.

"Point?" he snapped.

"Oh, yes, the odd thing. These wankers, who we think are with Turath Zanjibah, have chased us in a car, raided the hotel they thought we were in—where I saved our arses by insisting on a non-rat and bug-infested place, I should point out—and now chased us with a boat, yet what haven't they done?"

Grant growled. "What's your *point*, Charlie? I'm seriously in no mood for all the questions."

"How would you stop someone in any of those scenarios?" she asked.

"And, another question," he complained.

"Well?"

"With a gun. Happy now? I answered your blindingly obvious question."

"There's my point," Charlie declared.

"That you can make me answer your questions by being incredibly annoying?"

"No, you silly bugger. They haven't shot at us."

"And you're unhappy about that? I'm sure if we go back, we can talk them into firing off a few rounds."

"That's the odd part. They don't want to kill us," she said. "The only one who's tried to kill us—and by us, I mean you—was the giant with the machete. And he had something to do with the hotel, not the guys who tried to find us."

"Maybe they don't have guns here."

Charlie laughed. "Right. No bad guys have guns in East Africa."

"Fair enough," Grant admitted. "And One Headlight did have a gun, but didn't shoot when he had a clear opportunity."

"Ha!" Charlie declared, more than a little pleased with herself.

"So, what does that actually mean?" Grant asked.

"I've no idea," Charlie admitted. "I just think it's odd."

They walked in silence for ten minutes, both deep in thought. Finally, Charlie spoke up again, pulling her phone from her pocket.

"I'd better see if we have a signal. It'll cost a fortune to use cell internet, but we need a map."

Grant shrugged his shoulders. "This was the only road leaving the beach, so I figured we were going this way, regardless. Maybe we'll run into a store and can buy a map."

All they'd passed so far were block-built homes with tin roofs in varying states of disrepair and rebuild.

"There's a town ahead," Charlie announced. "And a resort back that way," she added, pointing down a road that forked into the trail they were on.

They both stopped and watched a shiny yellow Jeep approaching.

"Friend or foe?" Charlie muttered.

"Tough to tell," Grant replied under his breath. "I only see one guy."

The Jeep stopped ten feet from them, and the driver stood up. He was a brawny man wearing a New York Yankees T-shirt, mirrored aviators, and a well-worn baseball cap sporting an American flag. Charlie guessed him to be in his fifties. He removed a fat cigar from his lips.

"You two look lost," he said in a thick Brooklyn accent, and grinned. "Need a ride?"

"Where are you heading?" Grant asked.

"North," he replied. "Name's Baker. Get in, buddy. As long as you bring that beautiful young lady with you."

Charlie groaned, and Grant laughed. "I'm Chuck and my sister's Grace," Grant lied.

Charlie groaned again.

She let Grant take the front while she climbed into the back, from where she could watch the driver carefully. They hadn't had much luck with people driving them around so far, and she wanted to be ready for the next disaster.

Baker started down the road, with the cigar billowing smoke and one foot on the bar where the door would be if the Jeep had any.

"Where north, sir?" Grant asked.

"Heading into town," the man replied. "How about you two? Strange place to be wandering around." Baker glanced over and eyed Grant with a crooked grin.

"The boat we chartered ran into trouble and dropped us off at the beach," Grant replied. "We're staying with a friend south of Zanzibar City."

"Chukwani?" Baker asked.

"I'm sure you wouldn't know the guy," Grant replied.

"Chukwani's a town," Baker laughed. "It's south of Zanzibar City. West of the airport."

"Oh. Yeah, anywhere around there will do, sir," Grant said, and Charlie kicked the back of his seat.

"What is it you do here, Mr. Baker?" Charlie asked, shouting to be heard from the back.

"Anything I feel like," Baker replied, relinquishing another stream of cigar smoke, which Charlie ducked to avoid. "And it ain't Mr. Baker, doll, just Baker." He leaned over toward Grant. "They started calling me The Baker thirty years ago on account of me having the best bagels in New York. It got shortened to just Baker, which stuck. Now it's all anyone knows me by."

"Are you retired here?" Grant asked.

Baker laughed. "Nah. I fly over for a few weeks three or four times a year. Meet a few ladies, drink too much, fish, dive, have fun. Like I said, I do whatever I want, then I go home and sell more bagels and deal with three screaming kids and a wife who'll bleed me dry, given half a chance."

"You couldn't find all that closer to New York?" Grant asked.

"I could," Baker replied, pausing to exhale more smoke. "But the wife would wanna come then, wouldn't she?"

He turned and looked at Grant, then slapped his passenger's knee and laughed so loudly it made Charlie jump in the back seat. Grant smiled, and Charlie hoped her brother was playing along and appeasing the man rather than supporting his misogynistic lifestyle.

After traveling through the town, they were now heading east on a barely two-lane paved road with thick vegetation on both sides. Charlie hadn't seen a more major road heading north, but still realized that the man could be taking them anywhere. Although she wasn't sure why, something told her he wasn't out to harm them. He was an arsehole, no doubt, but she didn't think he was working for Turath Zanjibah.

"What are you two doing in Zanzibar?" Baker asked when he finally stopped laughing.

"We're touring around, spending a few weeks checking out Tanzania," Grant replied. "We'll go on safari after this."

Baker looked him over once more, but this time, he didn't smile. "With a carry-on bag and a backpack? That's a crock of shit, Chuck, or whatever your name is. But hey, I don't really care, my man. Live and let live, right?"

"Right," Grant agreed.

Charlie leaned forward between the front seats and took what she considered to be a calculated risk.

"You know a guy named Omar Al-Shomari?"

Baker's head whipped around, and his brow creased. "That's your friend?"

"So you do know him," Charlie said.

"No, I don't know the man, and that's okay by me," Baker replied, returning his eyes to the road. "I stay away from that kind of trouble."

"Trouble, how?" Grant asked.

Baker shook his head. The atmosphere in the Jeep had noticeably iced over with the drop of one name.

"What business do you have with Al-Shomari?" Baker asked.

"We think he has something that belongs to a client of ours," Charlie ventured, knowing she was saying more than she should.

Grant threw her a quick glance, and she registered the concern in his eyes.

"So, you're heading for his place?" Baker asked.

"That was our plan," Grant replied. "How far is it?"

"Sixty klicks, or thereabouts," Baker said, keeping his eyes straight ahead. "About an hour."

"Is it on your way?" Charlie asked, trying to recall the map they'd looked at before.

"Not exactly," Baker replied, then she noticed his shoulders relax. "Can you give me an idea of what you're up to here? I mean, I love a bit of fun and to break a few rules along the way, but I don't need to end up on a 'whatever happened to the New York Bagel King' episode of a Netflix documentary. You know what I'm saying?"

Charlie looked at her brother, who turned in the passenger seat and shrugged.

"I'm Charlie, and he's Grant," she said. "We're private investigators hired to return an item to the bloke it was stolen from last week. We were on that beach after outrunning men in a speedboat who we believe work for Omar Al-Shomari. Now we need to get to his house."

"Shit," Baker responded. "That's sounds like a bigger bunch of bullshit than his story." He turned and looked at Charlie. "But probably 'cos you're a hot doll and I'm a sucker for a pretty face, I believe you."

The man burst out laughing again, and this time, both Charlie and Grant laughed along with him, breaking the tension that had accumulated. Baker reached into his pocket and pulled out a business card, offering it to Charlie.

"Here, my cell number's on there. I'll drop you down the road from Al-Shomari's place, but after that, you're on your own. And by the way, it's more like a compound than a house. That guy's bad news I can't afford to be messed up with. But if you get your business squared away, and he hasn't fed your sexy ass to the sharks, then dinner and drinks in Zanzibar City are on me." He looked at Grant. "You too, hotshot."

Charlie took the card. "I eat my steaks rare."

"I bet you do, doll," Baker said with another laugh. "I bet you do."

25

———————

Grant watched the yellow Jeep disappear into the distance before joining Charlie on the beach, from where they had a better view of Omar Al-Shomari's mansion.

"Nice fellow," Grant stated when he joined his sister on the sand.

"I'm betting his wife has a different opinion," Charlie remarked.

"Eh, wives," Grant grunted.

"I'd bet Angie would have a different view of that," she noted.

"For sure," he admitted. "I don't think I'd be running around on vacation without her—especially if we were married."

"Not when?" Charlie asked.

Grant shook his head. "We are just working on being together again. I've got a lot of things to make up for."

Charlie nodded without comment. Grant appreciated that. His sister knew what a struggle he'd had with the pills over the last two years, and she wasn't the type of person to give him undue credit. He had tried a few meetings in the past, but they hadn't helped him. Not that he thought that was the case for all people. Grant needed to be more proactive, and the idea of giving up his control didn't work for him at all.

"How do we get in there?" Charlie wondered over the sound of crashing waves on the sand.

Omar Al-Shomari's house was on a stretch of beach at the southwest side of the point where the old Stone Town of Zanzibar City was located. It was a three-story structure that mixed the Cubist appearance of many of the homes they'd seen on their drive north through Zanzibar with elements from Western coastal architecture. In fact, Grant thought the house could have been lifted from Palm Beach and deposited there. Balconies and walkways lined the beach side of the house. Large single-pane windows looked out over the sea.

"We could go in like we're workers," Grant suggested.

"Are we wearing fake mustaches?" Charlie quipped. "Because I think Omar knows who we are at this point."

"There's a guard." Grant motioned toward a man walking along the perimeter of the property. Charlie cupped her right hand over her forehead to shield the late afternoon sun. The man wasn't obviously armed, but Grant suspected he carried something.

"You know, if your theory that Omar doesn't want us dead is accurate, we could just march up to the front door and invite ourselves inside," Grant suggested. "That might be the best way to scope out the place."

Charlie shook her head. "I'm not sure it's wise to test that theory quite so boldly."

"Probably true," Grant mumbled. "Wait, who's that?" he blurted, watching a pair of women setting up a table with a white cloth on the upper balcony.

"Omar's having a party," Charlie offered.

Grant smiled. "Maybe a catered party."

"What are you thinking?"

"Like I said, we can go in like workers."

Charlie shook her head again. "We'll stand out like Prince Andrew in a secondary school girl's changing room."

Grant wasn't altogether sure what that meant, so he moved on. "Wait, Charlie, hear me out."

His sister folded her arms and looked at him blankly.

"Oh, you're going to hear me out?" he said, surprised she was actually listening. "We just need to get past the door. We go in with the caterers—"

"If those are caterers," Charlie interrupted, reminding him he wasn't working with confirmed details.

"Right. If those are caterers, we slip in with them. If there's a party, maybe we can blend in with the partygoers."

"It's four now," Charlie told him as she checked her phone. "If it is a party, we can't go in until the crowd shows up."

"Back home, that would be around seven," Grant noted.

"Could be even later."

"I think the later, the better," Grant admitted. "We just need to know a little more."

Charlie pushed herself to her feet. "Give me a few minutes," she announced before trudging away in the sand.

Grant watched his sister vanish over the dune just west of Al-Shomari's beachfront mansion. He waited with some unease for twenty minutes until Charlie reappeared. She carried a bundle with her.

"I hope you can play the sax," she joked as she tossed him a folded garment bag.

"What's this?" he asked.

"A tuxedo."

"Where did you get a tux?" he demanded.

"Stole it out of a van. There were several in there."

"What the hell, Charlie?"

"Grant, bring it along. You're going in with the band. They're English lads, so if you don't talk too much, maybe no one will notice your atrocious accent."

"What about you?" he questioned.

"I'm going in with the caterers. They're too busy to notice anyone out of place. And we'll go in separately, which I doubt they're expecting."

Grant nodded. "Okay, let's do this." He reached for his bag.

"You'll need to stash that thing," she pointed out.

Grant rolled his eyes and dragged his luggage through the sand. When they reached the edge of the beach, he stuffed the suitcase under a shrub.

"Hope my clothes are still here when we leave," he stated. "My computer's in there, too."

"Next time, pack better," Charlie said. "Get changed, and you'll find the band's van at the front entrance. Once you're inside, we start searching."

"How do we link up?" Grant asked.

"It's a house, Grant. How big can it be?" Charlie rolled her eyes and left him in the bushes.

Grant stripped down to his boxers and began putting the tuxedo on, which was a little large for his toned frame. No one would mistake it for a custom-fitted suit.

"Dammit, Charlie," he cursed after tying the bow tie. There were no shoes with the suit. He could either go in barefoot or wearing the Nikes he had on. He chose the sneakers, slipping his feet into them as he pulled the jacket over his shoulders.

The van was parked right where Charlie had told him. A couple of young guys were dragging sound equipment out of the back. When they carried their gear into the house, Grant scurried up behind the van. He reached in and grabbed a case shaped suspiciously like a saxophone.

Disguise complete.

He took the same path as the two roadies and hoped he could get into the house before either returned for more speakers. He stepped into an entryway that fed into a gigantic kitchen. Grant paused to peer at a group of caterers plating canapes and hors d'oeuvres. No Charlie.

He turned away from the kitchen and walked down a corridor. Charlie's voice in his head reminded him not to speak in an American accent. He wondered if he could pull off an English one.

"Where is the band setting up?" he said aloud in his best Brit accent. He shook his head in disgust. At best, it sounded Australian. Just not very Australian.

Just don't talk.

His rubber soles squeaked on the marble floors, and each squeal sent a shiver up his back. It sounded like an alarm going off with every step.

He walked into what he would describe as a salon—although, in fairness, Grant did not exactly know what a salon was. In his mind, this open room with picturesque windows looking out over the beach fit that description. Amps and a soundboard sat propped against the two steps leading up to what would be the stage for the night. The two guys he'd followed inside from the van were busy running cables and setting up mic stands. While they focused on their jobs, Grant set the saxophone case down and continued through the room before either man noticed him.

When he reached the next room, he found round tables throughout the space. A white tablecloth covered each table, and the staff had set every seat with silverware. Folded napkins stood at each place like individual spires.

Catering staff flowed in and out of the room. A figure ascended a curving marble staircase—Charlie. Grant watched her climb the steps. He started to follow her when a man he recognized appeared across the room. Saleh Al-Maawali surveyed the banquet hall and curled his lip as he eyed the tables. A pair of female caterers came in behind him, and Grant spun on his heel to retreat to the salon before Al-Maawali spotted him.

Grant let out a breath when he escaped the banquet hall without an alert being sounded. He lingered in the salon as he waited for Al-Maawali to leave. When he returned to the door, the man was gone.

Grant hurried to the stairs and ran up, taking two steps at a time. When he reached the top, his thigh throbbed.

"Not now," he complained to his old injury.

Upstairs, he moved through a corridor lined with doors. He tested each one by opening it and stealing a glance inside. The first two were bedrooms with king-sized beds and matching dressing tables. Neither room had any personal decorations, and Grant assumed they were sterile guest quarters.

The third door opened, and he stared at the back of Charlie's head. She didn't hear the door open, and he stepped inside.

"What are you doing?" he rasped in a hushed tone.

Charlie jumped. "Bloody hell! Don't do that to me," she scolded.

"Pay attention. I just ran into Saleh Al-Maawali downstairs. It could have been him instead of me. Whoa!"

Stunned speechless, Grant stared at a mannequin inside a glass case. The male figure wore a long blue robe with a red sash across the front. A turban adorned its head with a gold and emerald brooch at the front. On its hip, a rapier with a gold and jewel-encrusted hilt hung down.

However, the centerpiece of the display draped around the form's neck. The gold necklace glittered in the last vestiges of sunlight streaming through the window. Glints of red and blue sparkled from the stones.

"Is that it?" Grant finally muttered.

"Looks like it," she replied.

"Great, let's grab it and get the hell out of here."

Charlie nodded. "Watch the door. I'll have to get into the case."

"Is it locked?" he questioned.

"No, just cumbersome."

"I can do it, Charlie," he offered.

"Don't start," she snapped. "I'm perfectly capable."

He lifted his hands in surrender. "Absolutely," he said as he moved back to the door. He cracked it open and peered down the corridor. It was empty. "I'm right out here," he told her as he stepped from the room into the hallway.

Nervously pacing, he waited. Footsteps came from down the corridor, and Grant turned to see a woman carrying a stack of linens. As the maid approached him, the older woman narrowed her eyes.

"The singer," he mumbled in his terrible Australianish accent. "She had a wardrobe malfunction." As he finished, he pulled on the lapel of his jacket to confirm the point.

The maid's expression didn't change, but she made a remark in Swahili. Grant smiled and shrugged to assure her he didn't understand her any better than she understood him. She stepped around him with a look of annoyance and entered the first bedroom he'd looked in.

The door behind him creaked, and he jerked around.

"Get it?" he inquired.

In response, Charlie pulled at her collar, displaying the necklace hiding under the white chef's coat she wore as her disguise. "We need to get out of here," she whispered, starting for the stairs.

"Keep an eye out," he warned as he followed.

Behind him, the door opened, revealing the maid again. She looked between the brother and sister. Grant gave her a polite, two-finger wave. She turned away from him and went to the second room.

"Did you put everything back in place?" he asked under his breath.

Charlie turned and shot him a glance over her shoulder. "Absolutely. I hung the fake version we brought with us around the mannequin's neck and cleaned off all my prints." She rolled her eyes. "No, dummy, I got the hell out of there."

Grant groaned. "We'd better hurry, then. The maid's going in that room in just a few seconds."

"Bollocks," Charlie muttered and picked up her pace.

No sign of Saleh Al-Maawali. That was good. If they could get out to the beach, they'd be home free.

Charlie led them through the dining room, where a man in a crisp black suit snapped out an order in Swahili. Charlie didn't pay attention to the command, and the man, who Grant thought might be the maître d', repeated his demand in a harsher tone.

"I think he's talking to you," Grant pointed out.

Charlie paused and looked at the man. "Sorry?"

His words came out again in a slurry.

"Nod," Grant urged.

Charlie nodded.

The maître d' let out a calmer string of Swahili words. Charlie nodded and took another step. She lifted her finger as if signaling for the man to wait, then she turned to hurry out the opposite side of the room.

This time, as Grant passed through the salon, the two sound engineers watched him walk past.

"Hey, isn't that one of the band's tuxes?" one remarked.

Grant froze for a second.

"Timothy said his was missing," the second man added. "Where'd you get that, mate?"

Charlie stepped forward. "Ahh, that explains it. They must have been switched. Maybe you guys got ours?"

The two men glanced at each other in confusion.

"We'll bring it right back," Charlie promised. "He can't just drop his drawers right here, can he?"

Neither man moved, and Charlie and Grant slipped out of the service entrance Grant had come through only fifteen minutes earlier.

"That was too easy." Charlie beamed as she caressed the lump under her jacket.

"Don't say that!" hissed Grant.

"We made it out," she announced, still grinning like the cat that ate the canary.

He was about to tell her not to count her chickens when shouts echoed loudly from inside. Grant turned around on the steps of the service entrance to see the bedroom maid dash toward the kitchen.

Grant and Charlie both locked eyes. Then they broke into a run.

26

───────

Voices yelled from all directions as Charlie chased Grant down a path leading to the beach.

"Wait," she hissed, and grabbed his shirt.

They stumbled to a stop.

"What? We gotta go," he gasped.

"Not this way," Charlie insisted. "We'll be trapped against the water."

Grant looked from the glimpse of blue water between the shrubs ahead back to the mansion's tall wall surrounding the property. "How the hell are we getting out any other way?"

"We'll nip over the wall," Charlie replied, then shoved through the hedge next to where they stood.

On the other side, trimmed grass led to the white stucco wall, which she figured was more than six feet high. Grant crashed through behind her and held his finger to his lips. Footsteps and raised voices rushed by on the path they'd been on moments before.

"Wall sounds good," Grant whispered.

Charlie took off, staying close to the hedge as a shield from anyone looking down from the top floors of the house. Ahead, a pair of tropical almond trees filled most of the lawn between the hedge and the wall.

"We'll go over there," Charlie said, pointing to the spot where the trees extended over the top of the mansion's boundary. She ducked under the cover of the low branches and made it to the base of the wall. "Give me a lift," she said, waiting for Grant to join her.

After bashing his head on several low limbs, he reached her side and leaned over, cupping his hands together. Placing her right foot in the step he'd formed, she used his shoulders to lift herself up and peer over the top.

"Bugger, this thing's—" was all she managed to say before Grant heaved, and Charlie had no choice but to scramble up the face. "—covered in broken glass!" she wheezed, precariously placing her hands between shards with one knee teetering on the edge.

"Go over!" Grant growled. "Hurry!"

"I'm trying, you prat. I wasn't ready, and now I'm stuck."

Balancing on the top of the wall, Charlie felt a sharp sting from the palm of her left hand and knew she'd found one of the vicious knife-like shards cemented into the top of the concrete blocks. With one hand pierced and her knee barely holding on, she couldn't move without falling and dragging her limbs across the glass.

"Bugger this," she finally groaned, and pulled her left hand off the shard.

Planting it on a clear space of concrete, she pushed for all she was worth. Her arms and legs cleared the glass, but now Charlie plummeted to the ground seven feet below, just getting her feet under her in time to land and roll to one side.

For a few seconds, she lay still and waited to see if any body parts screamed in pain, but more shrill voices from beyond the wall brought her to her feet.

"Your turn," she hissed.

"Yeah. About that," she heard Grant say.

"Should have bloody well thought of that before launching me," Charlie complained.

"You were lighter than I thought you'd be."

"Are you saying I look fat?"

She heard a groan and then scuffling as her brother attempted to scale the wall. "Fuck!" he yelped.

"Did I mention there's glass up there?" Charlie remarked snidely.

Grant's head appeared, and the toe of one tennis shoe. He grunted, groaned, and hauled himself atop the wall, carefully choosing contact points like a cat avoiding drops of water.

"Coming over," he warned, and jumped to the ground with a thud, bending his knees to absorb the fall before ending up on his back, staring up at the sky.

"Can we go now?" Charlie asked, grinning at him as he sat up.

"My bag!" Grant blurted.

Charlie offered him a hand and hauled him to his feet.

"Too late for that," she replied. "Besides, you look pretty James Bond in that tux."

"Really?" he said, dusting himself off.

"Maybe a Florida Man version," she quipped, and strode towards the road leading past the mansion. "Oh, dear."

A crowd of local men had gathered in the street and now stared at the two foreigners escaping over the Omar Al-Shomari's perimeter wall. Charlie held up her hands, smiled, and whisper-shouted to the group.

"We come in peace, lads. Nothing to see here."

One of the men leaned his bicycle against his thigh, cupped his hands around his mouth, and shouted something in Swahili toward the front gate of the mansion.

"I think something got lost in translation there, sis," Grant said. He bolted past her, angling around the group toward a small road leading away from the beach.

Charlie made a beeline for the crowd, who quickly parted as the crazy tourist rushed at them. The only person who didn't move was the snitch, who was too busy trying to get on his bike to escape. Grabbing the man's foot as he swung it over the bike,

Charlie launched the startled fellow backward, where he hopped a few paces before tumbling to the ground. His friends burst into a mixture of laughter and yelps of concern, which quickly subsided when Omar's men spotted the fracas and barked in Swahili.

Sparing the briefest of glances over her shoulder, Charlie ran with the bicycle, leaping onto the seat without slowing down. Pedaling furiously, she discovered Grant had paused just around the corner and was now standing in the narrow road between tall, faded white stucco buildings.

"Get on!" Charlie yelled.

"Get on where?" Grant called back.

"I don't know, but they're coming after us. Try the handlebars!" she shouted, braking to a stop.

"You're kidding me," Grant muttered, but turned and eased his butt onto the handlebars, his legs straddling the front tire. "I haven't ridden like this since I was eight."

Charlie began pedaling, struggling to get going with the extra weight and veering all over the road, much to the amusement of a handful of onlookers. From behind, she heard Omar's guards screaming at them and a gunshot echo off the walls.

"There goes your theory," Grant groaned, trying to wedge the edges of his tennis shoes on the front wheel hub nuts.

"Not unless they hit us," Charlie pointed out, huffing and puffing from the effort.

"I'll be sure to tell you I told you so if they blow my head off."

"Shut up and sing 'Raindrops Keep Falling On My Head,'" Charlie retorted.

"What?" Grant snapped, hanging on for dear life.

"Have you never watched *Butch Cassidy and the Sundance Kid*?"

"Oh, yeah. Mom made me watch it with her," Grant replied in a softer voice.

"Dad made me watch it with him, too," Charlie breathed. "Said it was his favorite movie."

"Mom's, too," Grant responded, and for a brief moment, they were both lost in the sad reflection of their recent loss.

Another gunshot soon brought them back to the moment with a jolt, and Charlie looked over her shoulder. A black SUV accelerated toward them with a man hanging out the passenger window.

"Charlie!" Grant yelped, and she spun around, stretching to peer around her brother.

The lane ended at a building. She turned hard left down a pathway far too narrow for a vehicle and pedaled as hard as she could, only to realize the walkway ended at another building.

"Right, Charlie, right!" Grant shouted, and she switched to looking around the other side of her brother.

Following his instruction, she swung right, brushing a shrub with the handlebars and grazing her right hand. The sting reminded her of the wound on her left palm she had yet to examine, but she noticed trails of blood had streaked around her wrist.

The bike began chattering when the asphalt path turned to cobblestones as they passed by a small square with a fountain in the center. Kids sitting on the side of the base watched wide-eyed as the two streaked by.

Meeting another narrow street, Charlie had to choose a direction. "I'm going right," she declared at the same time Grant yelled, "Left!"

She was already turning right when she saw the black SUV and wrenched the bars left. Unable to hang on, Grant launched off the handlebars, landed on his feet, and broke into a run, squeezing between parked cars and the buildings. Charlie scraped along the side of a battered old van but kept going. Behind them, she heard the SUV speed up. She passed Grant, who was dodging pedestrians and street vendors selling fruit from large baskets.

A moped zipped by her from the other direction, and the SUV laid on the horn, scattering people to either side of the narrow street. Shopkeepers poked their heads out of glass-windowed shops with colorful awnings, and power cables hung perilously low across the street in loose bundles. Up ahead, a tourist car backed out of a parking spot, mostly blocking the road.

Charlie aimed the bicycle at the tiny gap between the rear

bumper and the building, waving frantically at a man walking toward her. He jumped clear just in time for her to race by while Grant ran past the other end of the car, slapping the hood as he went. The driver raised her hands in fright, jamming on the brakes and remaining stationary in the street.

"Ha-ha!" Charlie yelped and slowed the bike. "Get back on!"

"I'd prefer not to," Grant said, out of breath, but he hopped onto the bars all the same.

Charlie strained at the pedals while the men in the SUV shouted and cursed the lady in the car.

"That won't keep them back for long," Grant warned.

"We need to figure out where we are," Charlie huffed.

"Doesn't much matter as we have no idea where we need to end up," Grant pointed out. "Losing them is about our only goal. Buy us time to come up with an escape plan to get us off the island."

"Hey, check that place out!" Charlie shouted, risking a hand off the bars to point to a building on her right.

"Freddie Mercury Museum?" Grant read off the sign as they zoomed by.

"I'd forgotten that his family was from Zanzibar."

"No shit?" Grant commented. "That's a stellar piece of trivia, Charlie, but how about focusing on where the hell we're going?"

"I'm focused!"

The street curved right a couple of times before facing a large and dirty white building, which presented the option of either taking an archway into the structure or a smaller lane to the left.

"Go left!" Grant yelled.

"No way. We'll hide in here," Charlie argued. She kinked right, shooting into the shadows of the arch.

Expecting some kind of courtyard, she was surprised to find it was actually a tunnel leading through the building. "See, shortcut," she said smugly.

"Car!" Grant shouted just as Charlie saw the vehicle entering from the other side.

"Oh, bollocks," she muttered, and steered against the left-hand wall, knocking paint chips off the stucco with the end of the handlebars.

The driver blasted the horn, scraping his side mirror along the opposing wall.

"I think this is a one-way street, Charlie!" Grant shouted when they cleared the car by a fraction of an inch.

"I was only going one way," Charlie replied defensively.

They exited into the late afternoon sunshine, and Grant looked behind them. "Oh, shit. Here come the goons. They're taking the *correct* road around the building!"

Charlie looked to her right, where an ancient stone tower and a long defensive castle wall blocked any chance of escape. Blue water peeked between trees and buildings on their left. She pressed on, catching a van that was slowing for what appeared to be roadworks.

"No!" Grant pleaded as Charlie dodged left and ran between the curb and the van, continuing past the next two vehicles in front.

Arms quickly pulled in from open windows as they brushed by until Charlie reached a larger delivery van. She braked hard to a stop, and Grant flew off the handlebars again.

"That's it," he growled. "I'm not getting back on there again."

"Hush up and stay behind the lorry," Charlie said, waving at him.

A man leaned out of the passenger window and barked something in Swahili to Grant, then softened his tone when he noticed Charlie. She shuffled the bike closer to his window.

"What's cooking, good-looking?" she said, and the guy, who was at least fifty, returned a toothless smile.

"That's your pickup line?" Grant scoffed.

Charlie pulled on his tuxedo jacket sleeve. "Will you get out of sight?"

A horn honked loudly from behind them, and she could hear Omar's men barking at anyone in the way. The driver of the lorry pulled left, bumping his front tire against the sidewalk as everyone made room for the SUV to come through. Toothless's expression had quickly turned from lecherous to nervous.

Charlie put her finger to her lips.

"Yeah, that really worked well last time," Grant hissed.

The black SUV squeezed by the roadworks and tore off down the road, which veered closer to the water up ahead. Charlie blew Toothless a kiss.

"Come on, Penguin, back on your perch," she told Grant.

"How about we switch?"

"Not on your life, mate," she said firmly. "You'll get those fancy trousers caught in the chain."

Grant gave up, hopped back on the handlebars, and Charlie pedaled away, dodging the piles of sand and broken pavement.

"We're going exactly the same direction they just went," Grant pointed out.

"Yup," Charlie replied. "Hopefully, they'll think they've checked this road."

"We need somewhere to hide for a while," Grant said as they cruised down the road, which now ran alongside the waterfront. "How about there?" he added, pointing to a large official-looking building on the right.

The place was in need of TLC, but the big black iron gate was open, and a sign out front read "People's Palace Museum." Charlie steered between oncoming cars and through the gate. Grant slid off the handlebars as they came to a stop, and Charlie leaned the bike against the low wall topped with a wrought-iron fence.

"Think it's open?" she asked, walking toward the entrance.

"Looks closed down," Grant commented, glancing at the road behind them. "Shit, get inside, quick."

Charlie scurried into an entrance hall, hiding in the shadows to watch the black SUV roll slowly up the road. Another one appeared from the left, and the two vehicles paused in front of the old museum, where the drivers began conversing.

She jumped when a voice said something in Swahili. Spinning

around, Charlie saw an old man in a uniform that may have fit him in his youth, but was now draped over his thinned bones.

"Closed," he said in heavily accented English.

"Okay," Charlie replied with a smile. "We just needed to get out of the sun for a few minutes, if that's alright?"

The old man looked Grant over, then turned back to Charlie. "Bad men."

"No, no, he's a good man. Most of the time," Charlie replied.

The old man pointed to the street where the two SUVs still lingered. "Bad men."

"Can't argue with you there, mate," she replied under her breath. "Yes, they're bad men," she added a little louder.

"We stay here until they go," Grant said, speaking slowly.

The old man nodded.

Charlie backed up farther into the entrance lobby, gazing around at the displays advertising the current exhibits. Or what was current before the place closed.

"Grant, look at this," she said, then turned to the old man. "This used to be a royal palace?"

He nodded again. "Second palace. First one, poof," he said, and by his hand gesture, she assumed it had been blown up. "You hurt?"

Charlie looked down at her hand and realized the old man had spotted the blood. She cautiously looked at her palm. It was more of a puncture wound than a cut, but it stung even worse now that she'd seen it.

Grant joined his sister, and they stared at the large text above an old painting of what must have been the original palace.

"'This is the site of the shortest war in history, which lasted 42 minutes on 27 August 1896,'" Charlie read aloud. "'The British Royal Navy bombarded the palace and its grounds, destroying the building beyond repair, and restoring a pro-British sultan to rule.'" She winced at Grant. "We were a bit naughty back then with all the empire stuff."

Charlie hadn't noticed that the old man had disappeared for a minute, but now he clutched a small first-aid box under his arm and beckoned for her to show him her hand. She held out her palm, and he sprayed it with an antiseptic.

"Bugger me!" she yelped, and the old man chuckled. He produced a square Band-Aid and placed it over the wound, pressing down firmly.

Charlie winced. "Thank you," she uttered before moving away in case he attempted any further steps.

She looked up at the next display, which described a related exhibit. She gasped and clutched a hand to her chest, where the priceless necklace lay hidden below her smock.

"Grant!" she whispered. "You need to see this."

He walked over. "We really don't have time for a history lesson. Oh…"

They both stared at the pictures of beautiful jewels and artifacts described as the sultan's treasure, but one picture in particular caught their eye.

"Lost during the Anglo-Zanzibar War of 1896, the Heart of Hürrem was the sultan's family's most prized piece of jewelry. A Tanzanian-mined thirty-six-carat ruby was the centerpiece…" Charlie trailed off. "Bloody hell, Grant."

"We need to get the hell out of here and think of something," he responded.

"What if we nick a boat?" Charlie suggested.

Grant shook his head. "As soon as word gets out, they'll be waiting for us on the mainland. Wait, I've got a crazy idea," he said, pulling his wallet and passport from his pocket. "Baker. I still have his card."

"You're right," Charlie replied. "That is a crazy idea."

"Gimme your phone," Grant said, ignoring her reticence and finding the card in his wallet.

Charlie reluctantly relinquished her cell phone, and Grant dialed the number, putting the call on speaker. It rang and rang until finally going to voicemail.

"This is Baker, the bagel king of New York. Leave a message."

Charlie rolled her eyes.

"This is Grant and Charlie," Grant said. "You gave us a ride north earlier. We could do with some help. Call us back as soon as you can."

Charlie looked out to the street. "They're gone," she said, seeing no sign of the black SUVs.

"Do we stay here, or try to get farther from Omar's place?" Grant questioned.

Before Charlie could answer, the phone rang in Grant's hand. He answered the call, putting it on speaker.

"Ready for that dinner?" Baker said, laughing.

"We may have to take a rain check on the dinner, Baker," Grant replied. "We need a little help with something."

"Okay, gimme an hour and I'll come meet you. Where you at?"

"We need help right now, I'm afraid," Charlie jumped in.

"Hey there, doll," Baker said, turning on what she was certain he considered to be his charming voice. "I'm about to do something with a young lady that my wife flat refuses to do, so you gotta give me an hour, doll. I already took the pill, if you know what I mean."

"Ew," Charlie spluttered, reeling at the thought.

"Baker, we need to get off the island. Like right now, buddy," Grant said, taking back over. "Boat, plane, strap us to a dolphin and swim us across, we don't care, but it's gotta be right now."

"Shit, guys. You did get yourselves in a pickle, didn't you?"

"Nothing that we can't solve by leaving," Grant urged.

"Alright. Look, I got a guy with a float plane. He could take you. But I'll have to work it out with my man."

"Can't you just give us his number?" Grant asked.

"No. He won't answer."

"Because he won't recognize our number?"

"Because he's busy in the next room right now, and he sure ain't gonna fly you nowhere if you interrupt what he's got going on right now."

27

"You the hot English lass?" the scrawny, grizzled man asked as Charlie approached the dock, which was more like a string of boats tied together. The man, who was in his fifties and shorter than Charlie, paused when he saw Grant following in the tuxedo.

Grant stared back at the man, who had an accent he couldn't quite place. It wasn't Australian or English.

"Not how I would have phrased it, but yes," Charlie answered. "Are you Dirk?"

"Aye, Dirk Visser," the man replied, extending his hand.

Charlie took it. "I'm Charlie. This is Grant."

"Nice to meet you," he greeted, smirking at Grant's tuxedo. "I don't have much of a dress code on my bird."

Grant smiled. "Did Baker tell you what's going on?"

"Only that you needed off the island, pronto."

Grant nodded. "And discreetly."

"Discreet is my business," he remarked with a mirthful grin.

"Can we go now?" Charlie asked. "Where's your plane?"

"She's tied up out there," he answered, pointing toward a mooring field in the water.

When Grant squinted, he could make out a yellow and white tail jutting out past a barge.

"Do you have anything?" Dirk asked.

Grant shook his head as Charlie lifted her backpack.

"He packs light," she quipped as she slipped her arm through the strap.

"Come on then," Dirk said, climbing down a ladder on the dock to a small wooden tender tied below.

"That boat has seen better days," Charlie mumbled under her breath.

"Just go, Charlie," Grant urged.

She climbed down, followed by Grant.

"You aren't from here," Grant noted when the man had pulled away from the dock.

"No, sir. But I've been on the island for thirty years or so. Born in Cape Town, but I landed in Zanzibar when I was twenty-one. Haven't left yet. Got married. Had too many kids. Can't ever leave now." He chuckled as he steered the tender with the tiller handle.

Grant caught Charlie's angry glare and remembered where the man had been plucked from for this unplanned trip. He hoped his sister would let it go for the sake of their chances of getting off the island in one piece.

As they moved through the mooring field, Grant soon saw the entire plane. He recognized the make as an old Piper. There was a guy in Marathon who flew a Piper, and when Grant had been on marine patrol, the man's neighbors had called about his reckless landings near their boat. Grant had ticketed the fellow at least twice while on sea duty.

"That a Piper?" he asked.

"Sure is. A '74 Aztec Nomad. Bought it off a guy who smuggled diamonds out of the Congo."

"Smuggled diamonds?" Charlie asked, casting an eye at Grant. He met her gaze, confirming the irony wasn't lost on him, either.

The tender bumped against the aluminum pontoon. Dirk

looped the dinghy's painter around the strut connecting the float to the plane's body. He climbed out and used a key to unlock the door to the cockpit. After disappearing inside, he reappeared and stuck his hand out for Charlie to follow him up.

She swung her bag onto her back and climbed onto the pontoon. Her feet sidled along until she reached the open door. Once she was aboard, Grant did the same.

There were four seats inside the Piper. The two in the cockpit had faded covers on them that likely concealed the worn seats on the fifty-year-old aircraft. The other two in the rear had been rearranged to allow more storage in the back.

"You sit up front here, baby," Dirk suggested to Charlie before glancing at Grant. "If you don't mind."

Grant smiled at Charlie and waved his approval. His sister narrowed her eyes at him before climbing into the co-pilot's seat.

"You ever fly in a floatplane?" Dirk asked her as he climbed back out onto the pontoon.

"Yes, once."

Grant watched him detach the line connecting the plane to the mooring ball. The pilot moved and tied the tender off to the ball, leaving the Piper floating free before returning to his seat.

Grant sighed, beginning to believe that they might make it off the island in one piece.

"Did Baker tell you how much this would cost?" Dirk asked.

Charlie sat up. "No, I thought this was a favor."

Dirk laughed. "I think the favor was connecting you to me. I run a business, little lady. While I like to ferry beautiful women around, if they bring a fancy date, it's gonna cost them."

"That's fine," Grant replied. "How much?"

"Thousand dollars. US. Plus fuel costs."

"Just to get back to Dar es Salaam?" Charlie questioned.

"If you pay for the fuel, I'll fly you anywhere you want to go. But it's a thousand a day. Doesn't matter if you fly an hour or eight. But this bird will go seven hundred kilometers on a single tank."

"We can go that far?" Charlie wondered.

"Sure. At some point, I'll need to make some fuel calculations to see exactly where and figure out if we can refuel."

"I think if we make it to the mainland, that would be sufficient," Grant told him. "But we can pay that."

Although Grant didn't really know if they had that much cash. Dirk looked at him and rubbed two fingers together. Grant looked at Charlie.

"Half now," Charlie responded. "And you'll have to take shillings."

"I don't have to take anything I don't feel like taking, little lady," Dirk replied. "But let's see it."

Charlie reached down and pulled out the wedge of cash from her backpack, unfolding it and fanning it out so it appeared to be more than she actually had.

"Lovely stuff." Dirk grinned. "Nothing works better than hard cash. You can pay me the other end."

Charlie shoved the money back inside her pack, which she then handed over the seat to Grant. He tucked it under the other rear seat for safekeeping.

The pilot started the engine, and after a quick check of the instruments, he slipped a headset on and motored the Piper away from the mooring field. Grant watched Charlie, who seemed to relax, but still moved her fingers up to check the lump under her shirt.

Dirk flipped a few switches and rambled off a string of pilot verbiage into the microphone, asking for clearance to take off from the air traffic controller at the Zanzibar airport. There was a pause before a red light on the radio flickered, and Dirk responded to whatever was said. From his reply, it sounded like they'd been given the okay.

"Can you land this on water at night?" Charlie asked as she watched the sun beginning to dip below the sea's surface.

After arranging with Baker to meet Dirk, it had still taken the pair a couple of hours to get to the harbor without attracting attention. A feat made more difficult with Grant sporting his penguin suit and the black SUVs showing up at the museum ten minutes after they'd left. Omar's men seemed to know their every move.

"Sweetheart, I can land this baby on a pinhead in the middle of the Indian Ocean in the pitch dark."

The answer seemed to satisfy Charlie, and she sat back as the plane began steadily accelerating.

Dirk took a quick look over his shoulder. "You been on a floatplane, too?" he asked Grant as if just remembering that Charlie wasn't his only passenger.

"I've flown one before," Grant answered. "Buddy of mine had a Cessna 185, and we'd fly down to Cayman for the weekend. I'd take the stick once we were underway. I've been meaning to get my pilot's license, but haven't gotten around to it."

"Flying is as good as fucking," Dirk joked. "Well, maybe better. I've had some bad fucks. Only crashed a plane once."

"Yikes. I think I'd prefer bad sex to crashing," Grant stated.

Charlie rolled her eyes as the pontoons lifted off the water and Dirk eased further back on the yoke, climbing above the darkening sea.

Grant turned to stare out the window. Looking back, he could see the island of Zanzibar receding into the distance.

"It's about half an hour to Dar es Salaam," Dirk explained after leveling off. "I'll have to land on the coast to the north. Especially since I didn't file a flight plan. But you can make your way to the city from there."

Charlie nodded, so Grant didn't comment.

Dirk continued, "If you want to go somewhere else, that's different."

"How far are you saying we can go?" Grant asked from the back.

"I assume you want to get back to the UK, or wherever you guys are heading?"

"Yes," Charlie answered.

"Victoria Lake is as far as I can go without a refuel. Even there, we'll be coasting in on fumes, but I've done it plenty of times. Usually with a full load."

"Can we catch an international flight from there?" Grant asked.

"You'll have to take a bus to the nearest city. We can land near Daraja, a little village on the southeastern coast. Or we can refuel and continue to Kampala in Uganda. Plenty of flights from there."

"That's a lot of borders that we'd have to cross," Grant pointed out.

Dirk shrugged as if that didn't concern him, but Grant didn't like the idea of facing more unwanted inspections. After all, they were a pair of foreigners carrying an expensive piece of jewelry they'd just stolen.

"Let's stick to Dar es Salaam," Charlie said, and Grant silently agreed with her.

"Sit back and enjoy the ride," Dirk said with a smile.

For the first time since they'd run from Omar Al-Shomari's house, Grant felt at ease. His index finger slipped under the bow tie and pulled the knot free. The ends of the black cloth hung down from his neck, and he let his eyes close, leaning his head against the window.

Given another minute or two, Grant may well have fallen asleep, but Dirk's voice on the radio brought him wide awake. The pilot had responded to something in Swahili.

"Dirk, everything okay?" he asked the pilot.

"Yeah, yeah. Right as rain," the pilot replied, but Grant noted a subtle change in the man's voice.

The radio light flickered again, and Grant noted the pilot's shoulders tense. He answered in Swahili once more, then gently eased the Piper into a turn. Grant peered between the cockpit seats to the dark expanse beyond the nose of the plane. The lights of the mainland twinkled in the distance, but the plane was banking to starboard. His eyes shifted to the compass on the panel.

"Our heading is now west," Grant pointed out.

"Redirected by ATC," Dirk replied seemingly nonchalantly, but he couldn't hide the tightness in his tone.

"I thought you didn't file a flight plan?" Grant asked.

"ATC can still move us around," Dirk explained, continuing to bank the aircraft.

"Northwest?" Grant questioned as they continued to bank. "You're turning us around."

Dirk stayed silent.

"What the bloody hell is going on?" Charlie blurted, now seeing the island of Zanzibar reappearing out of her side window.

"Wait," Grant said, tapping Dirk on the shoulder. "International rules require all ATC to communicate in English, don't they? Yet you were chatting away in Swahili. That wasn't ATC, was it?"

Dirk didn't respond, but leveled out and dipped the nose. The Piper immediately began losing altitude.

"Grant!" Charlie growled. "What's this wanker doing?"

"He's taking us back, that's what he's doing," Grant responded. "That was Omar's people on the radio, wasn't it?" he yelled at Dirk, cuffing the pilot's headset aside.

Dirk swatted Grant's hand away. "I've got no choice," he muttered.

Grant grabbed the man's shirt at his shoulder. "Why don't you set the autopilot and come back here?" Grant ordered calmly.

"Can't do that," Dirk replied.

"I think my brother phrased that poorly," Charlie explained. "Get in the bloody back!"

Grant unfastened his own seat belt and stood in the cramped plane, which meant crouching over at his waist.

"I have to," Dirk said through gritted teeth. "He said he'd visit my family."

"Fuck!" Grant cursed. "You *are* taking us back."

"It's my wife," Dirk snarled as he pushed the yoke farther forward and throttled back in preparation to land.

"Do something, Grant!" Charlie shouted.

Grant reached over and caught the pilot by the neck. Dirk struggled and released the yoke as Grant squeezed his forearm tighter. The Piper banked to port as the pilot's feet inadvertently kicked the pedals.

"Charlie, straighten us up!" he shouted at his sister.

She grabbed the yoke in front of her and wiggled it from side to side. The plane jerked around, violently waggling its wings, but continued losing altitude. It was now pointed north of the bay.

"No, back!" Grant screamed as he saw the landmass out the windshield. "Bank right!"

Charlie let out a growl and yanked the yoke right. The plane turned hard right, but as it was already rolled that way, it dived towards the black ocean below.

Grant continued tightening the chokehold on Dirk as his own body slammed against the side of the fuselage.

"Level us out, Charlie! Level us out!"

"I'm trying! What do the bloody pedals do?"

"They sort of steer," Grant groaned, using all his strength to hang on, with Dirk squirming and scratching at him.

The pilot's flailing began losing its vigor until finally, he fell unconscious and went limp. Meanwhile, Charlie brought the Piper out of his dive and somewhat leveled it out. The harbor lights glistened ahead. Lights from fishing boats were much closer than Grant would have liked, but he needed to get Dirk out of the way so he could take over the controls.

He pulled on the unconscious pilot, but couldn't budge him.

"His seatbelt, Grant!" Charlie reminded him.

"Dammit," Grant spluttered, reaching down and unfastening the buckle.

Taking hold of the man's shirt, Grant heaved, but all he accomplished was pulling the dead weight a few inches off the seat before hitting his own head on the fuselage above. There simply wasn't enough room to yank Dirk clear without bashing his body into Charlie, who was trying to fly the plane. Grant let Dirk go, then stretched over and pulled the man's legs clear of the pedals. It was all he could do for now.

"Okay, sis, you gotta fly this crate," he barked, searching the console for the altimeter. "Oh, shit," he muttered, seeing it read thirty feet.

"I think I'm getting the hang of it," Charlie said confidently.

Grant's eyes moved to the windshield. The lights in the bay were coming hard and fast.

"Pull up!" he yelled. "We're way too low! We need to gain height and turn…"

The light on the mast of a sailboat appeared dead ahead, followed by the awful sound of screeching metal from the underside of the plane, which violently dipped and banked to port.

"Pull up!" Grant screamed, wrapping his arms around the back of the pilot's seat.

Charlie pulled back, but nothing happened. "It's not responding!" she screamed just as the left pontoon hit the water.

Pieces of airplane exploded as the float ripped from the body of the Piper, which then cartwheeled before slamming to a stop.

The raucous sounds of the engine, the impact, and the plane being destroyed were immediately replaced with an eerie quiet. Stunned and disorientated, Grant felt hands pulling on him. There was a sensation of cold, and he realized the cabin was filling with water.

"Get up!" Charlie howled, her voice echoing around the metal cabin.

Grant's skull throbbed, and he touched his forehead. In the remaining glow of the instrument panel, he saw his fingers smeared with something dark.

"I'm coming," he announced, but in reality, he couldn't tell which way was up.

He was on his knees with water up to his waist. Reaching out, he touched the back of the pilot's seat. Up front, he saw Dirk's lifeless form slumped across the console, where red flashing lights illuminated the grotesque angle of his broken neck.

"He's dead," Grant commented.

"He deserved it," Charlie growled. "Come on, we need to get out."

Grant wasn't sure if the man deserved to die or not, but his opinion wouldn't change the fact that Dirk had made his last flight. As Grant's senses returned, he agreed with his sister on her second point. They needed to get out before they went down with the wreckage.

"There has to be a life raft back here," he said, moving aft now that he'd found his bearings and knew they were floating upright in the ocean. "Don't open the door yet."

Attached to the rear bulkhead was a bundle, and in the dim light, Grant read the words "Life Raft. Do Not Inflate Inside."

It took the flip of two ratchets on the straps to release the bundle, which he fumbled and dropped as his head swam. Charlie, seeing him falter, climbed back to help, but he waved her off.

"Are you okay?" she asked.

"Just dizzy," he admitted. "I'll make it."

Grant swept up the raft and shoved it forward, shuffling along on his hands and knees until he was between the front seats.

"Okay, open it," he told her, and Charlie groaned as she slowly forced the door open.

Water immediately gushed in, knocking her backwards, and Grant had to reach out and push her back toward the opening. With a determined growl, Charlie grabbed the frame and shoved her body into the gap, forcing the door open wider. Once she popped out into the ocean, Grant manhandled the raft bundle after her before clambering over the seats and grabbing the doorframe himself.

The plane was filling with more and more water, and the nose began to sink, tipping Grant forward and jamming him against the yoke.

"Grant!" Charlie screamed, and he felt a hand on his collar.

He pulled on the frame with all his might as he felt the Piper rotating beneath him. The air pocket was surging to the tail as the plane was being pulled down nose first by the mass of the water and the twin engines. Grant's foot caught on the yoke as he slithered out the door, urged on by his sister, yanking on his tuxedo. For a second, he was sure the plane wouldn't let him go, but he twisted to one side, and his foot suddenly released, freeing itself of the wreckage just before the door opening dipped under the surface.

With a loud whoosh, the automatic inflator triggered, and the raft filled with air, popping open like a jack-in-the-box. Charlie clung to the side and caught Grant by the arm. One by one, they hauled themselves into the raft, which quickly floated away from the sinking Piper. Two small LED lights attached to the side of the raft flashed in rapid succession.

Grant pulled himself to a seated position, leaned over the side, and vomited. The head wound, mixed with the adrenaline rush, had hit his stomach hard.

"What do we do?" Charlie asked after he slid back into the bottom of the raft.

"Paddle," he muttered.

"Paddle? We're in the middle of the bloody sea."

With a strained effort, he pointed over his shoulder. Charlie raised her head to see the lights on the shore, only a quarter of a mile away.

It took Grant a few minutes to recover, but he soon joined Charlie in leaning over the side and paddling with their hands toward Zanzibar City. With the help of the wind and waves, they reached the beach in thirty minutes. Neither of them spoke during the journey, except to ask the other to give them a brief break from paddling.

When they finally heard the waves hitting the sand, they knew they were close. Grant jumped out into the surf and found the water was only waist-deep. Charlie followed, and the two dragged the raft the rest of the way, stumbling up the sand before collapsing on the beach in exhaustion.

"I don't know," Charlie remarked with a tired but playful voice. "I think I've still had worse sex."

Grant, who stretched on his back in the sand, rolled his head over to look at her. "Oh, fuck you."

Suddenly, the beach was brightly illuminated, and Grant lifted his head to see six headlights charging at them over the sand.

"What's that?" Charlie asked.

Three black SUVs stopped on the beach. The doors flew open, and eight men poured out of the vehicles. Grant didn't move, and when he saw the silhouettes of the Kalashnikov rifles, he slowly lifted his arms.

28

———————

"Stand up," a man ordered, and Charlie squinted against the blazing white headlights.

"I'm good where I am, thanks," she muttered.

"Yeah, we'd better do what they say, Charlie," Grant whispered. "They've all got guns."

A rough hand grabbed Charlie and pulled her to her feet. "Alright, alright," she complained.

The wound in her palm stung from the seawater, but amazingly, the old man's Band-Aid had stayed in place. Charlie couldn't believe she didn't have a collection of other injuries after being in a plane crash.

Omar's guard frisked her, taking her phone, then quickly discovered the necklace still secure around her neck. The guard shouted something, and another man approached.

"Saleh Al-Maawali," Grant said, now standing beside Charlie, having been patted down by a second guard, who had found Mo's phone and kept it.

"Hello again," Saleh replied, his expression unmoved. "Care to try escaping now?"

"Sure," Grant responded. "Have these goons stand down, and how about you and me sort this out like men?"

The corner of Saleh's mouth barely rose, acknowledging the challenge before he removed the necklace from Charlie and walked back up the beach.

"That was pretty corny alpha male rubbish, Grant," Charlie groaned. "Now they'll kill us slowly instead of the old quick and easy bullet to the noggin."

"Shit, it was worth a try," Grant replied under his breath.

Saleh handed the necklace to a figure silhouetted by the head-lights. They briefly conversed in a language other than Swahili before Saleh turned and beckoned for his men to bring Grant and Charlie closer. The same rough hand shoved Charlie up the beach until she stood six feet from the men.

Saleh wore an expensive-looking gray suit with a tie, as though he'd stepped from a five-star restaurant. The other man was draped in a white kanzu, the traditional Tanzanian ankle-length tunic, and wore a gold kofia on his head, a brimless cylindrical cap with a flat crown.

"Omar Al-Shomari?" Charlie guessed.

"I'd say I'm pleased to meet you," Omar replied in perfect English. "But you've both been a significant inconvenience to me, so I'm afraid your company is unwelcome."

"Feeling's mutual, mate," Charlie rebutted. "But if you give us back the necklace you nicked, we'll get out of your hair."

Omar took a step forward, his brow creasing, and Saleh's hand moved inside his jacket to where Charlie guessed he holstered a gun. Omar took a beat to calm himself.

"Allow me to tell you a story about an important piece of our history," he began, his voice even. "In 1896, the British Royal Navy laid siege to the sultan's palace here in Zanzibar. Their ships were anchored very close to where you just made a less-than-perfect landing in the seaplane a short while ago. Their guns destroyed the palace, which once stood on the grounds you visited earlier today."

"Fascinating," Grant interrupted. "You think the necklace

belongs in Zanzibar, but our client has owned it for decades. So, what now?"

Omar stared at him. "I am not accustomed to people interrupting me, Mr. Wolfe. We consider it quite rude in our culture. It would give Saleh great pleasure if I allowed him to silence you." He turned his gaze on Charlie. "Or your sister."

Grant held up a hand and said nothing more.

"It has taken me decades on behalf of my Omani ancestors, the rightful rulers of Zanzibar, to trace the events of that day—and more importantly, discover the names of the naval officers who were intimately involved. Which led me to Captain Theodore Bamford.

"Teddy, as he was known to his family, wrote the manuscript for an autobiography of his life on the seas, which was never published. In this manuscript, the captain described how he was the individual who recovered the sultan's treasure, which he handed over to the commander of the Zanzibar army, Brigadier-General Lloyd Mathews."

"It must have been one or the other who removed the Heart of Hürrem," Charlie said, finding herself caught up in the tale despite their circumstances.

"I see you've done your homework, Miss Greene," Omar responded. "And indeed, this was my conclusion."

Charlie didn't bother telling the man that the extent of her homework came from a butler's comment and a synopsis of the shortest war in history on the wall in the museum lobby.

"Brigadier-General Lloyd Mathews' life is well-documented, and after many, many years following up on every available detail about the man, I concluded that he handed over the complete treasure he'd been given. Which left Bamford."

"Finding his descendants is easy," Charlie commented.

"Indeed," Omar agreed. "But of course, Theodore's memoir omitted the crucial detail of him stealing the Heart of Hürrem, and his family have long since held the secret close to their chests. As I'm sure you're aware, the necklace has been held in

Bamford's private office at the manor, where no guests are allowed."

"He found his way in there," Grant said, nodding toward Saleh.

"You have proof of this?" Omar rebutted.

"We can place him in the village."

"Thank you for confirming that you do not, in fact, have any proof, Mr. Wolfe."

Grant groaned.

"I can tell you this, as it is of no importance anymore," Omar continued. "My breakthrough was with the estranged son, Edmund Metcalfe. He is what you might call sloppy, and he has a habit of drinking too much. During one evening, which I doubt Mr. Metcalfe has any recollection of, we were able to not only confirm the existence of the necklace, but also its location."

Charlie rolled her eyes. "That bloke's an idiot."

Omar allowed himself a brief smile. "*Alhamdulillah* for this."

"If I may, sir," Grant said. "What happens now?"

His question brought Charlie back to their predicament, which Grant had seemingly done a better job of focusing on.

"How about we thank you for letting us know the complete story behind the necklace, which you now have back, and we find a place to clean up and get a change of clothes?" Charlie offered. "After all, we did just survive a plane crash."

"You're welcome for the story, but I'm afraid I must insist you come with us," Omar replied, and nodded to Saleh.

In an instant, guards took Grant and Charlie by their arms and led them to one of the three black SUVs, shoving them into the back seat.

"Got any bright ideas?" Charlie whispered as the doors slammed closed.

"Not at this very moment," Grant admitted. "But I don't feel great about our long-term prospects."

"Me neither. But they could have drowned us on the beach and made it look like our bodies had washed up after the accident."

"Is that supposed to make me feel better?" Grant scoffed.

"I'm just saying they had a great opportunity, so perhaps he'll let us live after all."

"That's uncharacteristically optimistic of you, sis, but I think we're a loose end he'll want tied up before this is all over with."

The front doors opened.

"Okay, but I don't see a way out at the moment, so let's see where they take us," Charlie whispered.

"Like we have a choice," Grant muttered in return.

Saleh slid into the driver's seat and turned around. "Give me an excuse," he growled, then faced the front.

Omar stepped into the passenger seat, holding the Heart of Hürrem in his hands, and once his door was closed, Saleh backed up and turned the SUV around.

The ride through the old town only took a few minutes, and before Charlie had time to straighten out her thoughts, they were slowing outside Omar's mansion. Which seemed like a positive in her mind. *Why murder them in his own home?* Far cleaner, both physically and figuratively, to take them somewhere remote and finish them.

Saleh braked to a stop while the big iron gates began slowly opening. Omar barked something to Saleh, who opened his door and stepped out, drawing his gun from inside his jacket. The two exchanged more words in what Charlie now assumed to be Arabic, the native tongue of Oman. Raising his voice, Omar began gesticulating animatedly at something down the road.

"Oh, shit," Grant muttered, and for the first time, Charlie noticed the crappy-looking yellow school bus parked just beyond the gates.

Except it was no longer parked. It was reversing toward them at an alarming rate of speed. Omar yelled even louder, then flung his arms up to protect himself, still clutching the necklace. Saleh raised his weapon and got off two shots before the rear end of the school bus smashed into the front of the SUV.

For the second time in less than an hour, Grant and Charlie were hit with a brutal impact. The now-too-familiar sound of crumpling metal shrieked in the night, and little explosions seemed to come from all around them as every airbag in the vehicle inflated. Charlie's head snapped forward and then smacked backwards against the headrest while all the air left her lungs in a gasp.

When she opened her eyes, all she could see was the twisted metal of the right rear corner of the bus, pressed against the broken windshield. The SUV had been spun at a forty-five-degree angle, blocking the narrow road, and the engine had died, leaving the dashboard beeping a series of warnings.

"You okay?" Grant asked, unbuckling his seatbelt.

"Yeah," she groaned, getting her breath back. "Should we run?"

"I think we should," Grant replied.

Charlie swung her door open, and gunshots immediately rang out, splintering pieces from the inside of the panel.

"Not that way," she squealed, wriggling closer to her brother.

Grant kicked his door open, and while a couple more shots rang out, they hit the bulletproof rear glass.

"We're shielded on this side," Grant said. "But stay low."

"He wasn't so lucky," Charlie said, nodding toward Saleh's prone body.

Blood pooled on the ground from a head wound, and both his legs had been broken from where either the bus or the door hit by the bus had clobbered him. Charlie didn't feel any sympathy for that man, either.

"Wait a sec," she called to her brother, and leaned forward between the front seats.

Omar hadn't moved, and she spotted the necklace on his lap. She reached over and snatched it away before he had time to come to his senses.

"Okay, let's go," she said, throwing a glance out the rear window.

Their SUV had been shoved back into the one behind it, and the third vehicle was now blocked from going anywhere. Doors were open, and stunned guards hid behind them with guns aimed forward.

Charlie followed Grant out the rear door, where they quickly moved closer to the bus. Feeling something wet, Charlie looked down at the necklace in her hand and realized why.

"Oh, that's yucky," she blurted, looking left through the open driver's door.

Omar's white kanzu was streaked with blood from where the airbag had slammed his hands, holding the necklace, into his face. The wound to his right eye socket was deep, creepily matching the shape of the thirty-six-carat ruby.

"Come on," Grant urged, and dropped to his hands and knees to crawl under the back of the bus.

Charlie scurried after him across the asphalt littered with broken plastic and car parts. Voices shouted from behind as Omar's men began organizing themselves. It would only be a few moments before they'd discover the boss was dead. She had no idea what they'd do then, but she doubted she and Grant would be invited in for tea.

Looking under the bus, Charlie froze when she spotted the silhouette of a figure appear, bent over and staring back at them. She winced and waited for the gunshot.

"Hurry, we must go," came a voice Charlie recognized.

"Mo?" she blurted. "Is that you?"

"Yes, yes, miss. Please hurry, and I'd be very pleased if you'd allow me to keep my *wengu*."

29

―――――――

"Mo!" Grant hugged the driver. "What the hell are you doing here?"

"I could not let these people hurt you," he explained.

Charlie stepped up beside the two men. "You followed us here?"

"Yes, it wasn't easy. But I'd given my word to help you."

Grant shook his head. "Man, I feel bad we ditched you back at the orchard."

Mo nodded. "Yes, but I understood why. Now we need to go before these men come after us."

"Omar is dead," Charlie told the taxi driver.

"That might buy some time. But in Zanzibar, someone else will crawl to power."

He motioned for the two to get on the bus. Grant saw Charlie wipe down the necklace with a rag before slipping it back around her neck, where she hid it under her wet clothes. He stripped the tuxedo jacket and dropped it on the ground. Without the sodden coat, he felt fifteen pounds lighter.

Mo pulled away from Omar's estate. The rear end of the bus

wobbled as he sped up, but it had survived better than Omar and his SUV.

"Where did you get a bus?" Grant asked.

"I had to do a terrible thing," Mo admitted.

Grant and Charlie studied him for a second before the driver said, "I borrowed it."

"That doesn't sound terrible," Grant responded.

"I am afraid they did not give me permission to do the borrowing."

Charlie snickered first, followed by Grant.

"I'm so sorry, Mo," Charlie told him. "I was thinking you were setting us up all along."

"Never. I am your friend."

The two siblings nodded. "Yeah, you are," they sang in unison.

"What do we do now?" Grant asked.

"The local police work for Al-Shomari. When they find him in the wreck, they will look for us," Mo explained.

"We could find another plane," Charlie suggested.

Grant touched his throbbing head. "No. Unless it's a commercial flight with peanuts and a lukewarm Coca-Cola, I don't want it."

"Can we steal a boat now?" Charlie asked.

"It's dark. Can we get across in the dark?"

Sirens sounded from somewhere distant, and the three people exchanged a nervous glance. "Doesn't matter," Charlie said. "If we don't want to get arrested for murder and grand theft."

"Mo, can you find us a marina?" Grant asked.

"Of course," he answered.

"I have my passport in my pocket," Charlie told her brother. "But my backpack went down with the plane. My cash was in it."

A sudden realization struck Grant, and he patted his pockets down, pulling his own passport out. "I have mine, but I lost my wallet."

"So, we're broke?" Charlie asked.

"Yeah, and no American Express to save us."

"What are we going to do?"

Grant thought for a moment. "We could call Bamford. If we have the necklace, he could wire us some money to get back to England at least."

"But if what Omar said is true, do we return the necklace to Bamford? His family technically stole it from the sultan."

"Charlie, that was over a hundred years ago."

"But it was still stolen to begin with," she argued.

"Look, we're being paid to return it to Bamford. We told him no questions asked."

"We didn't ask the questions," Charlie reminded him. "Those details came up on their own."

"It was still the deal," Grant responded. "And we can't know that Omar was telling the truth. Plus, if we don't, we're broke and stuck in Tanzania."

The bus stopped, lurching forward in three jarring jerks until it settled.

"I might have messed up the brakes," Mo remarked.

Staring out the window at a small dock with several tiny fishing boats, Grant turned to Charlie. "Those are smaller than the one Amani brought us over on."

Sirens continued to blare, but they were getting closer.

"We need to hurry, Grant," Charlie said. "I can't imagine there are that many stolen school buses running around the island."

"Can you call Bamford?" Grant asked.

"My phone drowned."

"Dammit, mine, too."

Mo smiled and handed them a small black mobile. "I had to get a new phone," he explained.

"Oh, thanks, Mo. I guess we owe you a phone, too."

He nodded in agreement as Grant took the device and passed it to Charlie. "You both speak aristocracy," he told her.

"Hardly," she said. "But I'll call him. You two get us a boat. The sooner we get off the island, the better."

"Come on, Mo." Grant waved for the driver to follow him.

As Charlie stepped off to call Bamford, Grant and Mo made their way out to the rickety dock that had been built from plastic barrels and old lumber. At least the wood felt sturdy. Most of the boats looked like the ancient outrigger canoes Grant had seen in *National Geographic*. Only these were modified with more modern conveniences—if an outboard motor that looked more like a weed-whacker counted as a convenience.

"We need something to get us across to the mainland," Grant noted, staring at the small crafts.

"That one might do it," Mo said, directing Grant's attention to a little boat at the end of the row.

It couldn't have been over twelve feet long, and it was built like a tiny tugboat. The fiberglass finish had once been turquoise, but the sun and salt had faded the clearcoat surface with cloudy patches of white. In contrast, Grant could see barnacles, and he realized that if he could make out the parasitic scourge in the dark, they must be covering the bottom of the hull. The plus to the craft was the relatively newer outboard. At least it was newer than the small ones on the canoes.

"The three of us should fit on board," Grant admitted. "But it doesn't have any lights."

Mo shrugged in response.

"Let's try it," Grant said, climbing into the vessel.

Mo followed him, and the pair went about checking the boat out. It became apparent to Grant that Mo at least knew his way around a boat. He went straight to the fuel tank in the back.

"It's full," he informed Grant.

"Lower the motor, and I'll get it started."

Mo found the manual tilt on the outboard and dropped the prop into the water. Grant found a key on a floating bobber in a watertight box attached to the helm.

"No need to hotwire it," he announced as he dangled the keys.

"Are you guys ready?" Charlie asked as she reached the end of the dock. "This thing is cute, but it's tiny."

"I can throw you a line if you want me to tow you," Grant joked.

She shook her head and handed Mo his phone. "Bamford is going to meet us in Dar es Salaam."

"When?"

"He says he'll have to make sure a charter's available, but he hopes to be at the airport tomorrow by ten local time." Charlie climbed into the tug as Grant turned the key.

The outboard turned over a few times, and Grant pumped the throttle up and down to send fuel through the lines. If the boat hadn't been started in a few days, the gas might have evaporated.

The engine fired up with a *putt-putt* before it coughed and died.

"Grant!" Charlie urged.

"Give me a second," he answered as he turned the key again.

Putt-putt. Cough.

Again, he turned the key. This time, the engine started with a steady rumble.

"Untie the lines," Grant commanded, pointing to a dock line on the bow.

Charlie proceeded forward and released the hitched rope, letting it hang from the dock cleat into the water. Mo did the same for the stern line, but tossed the excess length onto the wooden platform.

Grant pulled away from the dimly lit marina. When they got out of the harbor, the night sky surrounded them as the twinkle of Zanzibar City faded behind them. With only the thin line of a waning crescent moon, Grant used only the starlight to see ahead.

The tug's small size meant it pitched back and forth as the fifteen-horsepower motor pushed it through the waves. The propeller whirred as it caught air on the crest of each swell and dove down into the trough. Grant was in the small cabin, but there was only enough room for one person at the helm. Behind him, Mo and Charlie huddled at the stern as the water sprayed over the sides at them.

Without instruments or lights, Grant was relying on the general direction. He'd done an emergency celestial navigation course during some training with the sheriff's department, but he was on the wrong side of the globe to rely on it. Instead, he put the lights of Zanzibar to his stern and located a cluster of stars in the distance. That constellation—his mother would be ashamed that he didn't remember them—would move through the sky, but it gave him enough direction for now. Once the mainland came into view, he could follow the coastline.

The little outboard pushed them forward with all its effort, but Grant figured they were making six or seven knots. It was only twenty-five miles as the bird flies from Zanzibar City to the Tanzanian coastline, but then they'd have to make their way south. If he had a chartplotter, he might make it in three to four hours, but driving blind, Grant assumed this would be a long night's journey.

They were still motoring when the sun finally showed itself. Exhausted, Grant glanced back at Charlie, who was sleeping on Mo's shoulder. The taxi driver, now as drenched as the brother and sister were, only smiled and gave a thumbs-up.

Grant was now the driest of the three of them since the half cabin shielded most of the spray. Still, the night had been windy and cold. He'd stripped off his shirt, hoping it would be warmer without the damp material against his skin. Grant wasn't sure that had worked.

"There's Mbudya," Mo announced loudly, pointing at a small island. "It's the marine reserve. We are almost to the bay."

"About time," Charlie moaned over the drone of the engine.

An hour later, they pulled onto the beach at Ocean Road Park. The bow dug into the sand.

"Can we find a ride here?" Grant asked Mo.

"Absolutely," Mo agreed, climbing out into the surf.

Charlie followed the cabbie into the water as Grant grabbed his wet tuxedo shirt.

"I'm starving," Charlie said as they reached Barack Obama Drive.

"We only have an hour to get to the airport to meet Bamford," Grant advised her.

"I guess we'll show up soaking wet," she complained. "And hungry."

"Once he pays us, I'll go buy you whatever you want to wear."

"I might wear a hamburger," she muttered as she shuffled along the street.

"It's not far," Mo offered. "Two kilometers, I think."

"See, two kilometers," Grant repeated. "That's like a mile, right?"

Charlie rolled her eyes at him.

"We can find a bus or maybe just hike it. That's like a fifteen-to-twenty-minute walk."

"In wet clothes," she reminded him.

"Half an hour," he amended. "Lead the way, Mo."

"Let me call Juma. Maybe he can get us in the taxi." Mo pulled out his phone and tried to call. When he didn't seem to get an answer, he sent a text.

With no response from Juma, the trio moved through a park. They passed the National Museum and House of Culture and the botanical garden. Mo knew the fastest route, likely leaning on his years as a taxi driver. The trip took twenty-five minutes.

When they reached the fixed-based operator private flights section of the airport, Mo offered to find out where they needed to go. Grant and Charlie settled on a bench.

"I want a change of clothes, something to eat, and the first seat out of here," Grant stated.

"I agree," Charlie said.

Mo returned and motioned for them to follow him. "I've found your Mr. Bamford. He is landing right now."

Grant checked a clock on the wall. It was 10:05. "He said ten, didn't he?"

Charlie nodded.

"Pretty on the money. The man must have had a plane standing by. That's what you get when you're royalty."

"Bamford isn't royalty," she corrected him as they rose to follow Mo.

"There's a tarmac for private planes," Mo explained as they walked. "He should be there."

A Citation X aircraft taxied toward them as they came out of the building onto the asphalt. The plane slowed to a creep before finally stopping in front of a hangar. When the door opened, Cecil Bamford appeared in the opening. He was wearing a three-piece suit and holding a briefcase. Grant wondered if he'd changed on the plane or wore the outfit during the flight. He descended the stairs as Mo's phone rang.

"So sorry, it's Juma," he replied with a half-grin. "What do they say, 'Better late than never?'"

Grant and Charlie left the taxi driver to talk to his cousin as they approached Bamford.

"I truly didn't expect to hear from you so soon," Bamford praised. "You two would have made your father proud."

Charlie shot a wary eye at Grant before responding. "We found the necklace. Do you have our money?"

"Can I see it?" Bamford asked, shifting his eyes between the two siblings.

Charlie pulled the Heart of Hürrem from beneath her shirt. Sir Cecil sucked in a breath of relief.

"You found it," he sighed. "Who had it?"

Grant raised a hand. "No offense, Mr. Bamford, but we'd like to get paid and find a change of clothes."

Bamford stepped back and surveyed the two as if he'd just seen them. "Yes, you two are quite a mess. Here is the money. Two hundred and fifty thousand pounds." He handed the case to Grant.

When Grant cracked the seal, he saw stacks of pound notes. "Okay, Charlie."

"Did you count it?" she asked.

"Don't be crass. Cecil is a gentleman," he scolded as Charlie removed the jewels and passed them to Bamford.

"Bamford, you should know that this necklace was stolen from the sultan's treasure back in 1896. The people who took it want to repatriate it to Zanzibar." Charlie stepped back as she explained the Heart of Hürrem's history.

"Oh, I'm well-aware of the history, and as it is stated, 'History is written by the victors.' Time has a way of forgetting who owned what."

Grant and Charlie looked at each other.

"Would you two like to return with me to London? We'll be leaving promptly."

Grant shook his head. "I think we want to get some rest and clean up before we fly."

Mo stepped up beside them. "Mr. Wolfe, you might want to reconsider that."

Grant turned to the taxi driver. Behind him, three police cars screeched to a stop.

"Mo, what's going on?" Charlie asked.

"Cecil Bamford, you are under arrest!" Mo shouted.

Bamford's eyes widened, and he turned to run up the steps. Grant reached out and grabbed the man by his expensive custom-made jacket and jerked him back.

"Grant?" Charlie blurted out.

"Oh, reflex when a suspect runs."

"Thank you, Mr. Wolfe," Mo said, taking Bamford by the arm.

"Good job, Mohamed," Juma announced as he exited the first police car with three officers joining him.

"What the hell is going on here?" Grant asked, looking between Mo and Juma. "Are you cops?"

"We prefer the term 'inspectors,'" Juma explained. "I am Inspector Juma Membe, and you know Assistant Inspector Mohammed Sumaye."

"I demand you explain why I'm being detained," Bamford squawked, turning from scared rabbit to ferocious chihuahua.

"At the moment, you are being held for questioning concerning the theft of Tanzanian artifacts."

"I stole nothing," Bamford argued. "I demand to speak with the British Consulate."

"In due time," Juma confirmed. "Put him in the back."

Two of the officers escorted a grumbling Cecil Bamford to one of the police cars.

"Juma, what is going on?" Grant asked.

"Mohammed and I are part of a two-man task force that's been defined as the Department of National Treasures and Artifacts. Unfortunately, our investigations have been hampered by our boss, Al-Raisi, the Superintendent of Criminal Investigations."

"Were you able to speak with the senior superintendent?" Mo asked.

"Yes, we've arrested Al-Raisi early this morning. I have investigators inside Omar Al-Shomari's estate now. Already, we've found evidence that Al-Raisi was working for him. We've also arrested a low-level tech in our communications department. He's been feeding Al-Shomari your cellular location. That's how they've been tracking your movements."

"Wait, so you two aren't cousins?" Grant asked.

"Are you just now catching up?" Charlie asked. "They were undercover, right?"

"Right," Mo agreed. "We learned that Mr. Wolfe was detained in Turkey thanks to Al-Shomari's connections. That worked out because Juma was able to be in place when you arrived. Ms. Greene, however, was an unexpected bonus. We didn't know you were coming, too."

"But why the switch? That made us suspicious," Charlie asked.

"That's true," Grant agreed. "Why did Juma leave?"

"Unfortunately, the investigation into Al-Raisi hit a crucial point, and I needed support from—what's the phrase—up the food chain. Is that right?"

Charlie cocked her head. "Your English has improved."

Juma gave her a half smile.

"Why didn't you tell us you were coppers from the beginning?" Charlie asked.

Juma held up a hand. "My apologies, Ms. Greene, but we had no way of knowing if we could trust you. At the beginning, we believed you were simply here to steal back the artifact."

Charlie looked at Grant and cringed. "We sort of were."

Grant nodded. "What about Bamford?"

Mo stepped forward. "I just heard him admit to knowingly possessing stolen national treasures of Tanzania. By the time it's done, he'll go back to London without the necklace. But maybe we'll find out if he has any other stolen artifacts we don't know about."

Charlie asked, "What about us?"

Mo chuckled. "After being left to rot on Zanzibar, I should drag you in with Bamford."

"About that," Grant began.

Mo guffawed. "No, I talked with Juma. We won't do that to you."

Grant lifted the case in silent question.

"It seems Bamford hired you to deliver the necklace to him," Mo said. "You did that. His money has no place in this."

"Can we pay for your cab?" Charlie asked. "It was destroyed."

"It belongs to the government," Mo assured her. "There's no need."

"But we can go?" Grant asked.

"I'd advise you to get on Bamford's plane and leave now before questions arise that require you to stay," Juma said.

"Thank you," Charlie told the pair of inspectors.

Both men waved for them to go on, and the siblings wasted no time hurrying up the steps.

"Juma didn't mention Dirk or his plane," Charlie whispered.

"Nope. And let's get the hell out of here before he does," Grant replied.

They stepped into the cabin to find plush seats, a small galley, and a fully stocked bar. The pilot stood in the door to the cockpit.

"Is everything okay?" he asked.

"Yes," Charlie acknowledged.

"Let's get this bird off the ground," Grant told the pilot.

"Mr. Bamford?" the pilot asked.

"He's staying in Tanzania for a bit. We need to get to London, though," Charlie explained, plopping into a seat. "Bamford said we should ride with you."

Grant held up the case as though its presence explained everything.

The man cocked his head as he considered his new instructions. "The charter was for here and straight back."

"Straight back is in all our best interests, mate," Charlie urged. "Or the fellows outside with the flashing lights will keep you and your plane along with ol' Bamford."

The pilot took a last look outside and pulled the door closed. "We have a refuel arranged. Twenty minutes tops, and we'll be wheels up. Make yourselves comfortable."

"I believe we will," Grant replied, watching the pilot retreat to the cockpit.

"It's not a commercial flight," Charlie said. "But I can look and see if there's a Coca-Cola in the cooler."

"Screw that," Grant replied. "The man has a Dalwhinnie scotch in his minibar. That beats Coke any day."

Grant lifted the bottle of scotch and two glasses before dropping into the seat opposite his sister. He poured two drams and handed one to her.

"To our first case," he toasted, lifting his glass to hers.

Thank you for reading *Missing in Zanzibar*!

Wishing there was more from Grant and Charlie?
In return for joining our newsletter lists, we've written a fun bonus
scene you'll find by using this QR code…

The adventure continues for Grant and Charlie in
Missing in Hawaii.

Listen to Doug and Nick's entertaining podcast
The Two Authors' Chat Show.

ABOUT THE AUTHOR

Author of the Chase Gordon Tropical Thriller, Max Sawyer, and
Corsair series.

Douglas Pratt, a best-selling action author hailing from Memphis,
Tennessee, captivates readers with his unique blend of charm and
intensity, reflecting his Southern roots. His works keep audiences
on the edge of their seats, infused with a sense of adventure and
exploration. Beyond writing, Pratt's personal interests lead him to
sail the seas, exploring vibrant coral reefs and sunken shipwrecks,
which fuel his imagination and inspire enthralling adventures in
his stories.

For more information visit Douglas-Pratt.com

ABOUT THE AUTHOR

Author of the AJ Bailey Adventure series and Nora Sommer
Caribbean Suspense series

A *USA Today* Bestselling author, Nicholas Harvey's life has been anything but ordinary. Race car driver, adventurer, divemaster, and since 2020, a full-time novelist. Raised in England, Nick has dual US and British citizenship and now lives wherever he and his amazing wife, Cheryl, park their motorhome, or an aeroplane takes them. Warm oceans and tall mountains are their favourite places.

For more information visit HarveyBooks.com